I0700950

ACCIDENTAL MISTRESS

FILTHY BILLIONAIRES

EVELYN AUSTIN

SILVER GRIFFON ASSOCIATES
ORANGE, CA, USA

CHAPTER 1
THE DEVIL HIMSELF

THIS IS SERIOUSLY CRAZY. MY HEARTBEAT IS HAMMERING in my throat as I stare out across the gathering in the private room section of a high-end Malibu restaurant Isca Dumnoniorum. The uber-rich elite of Los Angeles litter the place like shattered glass.

And I'm here among them in a designer gown I splurged on with the help of my mom's credit card. It's tighter than I'm normally comfortable wearing—black with golden sparkles that accent the plunging neckline, revealing more than just a hint of my breasts. My God, the underwear I had to select specific to the dress was enough to buy a semester's worth of graduate-level cryptography textbooks.

Not that I'm budgeting these days, thanks to Mom and her guilt money.

My date, David, slides his hand partway down my back as he guides me to a table and pulls out a chair. I smile up at him and angle myself so he gets a good view down my cleavage.

I'm not normally so brazen—nor so obvious—but David and I have been dating on and off for about five months and I'm hoping this sexy dress, along with a few other tricks I have up my sleeve, will seal the deal with us. I'm angling for us to be exclusive, then, eventually, engaged. It's all a part of my two-year plan.

David takes his seat across from me and flashes me a fetching smile. He's good-looking, young and successful. He's got plush, dark-blond hair and light-blue eyes and a well-defined jaw. More importantly, for me… he's perfect husband material. I bite my lip and smile back at him.

He leans forward and touches my hand. "Thirsty?"

I widen my smile so that my teeth show. "Parched."

He returns the smile. "I'll be back, then."

I turn to watch him go, wishing he had the type of backside I could admire, but with so many other fantastic qualities, it would be greedy to ask for more. David reeks of stability, rationality, and he's just what I need in my future.

As he recedes from view, heading out to the refreshment table, I look around me. My eyes gravitate to the couple hosting the elaborate engagement party: my dear friend and, until recently, roommate, Maddy Swanson and her over-the-top gorgeous fiance, tech billionaire Evan Kohl. They are the picture of wealth, beauty and brilliance. My eyes rake Maddy's pretty sparkly gown from head to toe, aching with envy. She has everything that I want. But I've always been a girl who's gotten what she's set her sights on, too.

Am I not a student about to graduate from one of the most prestigious technical institutes in the country? I have everything my mother wishes she had. Yes, she has the looks and the body that makes men sniff after her wherever she goes. Not only have I inherited those things from her, but I also have smarts and determination that don't let me settle for anything less than my perfect vision for the future.

I'm so lost in my thoughts that it takes me a minute or two to become aware of a new presence sitting beside me at the table. I don't look up from my phone, but I can smell his expensive cologne and I can feel his eyes on me.

"Are you waiting for someone?"

A British accent rolls off his tongue, smooth and sexy. Instinctively, I look up and into a pair of eyes, dark like midnight. For a minute, the air is caught in my throat and I can't breathe. He's *gorgeous*—at least six feet tall with dark, wavy hair, a strong, angular jaw and a chin dimple. But it's his eyes I'm drawn to, mysterious pools of darkness. My heart pounds at my throat and temples, and I'm suddenly perspiring under my dress.

The visceral reaction to this gorgeous specimen is powerful and immediate.

He's doing the same as me, checking me out. His gaze slowly rakes up my body and settles on my breasts, which are practically falling out of my dress. This is the sexiest dress I've ever worn, and I chose it specifically to tempt David into finally taking me to bed. I want to tease him, make him pant for me and then make me his lover. Make this a real relationship instead of an occasional pleasant date that doesn't go anywhere beyond a little making out on the front step.

And anyway, I could really use a good fuck. It's been way too long. Over a year, honestly. My body is hungry for it, but not so hungry I'd take a stranger to bed.

The way the stranger's eyes are devouring me, however, I can tell he has no such reservations.

I place my phone on the table and smile. "I am, actually. He's getting us some drinks."

"What will you drink? I'll have something brought over at once." And much to my shock, he pulls out his phone, starts to text. "An appletini, I think? Their martinis are excellent."

Before I can reply, he presses a button and sets his phone down, smiling at me cockily.

I blink. "I have one coming already."

"Yes, I know. A glass of champagne from the refreshment table. I texted the bartender to send me drinks straight away. Should be here in just a few minutes. I wager it will make it here before what's-his-name can even get his hands on a glass of champagne."

My eyebrows dart up at his brazen confidence. And while he's to-die-for handsome, his brash boldness is almost frightening in a worldly way. I immediately peg him for the type of guy a nice girl doesn't date. I've avoided those guys for so long, I can spot them pretty quickly.

The handsome stranger signals to the waiter quickly approaching our table with two drinks on his tray. He bends and places what looks like Scotch on the rocks in front of him and the bright-green appletini in front of me. "There you are, Mr. Grayson. Please let us know if you need anything else."

"Thanks, Charlie," Suave Stranger, aka Mr. Grayson, grins at the waiter and slips him a tip, which he quickly pockets with a smile.

I take a sip of the drink—may as well. It's my policy to never refuse a first drink. But I hardly ever accept the invitation for a second one. Mr. Grayson doesn't know that, so I may as well nurse this until David gets back. I'm immune to slick moves and suave playboys and have no intention of giving this one anything more than the time of day.

The drink's tartness makes my lips pucker, and he laughs.

"What's your name?"

"Lexi," I say just before taking another sip.

"Short for Alexandra? I'm Ash," he offers back.

He leans back with an air of self-confidence that few men possess. With a long finger tracing the rim of his glass, he watches me. "You're on what...your fifth or sixth date? But things haven't been moving fast enough for you."

It's not a question or a judgment. It's an observation, and his accuracy startles me. I blink but try to play it cool. "Maybe we're on a blind date." I shrug.

"I'm guessing you're a nice girl. And nice girls don't wear dresses like *that* unless they're hungry for a good fucking." I suck in a sharp breath, shocked by his crude words. He smiles. "And you don't look like the type of woman who fucks on a first date."

I arch a brow, annoyed that a complete stranger would presume to know anything about me. "You seem awfully confident about that."

Reaching out, he touches his finger to my necklace, just above my collarbone. It's a double strand of pearls interspersed with pale pink and green gemstones.

"Pink pearls." He smiles to himself and drops his hand. "Expensive. More than someone in their early twenties can usually afford. I'd wager they're a gift from your mum."

My brows arc. Actually, they were, but I'm not going to admit it to this smooth operator. No need to feed his cockiness. I touch the cool strand with my fingertips. "What does my pearl necklace have to do with my unwillingness to fuck on the first date?"

"It speaks to your innocence," he says simply. "Your purity. Your vulnerability."

There's something smoldering in his eyes—a dark hunger that sends tingles down my spine. My nipples tighten and heat spirals through my veins. I try to push the feelings away, but they won't budge. This man does something to me—something I can't quite explain. Even to myself.

That doesn't mean I have the least bit of desire to follow through on that, however. That way leads to disaster.

My phone vibrates, breaking the spell. I glance down as the screen lights up. It's a text from David.

Sorry, babe. Got waylaid on my way back from the men's room. Tipped a waiter to send you a drink. Be there soon as I can.

Disappointment washes over me. Damn. How long will that take and who waylaid him? Perhaps it was an associate. He'd explained to me on the way over to the party that he was trying to get his own membership at Exeter House—LA's most exclusive private club—of which this elegant restaurant is the public face.

The club is notoriously difficult to get membership into—the waiting list is said to be decades long. But David is an associate who is sometimes able to rent a room here and was excited about possibly moving up for consideration as full member.

I take another sip of my drink to cover my irritation. How can I seduce a man who refuses to sit still for more than five minutes?

Hopefully the night will still be young by the time he gets back here, since he's hinted that he might be able to get a room here tonight. And I'm quite certain he didn't just let that tidbit drop by chance. He meant he'd take a room for us to share and—hopefully, *finally*—consummate this relationship.

I bite my lip, texting back.

Don't dawdle. I've barely had a chance to see you tonight...

He replies immediately.

Not a chance. I'll hurry back to you ASAP.

I sigh and stuff my phone into my tiny, wallet-sized clutch.

"Everything okay?" asks the oh-so-sexy Ash over the rim of his tumbler.

I look up into those midnight eyes and shrug. I should probably be irritated by his curiosity, but I actually think it's kind of sweet. "He got waylaid."

Ash nods and smiles faintly, which puzzles me, but I dismiss it. "Well it's a good thing you have something to drink now, isn't it?"

My mouth curls up. "Yes, indeed. Thank you." And I punctuate my gratitude with another sip of the tart drink.

Suddenly, Ash reaches up and traces his index finger along my jaw, and down my neck. I don't stop him. I don't even move. I can only watch in shock. My heart is pounding hard, like it'll hammer right out of my chest.

His eyes meet mine, stare right into the depths, and I'm mesmerized.

"So damn beautiful," he murmurs. His voice is so low I wonder if I misheard him. In fact, I'm sure I did. David hasn't said I'm beautiful yet, not even when he picked me up tonight. Mom always said I'd never be as pretty as her. I guess I'm not used to a complete stranger coming on to me like this.

I swallow as his finger trails down my bare arm, sending tingles up my spine. I run my tongue along my bottom lip nervously. "I, ah, see someone I know over—"

"I have a suite upstairs," he interrupts with that voice like a purr. "Come up with me. I'll mix you another cocktail."

I imagine that the "cocktail" he wants to serve doesn't come in a glass mixed with fruit juice over ice.

God, yes. I swallow, startled by how much I want to be under this man. The image of him naked, on top of me, poised to plunge himself into me. *Oh god, yes.*

But he's right. Deep down, I'm a good girl. I've never had a one-night stand. That's the sort of trashy thing my mother does all the time and it never ends well for her. *Ever.* I've learned enough from her foolish mistakes to never repeat them. My eyes flick to the hauntingly gorgeous man in front of me. As tempting as he is, I'm not about to start doing something like that now.

Especially not when I'm on a date with another man. And there's also my plan of taking things to the next level with

David…. I still have every intention of seeing that through tonight.

"You said it yourself—I'm not the type of girl who fucks on the first date."

He sends me a wicked smile. "Ah, but this isn't a date."

Well, he has me there.

When I don't respond, he leans close, and his warm breath brushes across my cheek. "Have you ever truly surrendered yourself to a man, Lexi? Experienced the freedom of complete submission? I want show you how fucking good it feels to be bad. I want to tie you down, make you beg, then moan and scream with pleasure. I want to take you to the edge."

The words are said with such dark, hungry desire that my nipples harden painfully. I should probably be horrified that a stranger is talking to me this way, but I'm not. Not even close. My breasts feel heavy, and my core is wet, aching to be filled. I want him to fuck me hard and fast. For a split second, I'm tempted to follow him up to his suite and let him do just that.

"Hey, sexy." A woman in a tight, low-cut dress sidles up on the other side of where Ash is sitting. She runs her hand along the back of his neck, twining her elegant fingers through his dark hair.

Silky blond curls spill down her bare shoulders, past her perky, rounded breasts. Every inch of her is waxed, plucked and sculpted to perfection. She's my exact opposite in just about every way, and I suddenly feel…inadequate.

She doesn't even glance at me as she leans down and coos seductively in his ear, "I've missed you."

Wait, *what?* Who the hell is this woman?

As her fingers gently stroke his hair, it becomes apparent that she's someone he's fucked. Someone he's currently fucking, by the looks of it.

He glances up at her, and I take that as my cue to exit stage right. I'll find David myself or text him from wherever I settle. This guy can move on to greener pastures. Deadly gorgeous as the devil himself, sure, but that's not what I need tonight…or any night.

I bolt to my feet, shoving the chair back. "Thanks for the drink." I spin and make a beeline for the nearest exit.

CHAPTER 2
ALL BETS ARE OFF

"HEY! YOU'RE NOT LEAVING ALREADY, ARE YOU?"

Gwen, one of my roommates, who's also in attendance at the swanky party, has caught me by the shoulder and stopped my flight from the private reception hall of the restaurant.

I signal for Gwen to follow me to the bathroom, before throwing a worried glance back toward the table. Ash is still talking to the blonde, but he's standing and seems to be looking around, in my direction. Before he can spot me, I grab Gwen's arm and practically drag her to the ladies room.

"What's going on, girl?" Her dark eyebrows are scrunched in concern.

"This evening is a complete fail. David left half an hour ago to go fetch drinks and then got 'waylaid' by someone, and I have no idea where he is. While I was waiting for him to come back, I got hit on by a gorgeous asshole."

She laughs. "That doesn't sound like a fail to me."

I gesture to the dress as I brush lint off the skirt. "I sank way too much money into this dress just to impress David, and instead it's attracted the player to end all players."

Her brows shoot up. "*Yes, please.*"

I sigh. "But...David. If I didn't know any better, I'd think—"

"He's just not that into you?" Gwen said, nodding knowingly.

Now it was my turn to frown. "Umm, no. That's not what I was going to say."

Gwen draws back in obvious surprise. "Well…I mean. You guys have been dating off and on for months, right? Like almost six months."

"Five, but yeah. He keeps asking me out. We text from time to time. But…things stall out every two or three dates and we don't talk for weeks. He's just *so* busy and I've got school and well—"

"Maybe it's a sign that you two just aren't…clicking, you know?"

My eyebrows come down, and I glare at her. "No, I *don't* know, as a matter of fact. I have every intention of taking this relationship to the next level."

She puts a hand on my shoulder and squeezes. "Don't overthink it, Lex. It'll be fine. Maybe just go out and ask around for him? He's probably out there looking for you right now."

I nod, knowing she must be right. And when I poke my head out of the bathroom and look down the long hallway that leads to the entrance of the members-only section of Exeter House, I see the top of someone's head who *could* be David, so I venture out into the fray once more, on the hunt.

I've had enough of being sidelined, damn it.

Weaving through the crowd and trying not to jostle people's drinks or bump into anyone, I finally make my approach toward David, only to have him turn in profile just before I reach him. I see that he's definitely *not* David. Damn it. Where did he vanish to?

I make an abrupt right turn and almost crash into a couple coming around the corner. Much to my surprise, I almost collide with the couple of honor, newly engaged Madeline Swanson, my former college roommate, and her hunky man, brilliant tech billionaire Evan Kohl. Talk about a match made in heaven. The two of them are gorgeous together and obviously happy. Once again I ache with envy at what they have.

I'll have it soon, too, if I play things right. For some reason, tonight feels very critical to the turning point of my relationship with David. It's a do-or-die kinda night, and what I want us to do is a whole lot more pleasant than dying.

"Maddy! Mr. Kohl—!" I start.

"Call me Evan, please," He smiles down at me. He's fused to Maddy's side. She's wearing a gorgeous designer gown in blush pink and he's in a deep-gray suit with black tie, but a silk handkerchief in his front packet matches the exact color of her dress.

"I'm so glad I ran into you so I can give you my personal congratulations."

He'd proposed to her just a month ago, on New Year's eve. At an intimate party in their apartment with all of our friends present. Unfortunately, I'd missed it because I'd had to run out early.

I'm sure it would have made me even more envious than I am now, which is tough to imagine, honestly. But envious or not, I'm also thrilled for my friend Maddy who has never been anything but kind and open toward me ever since I met her three years ago. She's been through some tough times and deserves every bit of this happiness.

I'm just hoping a little of that engagement dust will sprinkle over my way and that David will be inclined to put a shiny diamond on my finger sometime this year.

But before we get there, we have to become an actual couple first.

And in order for me to carry out my plan to take this to the next level, I've got to *find* him!

After returning my hug and thanking me for my well wishes, Evan turns and starts talking to a friend who's passing by. I take the opportunity to ask Maddy. "Have you seen David, you know, the guy I came with?"

She frowns. "No, sorry. But Gwen and Avery are here. Maybe they've run into him. Should I text them?"

I shake my head. "No, no. Go enjoy the rest of your party! I just saw Gwen, but I'll hunt down Avery and see what she knows."

Maddy heaves a long sigh and gives me a tired smile. It's only now that I notice how exhausted she is. "I'm not sure how much more enjoying I'll be doing tonight. I'm about to turn into a pumpkin!"

"Ah." I rest a hand on her shoulder. "It's barely ten p.m. The night is young!"

She almost wilts. "I've been up since oh-dark-hundred organizing this whole thing. I'm spent."

After kissing her on the cheek and wishing her courage to face the rest of the evening, I find myself suddenly wanting out of the private rooms of the engagement party. I've scoured every one of them anyway, and David is very clearly not here. In frustration, I wonder what to do.

Did he stand me up? I check my phone for the hundredth time and still no texts from him. My last text to him asking when he was coming back, was sent over half an hour ago, and it's still there, glaringly unanswered. I'm not about to send another one.

I'm about to turn and walk out the door when, to my surprise, I'm approached by a uniformed member of the waitstaff. He's young and babyfaced in a white coat and black slacks.

"Miss Anderson?" he asks.

My eyes widening, I nod. "Yeah, that's me."

"I was told to deliver this to you."

He hands me a note on heavy cardstock with the emblem and logo of Exeter House on the top. It's been folded in half but there's no envelope, as if it's been hastily scrawled out.

I thank the man, only realizing after he turns and walks away that I forgot to tip him. I don't have any cash on me anyway.

Stepping into a nook beside the marble stairs up to the mezzanine of the building, I unfold the card with shaky hands, hoping it's from who I think it's from.

The handwriting is messy and hastily scrawled, but my heart leaps with hope.

Apologies for tonight. Let me make it up to you.
Suite 403
I'm waiting...

I refold the card and tuck it into my purse, allowing myself to acknowledge the little thrill inside, cheering like crazy. Well, this is an amazing plot twist. Just when I was about to walk out of here and call it quits with David, he's got us a room here. *And* it's clear he wants to use it. The seduction can happen as planned.

If I weren't wearing four-inch Jimmy Choos, I'd be jumping up and down and doing a little dance across the expensive carpeting in the front reception hall. But I have to play this smart. I bite my lip, thinking while I scan my surroundings under my eyelashes.

Instead of heading toward the elevators to get to room 403 as quickly as possible, I opt instead to cross the front hall toward the house bar just adjacent.

Hasn't David made me wait for hours? Sure, sending the mysterious note via waitstaff was a nice touch, but I'm inclined to make him wait for me for a change. He got a good hot look at my bod in this tight and sexy dress. Earlier, I was aiming to make him hungry and begging for it by the time we finally consummated things. If I go racing up there now, it would reek of desperation.

No. Better to let him sit and wait until I'm good and ready to go up there. Let him stew in his own lust. For a little while, at least.

Besides, I need a little liquid courage to carry out the full plan. So I plop myself down at the bar, tuck my clutch beside me. Then I purposely set my phone face down –in case he texts asking where I am. If I don't see the message come through, I won't be tempted to shoot back an answer right away.

"Scotch and soda, please," I say to the bartender when he comes my way. Minutes later, he places the drink in front of me. I scoop it up and take a sip.

Oh yes, tonight things are going to change. Big time.

Once I get up to room 403 and find David in his room quietly drinking alone...all bets will be off. Along with this very expensive dress.

CHAPTER 3
HIGH EXPECTATIONS

IT'S JUST BEFORE MIDNIGHT WHEN I SET DOWN MY THIRD empty glass of Scotch and soda, hazily pondering whether it's a buzz or something more. There's a warm glow coming from within, and I feel ready to take on the world.

It's been nearly two hours since David sent me the note via waitstaff, so now is the perfect time to set my plan into motion.

Hopefully David's *also* good and buzzed by now. I've been imagining him up in the room, nursing a few drinks while he waits for me. Hopefully, with both of us nice and buzzed, it won't take long before we find our way to the bed…

I pay my tab, slip off my barstool and pull the note out from my purse to double-check the suite number. Then, on less than steady heels, I make my way across the polished marble floors toward the bank of elevators. The bottom floors of Exeter House are open to the public, but only members and aspiring members are permitted to take rooms here. With a thrill, I press the button for the fourth floor, excited not only for the inevitable hookup but also that it will be taking place *here*. David has outdone even my high expectations.

The elevator car is elegant, with shiny gold and mirrored finishes. I straighten my attire in the polished reflection, ignoring the fact that my heart feels like it's about to erupt out of my chest. I take out my lipstick and have just enough time to apply it in the door's reflection before it slides open, revealing the sleek black marble and white carpeted hall of the fourth floor.

The hallway is empty and my shoes are muffled on the carpet as I quietly make my way to suite 403. But when I lift my hand to knock, I notice that the door is ajar, opened to just a crack. I smile at the thought of him patiently waiting for me, listening for my footsteps. I'm praying that means his frustration has grown to a fever pitch.

I'll soon find out.

But when I push the door open, the room beyond is cloaked in near darkness. There's a small lamp in the corner of the sitting area, casting the room in a pale amber glow—just enough light to see by. As I cross the room, I note the nearly empty bottle of vodka and a single empty tumbler beside it, which is a little strange. I've never seen David drink vodka. He once said he hated it, but maybe he needed a little extra courage tonight?

Beyond the sitting area is the bedroom. I peer into the darkened doorway, and in the shadows, I make out a figure lying in the massive bed. It's so quiet, I can hear the slow, steady rhythm of his breathing.

Looks like David had a little too much to drink and fell asleep while waiting for me. Hopefully, he hadn't had *too* much to drink. I want him to remember this in the morning.

I lick my lips, quickly formulating a new plan.

I've come too far to let some alcohol and a catnap stop David and me from *finally* consummating our relationship. I'll just alter how we'd segue into it. What I have in mind is *definitely* not something a nice girl would do, but it's for the greater good, and sometimes, the good girl has to step aside and let the bad girl take over.

I kick off my heels next to the coffee table and set my purse on the nearby armchair, then slowly approach the bedroom. Inside, it's completely dark, the only sliver of light coming through the open bedroom door. I can hardly see, but I stare at his outline on the bed for a minute, a knot of foreboding in my stomach. I'll know soon enough whether or not he's on board with this.

Why wouldn't he be, though? Isn't that why he took the room for tonight and sent me the invite in the first place? Likely he'll appreciate my forwardness. There's a chance that he's had too much to drink, but I'm not expecting mind-blowing orgasms from this. That isn't the goal. There's a slim chance this wasn't what he had in mind at all, though. He might even push me away...

But, thankfully, the odds are in my favor.

Sucking in a fortifying breath, I shove the doubts aside and unzip my dress. This is our chance to take things to the next level, to make things official between us.

I slither out of my pricey black dress, then shed my lacy bra and panties. I bought them specifically for tonight's seduction, because he once told me he loves lace panties, and I knew they'd make him drool. Too bad he isn't awake to enjoy the show.

Eye on the prize.

As I slide under the covers, the warmth of his body beckons me. He's lying on his side, facing away from me, so I move in to spoon him. Then I reach over to trail my hand across his hard, muscular torso. *Whoa...*I had no idea that David was this well built. I'd never even seen him with his shirt off. He's far more toned than I'd imagined.

In fact, this close and in the dark, his shoulders seem broader, too. My hand roams across his flat stomach, relishing the feel of his hard six-pack and the creases under his hips. *Mmmm.* It's sexy as hell, and I moan in approval. Where our skin is touching, the heat of our bodies fuses us together, and the tingle of arousal seethes in my core.

God damn. A good girl does *not* do naughty things like strip off her clothes and slide into bed with a guy she's never been with before. But if all goes well tonight, then the ends will definitely justify the means.

And, honestly, if I'd known he was this yummy underneath his clothes, I'd have jumped his bones weeks ago.

Sliding my hand lower, I find that he's also shed all his clothes, too—most likely hoping I'd do exactly what I'm doing. My hand brushes lower and…he's already hard. I take his thick cock into my palm and whisper in his ear, "Wake up, sleepyhead."

He's awake in seconds. With a low, predatory growl that sounds nothing like his normal voice, he flips around and ducks his head to fasten his mouth on my already-erect nipple. My entire body comes alive in fire and steam as he suckles me hard. Letting out a long breathless moan, I throw my head back and thread my fingers through his hair.

Oh God, this is turning out to be a whole lot hotter than I thought it would be.

I'd been hungry for a hot fuck, hadn't I? And that's just what I'm about to get. His mouth travels down across my belly and settles on my sex as he spreads me open.

Holy shit. Thank God for that whiskey. I'd never be brave enough to let him do this to me in real life. Well, maybe I would, but I'd be a lot more bashful about it. Now, I just want him to devour me, and I couldn't care less how slutty it makes me look.

Soon his mouth is settled over my clit and I'm gasping as his mouth does the same thing to me there, licking, teasing, pushing inside me. When he sucks gently, I nearly shoot off the bed, but his strong hands reach out to grab my hips, holding me down, keeping me pinned to the mattress.

"Holy shit," I hiss, practically coming out of my skin.

He groans against my hot center, and the vibration nearly sends me over the edge. Reaching out, I thread my fingers through his hair, tugging as he sucks gently on my clit.

Oh damn…who knew he'd be this talented with his tongue?

"Oh God," I moan as the heated pleasure and tension spreads across my belly, down my legs to encompass my entire body. I'm gasping for breath and moaning with ecstasy as an intense wave of heat slams into me. It hits me so hard I actually scream out.

But before I can even catch my breath, his large hands encircle my waist, and he roughly flips me onto my stomach, like he can't wait another second to fuck me. With a hungry growl, he presses his erection between the globes of my ass.

Wow. Who knew it would be so easy—and so fucking hot—to seal the commitment deal?

My heart races as he nudges my thighs apart with his knee, and places the tip of his cock against my entrance. I'm panting so hard, and so fast, that I can barely catch my breath.

His lips and teeth are on the back of my neck, his fingers threading through my hair, tugging my head back so he can kiss me roughly.

Holy fuck, his mouth feels so good on mine. David isn't usually this way—so powerful and assertive—and surprisingly, it feeds something inside me. Something hungry and desperate. I'm completely at his mercy, and it's so fucking hot I wonder if I'll ever get enough.

When he breaks the kiss, my body instinctively tightens, bracing for what comes next. His cock is pressed against my wet entrance, and I have the sudden, inescapable feeling that after this, there's no turning back…

CHAPTER 4
POINT OF NO RETURN

I ARCH MY BACK AND SHIFT MY HIPS A LITTLE, TRYING TO GET him to hurry the fuck up. I *need* him inside me like I need my next gulp of air.

"Please," I say on a breath. "Please."

He knows what I'm asking for. He knows what I want. Still positioned at my entrance, he slowly pushes inside me. Oh, fuck, yes. He feels *glorious*, his cock stretching me to capacity. He's balls deep when he stops, pausing briefly to allow my body to accommodate him.

The pain-pleasure combo is fucking amazing, and when he begins to rock his hips, my body immediately comes alive beneath him. His cock glides in and out so fast, and so hard, it leaves me breathless.

He's not gentle. Thank God. I don't want gentle now. I need it hard and fast, just like he's giving it to me. I want a *savage* fucking. And it appears he's more than happy to deliver.

Dipping his head, he moves to kiss the back of my neck, but instead sinks his teeth into my nape with a low, guttural growl. Then he threads his long fingers through my hair, takes a handful and tugs my head back.

He's in control, and he wants me to know it.

With my legs spread and my head back, he begins to move again. Roughly. Unapologetically. And I fucking *love* it. He quickly finds his rhythm, pounding into me with long, harsh strokes. His cock is huge, stretching me to my limits and I moan, relishing the feeling of tightness and pressure where we are joined. I can hear his breathing intensify as he continues to fuck me, his grip on my hair getting tighter, almost painful.

Finally, he releases my hair and reaches beneath me to stroke my clit. I'm practically launched into the stratosphere. The intense pleasure of him fucking me from behind and rubbing my clit is almost too much to bear. I'm pinned down, so I can only move my hips a little. That's the true torment. I'm completely at his mercy, unable to hurry my orgasm along, even if I wanted to.

But in just a few seconds, that familiar pressure begins building in my veins, centering on my hot core. It's too much. My head thrashes from side to side and my hands fist the sheets. His head dips so he can speak directly in my ear, "That's it, kitten. Come for me. I want to feel you come on my cock."

In my haze of ecstasy, it takes a half-second to register, and then I realize the voice growling in my ear is deep, seductive...*accented*—and most definitely *not* David's.

But it's too late, my body is already careening toward the edge, ready to plunge into the abyss. I can't think. I can't cry out. All I can do is *feel* the intense orgasm as it slams into me. Hot waves of pleasure course through my veins, spreading throughout my entire body, making me gasp. My whole body contracts, gripping his cock as he moans his approval. Lightning and heat zing through me on a wave of euphoria. I've never felt this good, and it's all I can do not to scream.

With one last, powerful thrust, he stiffens and pours himself into me. It feels so fucking good, and…*right.* I'm momentarily transported outside my body. It's unreal. I've never felt anything like this in my entire life.

As soon as I reenter my body and that amazing orgasm begins to fade, I remember that I'm pinned beneath a complete stranger. I have no idea whose cock is still inside me.

With a cold rush of fear, I scramble out from under *whoever this is*, searching blindly for the lamp on the nightstand. When I find the switch and turn it on, the room floods with bright white light. The second I turn back toward the man who just fucked me, I feel faint.

A pair of dark, fathomless eyes stare back at me.

"Ash," I breathe in shock as I pull a corner of the comforter up to cover my body. It's the hot British guy who hit on me at the bar earlier in the evening—the *gorgeous asshole*, as I'd described him to Gwen.

I stiffen in shock. "What the fuck are you doing here?"

His mouth curves up in an elegant smile. He's not even fazed by my question. "This is my room," he replies evenly.

I shake my head as I pull the comforter up even higher. "*No.* This is David's room. He sent me a note." Was it possible I'd read the wrong room number? "This is suite 403, right?"

Ash's lips twist up into a handsome grin. "Your boyfriend didn't send you that note. *I* did."

"*What?*" I blink at him, a rush of anger flooding me. "You used David's name to lure me here?" No, that can't be right. I have a hard time believing someone could be so outright manipulative.

He has the decency to look appalled by my accusation. "The note was from *me*. There was no name signed. Mine or David's."

He spits out the name like a curse that leaves a bad taste in his mouth.

I shake my head and glance around for my purse, before remembering I left it in the other room. "Grab my clutch. It's in the armchair in the sitting room."

With an annoyed growl, he stands, unfurling his full six-foot-something frame, and moves toward the door. He's magnificent, his chiseled backside on full display, and I can't help but look. His body is perfect, like the statue of a Greek god prefect. *Damn.*

My thoughts skid to a halt. *What the hell is wrong with me?* What just happened was the worst mistake of my life. I shouldn't be looking at him like this. Good girls don't fuck complete strangers in the dark.

Seconds later, he re-enters the room, and I quickly glance away. He sits on the bed and tosses my clutch at me. I open it and pull out the note, my heart racing—hoping I'm the one whose right and he's wrong. But as I read it, my heart sinks and nausea roils in my belly. I'm going to throw up.

Apologies for tonight. Let me make it up to you.
Suite 403
I'm waiting...

He's right. David's name isn't mentioned. That had only been my stupid assumption. Perhaps because I was hopeful I wasn't being truly ghosted by my date.

"*Omigod.*" How in God's name am I going to explain this to David? I'm such an idiot. "Fuck. I have to go."

I move to climb off the bed, but he leans over and places one hand against the headboard, just above my head, trapping me. The scent of him surrounds me, and despite my rising panic, I actually suck in a lungful of air. He smells so good—just a hint of cologne and something musky. Sweat maybe. Whatever it is, it's making my head swim and my body come alive all over again.

"You're not going anywhere until you promise me you'll meet me for dinner tonight," he says.

I'm a little taken back by his demanding tone. All my defenses are suddenly up. "I told you, this was a mistake. I thought this was David's room. That *you* were..." My words trail off as a thought comes to mind. "Why didn't you include your name on the note? You knew I was waiting for someone. Was it your plan to trick me?"

He leans back, a muscle in his jaw twitching. He says nothing. Of course he doesn't. If anyone needs to explain, it's me. I'm the one who accepted his invitation—which, for all he knew, was to come up and share a drink in his suite before giving up and going to bed after I'd made him wait for hours. I was the one who slipped into his bed naked and grabbed his cock. There's no possible way he could have known that I assumed he was David.

I shake my head. "I'm sorry, I shouldn't have accused you. I'm just freaked out."

I'm still trying to absorb everything that's happened.

He leans forward to lift my chin. Our gazes collide, and for a second, my breath catches in my throat. There's something about this man that causes every rational thought to flee my brain.

"Maybe it was fate. Maybe we were meant to meet here, in the dark. You won't deny that what just happened was searing hot. I won't deny it either." His voice is rough, growly. "And I want *more*. I want to take you to the edge, Lexi. To show you the pleasure of surrendering to your darkest fantasies."

Oh, *Jesus*. The way his dark eyes drill into mine when he says those last two words makes my channel pulse instantly with need. Like I didn't just ten minutes ago have the most intense orgasm of my life. But I can't go to that place he's describing. Not with him. Not with *anyone*. I need stable, dependable. Predictable.

Surrendering to dark fantasies is my mother's territory.

Then I remember the woman from earlier, the woman who approached us and couldn't keep her hands off Ash. "And what would your *girlfriend* say about that?"

He lifts an elegant brow in question.

"The woman who came to the table where we were sitting…" I clarify. "The blond who couldn't keep her hands off you…"

"Rebekah." He rubs a hand over his face. "She isn't my girlfriend."

"Really?" I say. "Maybe you should tell *her* that."

He laughs and shakes his head. "I don't have girlfriends, Lexi. I'm not that kind of man and she knows that."

It's on the tip of my tongue to ask him what kind of man he is, but I can't seem to get the words out. Maybe I'm afraid of what he'll say. It really doesn't matter anyway. This was all a mistake— a horrible, erotic, mind-blowing mistake. On my part, at least.

He dips his head, his mouth hovering dangerously close to mine. I can feel the heat of his breath on my mouth, and I'm tempted to take his plump bottom lip between my teeth. Inexplicably, I want to make him bleed, leave my mark. I want to taste his blood on my tongue.

I blink, shocked at my own thought—that I would imagine doing something so...dark and twisted. This isn't me at all. I'm getting my graduate degree in Computer Science, for God's sake. I'm smart, well-adjusted. *Rational.*

I don't sleep with strangers, and I certainly don't fantasize about biting them. What is this guy doing to me?

"I have to go," I manage to say.

He doesn't move. "No, you don't. You can stay right here with me."

Before I can argue, he dips his head and captures my lips in a hot kiss. His tongue boldly sweeps into my mouth as his free hand slips around my waist. I don't even try to pull away. I'm drunk with the taste of him. This is all I want right now—his mouth devouring me, his hands on my body. I don't care how wrong or stupid or reckless it is.

I press my hands to his chest, needing to touch him. He's all honed muscle, and I skim my hands over his hard body, soaking in the feel of him. He's so beautiful, so rough and so unlike the guys I usually date.

His lips never leave mine as he shifts his body so he's on top of me, positioned between my open thighs. I thread my fingers through his hair, pulling the dark strands roughly as I rock my hips, grinding against his cock. Even with the sheet and comforter still between us, the friction is amazing. I can't get enough.

The loud ring of a cell phone fills the room, and I freeze.

I glance down at myself, entangled with this stranger. *What the hell am I doing?*

I scramble out from under Ash and grab my clutch, pulling out my phone.

It's David. The *real* David.

Shit. Tossing my phone down, I rush around to pull my panties and dress on, leaving it mostly unzipped in the back. I grab my heels, my clutch and bolt for the door.

Ash is off the bed in seconds. In two long strides, he meets me at the door, grabbing my wrist just as I reach out for the handle. I suck in a breath as he pushes me up against the wall, pinning one hand above my head, smoothing his free hand around my waist as he presses his naked lower half against me, fixing me in place.

"Are you running away, Lexi?" he asks.

Licking my bottom lip, I blink up at him. *Am* I running away? Maybe I am. But I don't know what to think, what to feel. This is just all too much to take in. I need some time to process everything that's happened. My heart is hammering, and I can barely catch enough breath to speak.

"I just…I need to go."

He brushes his thumb across the line of my jaw. "You can't escape this, Lexi. You can't run from what this is between us. I won't let you."

I shake my head, but deep down, I know what he's saying is true. It doesn't matter. I can't allow myself to give in to the temptation that is the very sexy Ash. He's far too dangerous for someone like me.

"I have to go," I repeat.

He leans in, the gaze in his dark eyes intensifying. "This isn't over," he growls. Then, he nips at my bottom lip and pulls away, opening the door to let me out. "Until we meet again, Miss Anderson. I'll leave a candle burning in the window for you."

I stumble into the hallway and blink, dazed, and so fucking confused. My mind is racing about what to do and I think of my friend, Maddy. I was just at her engagement party, and I know she must be back at her place by now. I need a friend. I need *someone*. Gods...I scramble down the hall, thoughts jumbling against each other in a perfect recipe for an anxiety attack.

It isn't until I make my way to the elevator that it occurs to me—I never gave him my last name.

CHAPTER 5
BACK FOR MORE

GWEN TAPS HER CHIN THOUGHTFULLY. "MAYBE YOU mumbled it under your breath or something."

I think back through my conversation with Ash at the bar, then later in the suite and shake my head. "I'm positive I never mentioned my last name."

God, this is so fucked up. Thank heavens for Maddy, though. Last night, I had rushed up to her room in tears, and she'd talked me down off the emotional ledge. We talked well into the morning, until we were both so tired she finally called me an Uber.

When I came stumbling into Hill House, Gwen was still awake, watching a Cary Grant movie on TV, and I'd immediately told her everything. The whole sordid tale.

I, a brilliant Caltech graduate student in Computer Science, had mistakenly walked into a hotel suite and fucked the wrong guy—a stranger, in fact. And it had been by far the hottest encounter of my short twenty-three years.

Gwen leans back on the couch and takes another bite of the cheese pizza she'd ordered from the all-night delivery place near the campus. It's nearly three in the morning. "Well, someone must have told him," she says, chewing slowly. "Why don't you just…ask him?"

I shake my head as I pick up the last piece of cold pizza. "Yeah, *no*. I'm not that curious. I'm not going to see him again."

Except that I actually *am* curious.

Gwen frowns. "But why? The guy gives you the best orgasm of your life and you're just going to walk away? That's...tragic."

I widen my eyes in disbelief. "Oh my *God*, Gwen! He's a complete stranger." I toss a throw pillow at her, which she dodges with a laugh. "You know me better than that. I'm classy. I don't do this type of thing on purpose."

She shrugs. "So. Who cares? What's wrong with an anonymous hookup? It'll be good for you. Well, it obviously already *was* good for you. But more of the same? Even better."

I blink at her. Is she serious?

"Sex with a complete stranger is *good* for me?" I repeat, disbelieving.

She shrugs. "Sure, why not? Seriously, Lexi, you're twenty-three. Live a little. It's better than waiting around for the dude who barely pays any attention to you and doesn't treat you like you deserve. I mean...where was David all night?"

Just then, Sam emerges from her bedroom in her cutesy pink pajamas, curly blond hair tied up in space buns. She's rubbing sleep from her eyes.

"What are you two doing still up?" she asks.

Gwen chews her last bite of pizza and swallows. "Discussing the merits of hot anonymous sex. What's your opinion?"

"Yum. I'd say yes to rough, no-holds-barred, stranger sex," she says on her way to the kitchen to fill up a glass of water. "Is this just random talk or is someone actually contemplating it?"

I stiffen. "I'm not having stranger sex and that's the end of it."

"You mean you aren't having *more* stranger sex after having the hottest sex of your life…with a stranger," Gwen corrects, throwing her crust down into the empty pizza box.

Suddenly Sam is wide awake and settling in on the couch, sipping at her glass of water while Gwen fills her in, and I correct the mistakes as she recounts my shameful tale of woe.

"That's…incredible, Lexi. What are you going to do now? Go back to David?" She scrunches her nose, like the suggestion has left a foul taste in her mouth.

I blink. "We never broke up!"

She frowns as if confused. It does sound horrible, I know. "I was under the impression that the two of you weren't really that serious yet. Are you two exclusive?"

I swallow, ashamed to tell her that I have no idea. I hadn't even gotten far enough to ask David if he was seeing me exclusively.

"So…are you going to call David back?" Sam asks.

I blow out a breath. "I'll call him tomorrow. I'm sure he had a perfectly reasonable explanation for disappearing last night."

"Yeah, the explanation is that David is a bastard." Gwen smiles brightly. "I hope he chokes on his own vomit for having the nerve to ghost my girl at an engagement party. Who does that shit?"

"Great," I say, getting up. I toss her my uneaten slice of pizza. I'm not hungry, anyway. "I'll give him your love when I talk to him."

"Please *don't*," she mutters.

***

"*Shit.* It has to be around here somewhere..."

The following morning after the engagement party, I'm dumping out the contents of my clutch onto the bed and sifting through them when Gwen walks into my room, sleep-drenched and irritable.

"If you're going to freak out, can you please be quiet about it? It's eight in the morning and you've been tearing the room apart for the last twenty minutes. People are trying to sleep."

I whirl around to face her, panic clawing at my throat. "I can't find my cell phone and I double-checked at the bar. I keep hoping it's here somehow."

"Didn't you have it with you when you came home last night?"

"No. Actually when I wanted to run and go see Maddy and tell her what happened, I'd tried to call her first and couldn't find the phone. I checked at the bar and it wasn't there. I left my name and contact info at the reception desk just in case it turns up. But I was thinking I probably left it in my purse, or my jacket or something. I was pretty tipsy last night."

"Well...where were you when you last used it?"

I take a deep breath, thoughts racing. In the haze of wishing everything that had gone down last night had been a bad dream, I'd blocked a lot of the details from my mind.

Then I remembered Ash on top of me after that first time, him kissing me, and I'm melting underneath him and thinking this will likely lead to a second round...

The phone rang then. A call from David and in my panic, I'd thrown it down on the bed, grabbed my clothes off the floor, dressed in thirty seconds flat, scooped up my clutch and ran for the door.

In my blind panic, I must have left my phone on the bed.

My stomach sinks, and I can barely form a swallow. "I think I left it in the hotel room last night."

Gwen perks up. "With the sexy stranger?"

"*Yes!*" I squeak, throwing my hands in the air like a lunatic. "What the hell am I going to do?"

With a smile, Gwen shrugs. "Well, looks like you're going to see Mr. Sexy again after all."

My mind scrambles for a solution. "What if I tell my provider my phone was stolen? I can just get a new one, right?"

Gwen snorts. "Isn't your phone only a few months old? That will cost you some big bucks."

I bite my lip, thinking. The cost might even be worth it…but I did just spend five hundred bucks on this one…

"Besides that…there's the security risk. With a little know-how and a wad of cash, a phone can be hacked into. All your text messages, photos, contacts. Do you want to leave those in this guy's hands?"

I cover my eyes and groan. "I'm such an idiot."

She frowns, crossing her arms across her chest and leans against the door jamb. "I thought you liked this guy. So you see him again…. What's the big deal?"

I rub my forehead, suddenly feeling flush with the memory of him on top of me, the way it made me feel…. "You don't get it. This guy is…" I gesture with my hands to find the right word. "*Intense.*" That's putting it lightly, to be honest. With just a look, he made me melt. The minute he touched me…well, it was game over. "If I see him again, he's going to fuck me. No question."

And worse, I'll be begging him to do it.

Gwen's enthusiastic smile and nod do not reassure me in the least.

I'm so screwed. *Literally.*

***

I'm standing at the front desk at Exeter House. The same front desk that I stood at last night when I left my info for the lost phone. Only this time, I'm asking them to contact the man in suite 403 and bring my phone down to the lobby.

That's my plan. Meet him in public, get the phone and walk away. It's the only safe way.

"I'm sorry, there is currently no occupant in suite 403."

"That's where I left my phone last night—I mean, early this morning. Did the cleaning crew find it, by any chance?"

The woman checks her computer for a moment and then looks up. "I do see a note here. One of our founding partners, Mr. Ash Grayson, sent down a message that he has the phone. I can have one of our bellhops escort you to his private suite to get the phone from him *personally.*" She says this last part with a breathless sort of giddy grin that lets me know what an incredible and rare privilege I've been afforded.

But alarm bells and alerts have gone off all over my brain. *Do not engage target on his home turf. Do not engage!*

"I'd, um, rather the phone be sent down to me. But...since I know he's such a busy and important man, maybe a messenger can bring it down?"

She gives me a skeptical look, but my hopes soar when she picks up the phone to call this very important *founding partner.* In those few moments, I've figured out that he must have highly elite status here. Waiters brought him drinks at the virtual snap of his fingers last night, and he'd gotten that suite in the public section of the hotel.

I guess if he was close enough friends with Evan Kohl and also a partner here, did that make him also a fellow billionaire? *Note to self: Google Ash Grayson as soon as I have my phone back.*

After a short conversation that I'm hardly paying attention to, the receptionist turns back to me and with a bright smile. "I just spoke with Mr. Grayson himself, and he's very insistent that you get the phone directly from him. He wants to make sure he puts it safely in your hands. He's *such* a kind man."

Kind, right. I blink. "Can't he just bring it down to me, then?"

She says nothing, but behind that wide smile, her eyes harden. It's like I can read her mind. *She's turning down the chance to see a billionaire's penthouse?*

Except I'm mentally revising that supposed thought I'm reading, adding such adjectives as *sinfully tempting, devilishly seductive* and *irresistibly alluring.*

"The bellhop will see you up. It's just a short elevator ride to the top floor. Won't take you more than five minutes." The frostiness of her glare is unmistakable as she turns and asks a nearby bellhop to do just that without even waiting for my response.

Well, okay...so what harm will it be if I have someone with me while I get the phone? Safety in numbers and all that. The bellhop can be my shield against temptation. That's it. He'll be my protector, my knight in shining armor—and he won't even know it.

Following the bellhop toward the bank of elevators, I steel myself for what's to come. I'll be in and out like a flash. Knock on the door, grab the phone, smile and a quick thank you, and then off again as fast as I can. Less than three minutes, tops.

I just pray he answers the door fully-clothed. If he isn't, there's no telling what I might do. Or what I might let *him* do to *me*.

Just as we get to the bank of elevators, one of them opens with a loud *ding.* The doors open, and a man steps out, almost colliding with me.

"Oh, sorry," I murmur, stepping past him.

But suddenly he reaches out and takes my arm. "*Lexi?*"

I glance up at the man and instantly do a double-take, eyes widening. Neat blond hair in a slicked-back hairstyle, pale blue eyes. Good-looking features, pale-gray designer suit. It's David.

Suddenly, I screech to a halt, the bellhop forgotten.

"*David,*" I breathe, stepping back in shock. "I was just...here to...see if you were around..."

He bends down and kisses me warmly on the cheek. A hand glides down my back before settling on my waist. When he pulls back, it's easy to read the concern in his eyes. "I am so sorry about last night. You'd never believe what happened. I've been trying to call and text you since early this morning but no answer. You have every right to be upset but...are you okay? I was honestly getting worried."

My chest feels tight, though I can't tell if it's from guilt for my searing hookup with Ash or because David vanished from the party, leaving me alone. On the other hand, had he not ditched me last night, I would never have ended up in a stranger's bed.

My face heats. Yeah, I'm annoyed with David but shame is winning out—probably because I enjoyed that accidental hookup way more than I should have. Even after discovering Ash wasn't

David, I'd stayed. I allowed pleasure to overwhelm me, blotting out all thoughts of David.

I flash him a tight smile. "Yeah, sorry, I misplaced my phone, but it ran out of battery long before that."

He just nods, accepting the lie at face value. I'm eager to change the subject before he asks questions. I smile. "So, um, you stayed here last night?"

"Yeah, it's wild. I was doing a little networking, you know, schmoozing with some of the partners to help ease my membership interest along. Got invited to go have some Scotch in the cigar lounge they have here. It got late and one of them reserved me a room for the night. I called to see if you were still around. I wanted you to come up and hang out, but, ah, I guess it was too late for you. You'd probably gone home to bed by that point."

I gulped, avoiding his gaze. I'd gone to bed alright. The *wrong* bed.

"Wow, that must have been something." I avoid his gaze. "You stayed in one of the suites here? You must be making some pretty valuable connections."

He flashes me that charming, all-American smile. "Clearly my charm is getting me somewhere. I'm hopeful." His grin widens.

He steps closer, his blue eyes focusing intently on me. "So…assuming I can keep the room for another night, do you think you'd like to, ah, hang out with me tonight? I'd love to take you on a special date. Make last night up to you. Then we could come back to the room and, you know, just hang out."

There's a heavier meaning to his words. Clearly he wants us to spend the night together. I lick my lips, surprised that the realization doesn't make me more excited after all my planning and maneuvering to get us into bed together last night.

I plaster on a fake smile and nod speedily like an insane woman. I'm completely at a loss for how to respond.

Less than twelve hours ago, I was upstairs in bed underneath another man, delirious with pleasure as he pushed himself into me and brought me to the best orgasm of my life. Since then, all I've thought about is Ash—his hands on my body, his tongue stroking me to climax.

But David…I had such great plans and we have a future that could last longer than a hot physical affair. David could be the one. The one who puts the diamond on my finger and buys us our dream house.

We're easy together. Our life could be amazing. Uncomplicated. That's been my goal from the start.

"I'm on my way to a meeting," he persists. "Meet me tonight?"

"Um, here?" I glance up at him. "What time?"

"How about nine? We can have dinner at Isca."

I swallow and force more enthusiasm than I really feel by nodding like a crazy woman. "Sure. That sounds great."

"Perfect." He places a quick kiss on my forehead. "See you tonight."

I watch him walk toward the main lobby and disappear before I turn back to the bellhop who has been patiently waiting for us to wrap it up so he can carry out his errand. Stepping in beside him, I suck in a shaky breath as the elevator lurches upward, shooting us to the very top floor of the towering Exeter House.

"Mr. Grayson is on the top floor, south wing. If you'll follow me…" He leads me from the open elevator and turns left down a short hallway all of glass. There are chairs and lounges arranged to take in the stunning view of the shimmering Pacific Ocean below. Off to the left, I can see the roller coaster and Ferris wheel at the Santa Monica Pier. The primest of the prime real estate in all of Los Angeles on one of the most famous beaches in the world…Malibu. My jaw drops. This place is amazing.

My escort halts at a darkly polished set of wooden double doors and knocks. Nervously, I smooth my hands down my pale turquoise skirt and take a deep breath.

A stern mantra is running through my head…

Go in. Grab the phone. Leave. Do not, under any circumstances, have sex with him.

Suddenly, the door opens. My heart lurches when I see the darkly handsome form framed in the doorway, shirtless with gray pajama bottoms hanging low on his lean hips.

Ash.

My eyes rake down his tanned, chiseled body, and I feel my resolve slowly start to slip away. Ash turns and nods to the bellhop, handing him something with a brief thanks… And just like that, my supposed stalwart knight in shining armor fades into the background, deserting me without a word.

I'm frozen in place, unable to take my eyes off this perfection in male form. Ash has abs for days and that V-shaped muscle that curves below his hips and dips into his pajama bottoms. His skin is lightly tanned and dusted with dark hair. My eyes glide down that happy trail from his navel to his low-slung waistline. He's utterly drool-worthy, and my pulse shoots into overdrive.

He props one arm above his head against the door frame as he leans into it, and my eyes are suddenly caught by something I never noticed before. On the inside of his forearm is the tattoo of a skeleton key over perfectly formed muscle and sinew.

Gulp.

I'm biting my lip so hard it's bound to start bleeding at any moment.

As soon as the bellhop is out of earshot, Ash turns to me, eyes sliding down my body appreciatively while a sexy smile plays about his mouth.

"Hello, Princess. Back for more?"

CHAPTER 6
SURRENDER TO FEEL FREE

Y HEART FEELS LIKE IT'S GOING TO LEAP OUT OF MY body.

"You have my phone," I blurt out in a rush.

With one hand resting on the door frame, he flashes a smile and opens the door wider, inviting me in without stepping aside. I duck under his arm and enter the room. With folded arms across my chest, I pivot back to him.

"Keep that door open. I won't be staying."

Without hesitating even a second, Ash turns and firmly closes the front door behind him. He doesn't even have the decency to look defiant when he does it.

"I like my privacy," he says in that sexy-as-fuck baritone.

I swallow. *Do not have sex with him. Do not have sex with him.*

I flash him a tight smile. "My phone?"

He leans over and grabs it off a nearby side table, then holds it out to me. I swipe it out of his hand and glance down at the screen with a sigh of relief. Several texts from David light up the screen, and the battery is at one bar, almost dead. Of course.

I slip it into my purse, then glance up at him. "Thanks," I say awkwardly, stepping forward to leave. I'm not taking a moment to look around. What I've glimpsed already is gorgeous, opulent.

I'm not taking a tour or the scenic route, and I'm sure as hell not going near his bedroom.

Do not pass go. Do not collect $200. I am out of here.

He points to an open door, and I follow his gaze. From here I can see it's a bedroom. "Go in there and get on the bed," he says.

I draw back, blinking up at him, certain I've heard him wrong. "Um, what?"

He doesn't move a muscle, not even to blink. "Get on that bed." He's dead serious.

"I, um…" I clear my throat. My heart is beating hard beneath my ribs, at the top of my throat. "I just came here for my phone."

He shakes his head and looks down at his feet, laughing to himself. Then, he glances back up at me, and I swear to God, his dark soulful eyes pierce right through me—stripping me bare. "No, you didn't."

I swallow again. "Of course, I did."

Pushing off the wall, he advances on me. "You can lie to yourself, Lexi. But don't ever lie to *me*. There must always be honesty between us."

I shift from one foot to the other, suddenly nervous, a rabbit cornered by a fox. "I'm not sure what you mean."

He's standing right in front of me now, and all I can think about is reaching out and tracing my fingers across the ropes of muscle lining his stomach. His skin would be hot, like mine is now.

Reaching out, he takes my purse from my shoulder and tosses it onto a nearby armchair. Then, he brushes his finger along the low neckline of my dress.

"You came here because somewhere deep down, you realize I'm the only one who can give you what you need," he says.

My nipples tighten, and my breasts suddenly feel heavy, sensitive. I suck in a breath. "And…um, what's that?"

His eyes return to mine, pinning them down. "You need to be dominated, cherished." His finger dips into my bodice and brushes against my tight nipple. That one touch burns me with a searing heat. His voice is low, hoarse. Seductive. "You need to be *worshiped*."

I can hardly catch my breath, entranced by his rough, erotic timbre. I want everything he just described—as long as it involves his cock buried deep inside me. After last night, my entire body feels like a live wire, humming with electricity. Never before have I felt so on edge. So turned on. Everything inside me tightens. My body is begging for release.

Briefly, my mind wanders to David. I shouldn't be here. I shouldn't allow Ash to touch me like this, but I can't stop him. I won't stop him. Like a junkie, I crave his touch, the feel of his skin gliding against mine. I don't think I'll ever get enough.

The shrill ring of a telephone fills the room, cutting through the silence. Ash doesn't move. His finger continues to stroke my nipple, sending little waves of pleasure crashing through me.

My eyes flutter closed, savoring the erotic sensation. Everything inside me heats.

"Shouldn't you, um, answer that?" I ask breathlessly.

He shakes his head, and his finger never stops moving against my nipple. "Whatever it is can wait. My full attention is…elsewhere."

Suddenly, my thoughts are cast back to the woman from last night—Rebekah. Is that her on the other end of the phone, I wonder? It was painfully clear just how much she wanted him. Is she calling now, hoping to set up a booty call?

The phone abruptly stops ringing.

I shake my head. "You can have any woman you want. Why me?"

He smiles. That half-smile that makes my core pulse and my knees go weak. "I don't think you quite understand the power you hold over men, Lexi."

I nearly snort at that. Is he serious? "I have no power over men." If I did, David and I would have been sleeping together from the start and happily engaged by now.

In all of my twenty-three years, I've had two boyfriends. Only one of which I'd ever had sex with. I'd hardly call that having a powerful hold over men. In fact, they tend to ignore me—especially if Gwen is anywhere in the vicinity.

"That's where you're wrong." He pinches my nipple, and the sharp sting makes me gasp. "See, there. Just that small, breathless sound could bring a man to his knees." His fingers move to my mouth. "And these lips…" He sucks in a breath. "These lips could haunt a man's dreams."

"You're delusional."

"Actually," he says quietly, his gaze resting on my lips. "I've never been more clear-headed in my life."

There's a heaviness in his voice that makes me wonder if he's talking about something else completely. It's on the tip of my tongue to ask him what it is when his hand falls away from my mouth, the moment is gone.

I shake my head. I'm so fucking confused by all this—me and Ash. "Just tell me something," I say. "What do you want from me? I mean, *really*."

"Everything, Princess. I want everything you have to give."

"Oh, is *that* all?" I quip. "And after giving you *everything*, what would you give me in return?"

"The freedom of complete surrender," he responds.

My lips suddenly feel dry. I push my tongue out to moisten my mouth. "I don't need to surrender to feel free."

He looks into my eyes, and I see my own desire reflected back at me. He flicks his chin in my direction. "Take off your dress." His words are soft, powerful. *Commanding.*

Indecision wars within me. If I'm going to leave, this is the moment. And yet, I'm rooted to the spot, unable to move. Something in me wants to stay. There's a strong, undeniable compulsion within me to obey this man. How does he do that to me?

The gaze in his dark eyes intensifies, zeroing in on me. "I said, *take off your dress,*" he repeats with more force behind the words.

Only another moment passes before I reach behind my back and slowly pull down the zipper of my dress. The pale-turquoise fabric pools at my feet, and I step out of it. Cold air bushes over my heated skin, making me feel vulnerable and exposed. I shiver.

His gaze rakes over me greedily. "Now your bra and your panties."

I swallow and do as I'm told, stepping out of my heels, I fling my black bra and lace panties aside. As I stand there, naked in front of him, all I want to do is grab a blanket to shield myself from his hungry gaze. Instead, I lift my chin and look him straight in the eye, trying to convey all the courage I don't feel.

"Excellent." He sounds pleased, and a little tendril of happiness coils through me. He takes my hand and leads me through his palatial penthouse, guiding me into the nearby bedroom he'd pointed out to me before. A quick glance down, and I can easily make out the bulge of his huge erection under the thin fabric of his pajama pants. I'm already aching to be filled by that large, girthy cock again.

"*Now.* Get on the bed."

This time, I don't hesitate. I climb onto the massive bed and wait.

He steps toward me. "Lie flat on your back, hands above your head."

I ease back, my legs pressed together, my hands gripping the headboard. My entire body is quivering, hungry for his touch, and my nipples are tightened to aching, painful points. The distance between us is agony. I twist on the bed restlessly, awaiting his next command.

"Close your eyes," he whispers.

I shut my eyes, and a few seconds later, I feel the mattress dip under his weight. The subtle scent of his cologne lingers in the air between us, and I draw in a shaky breath.

"You have a beautiful body, Princess." His fingertip circles around my nipple achingly slow, and I thrust my chest upward in response. "I could worship you all night." I can hear the smile in his voice. "Perhaps, I will."

Oh, yes, please.

His hand trails down over my ribs, my stomach, his touch feather-light and teasing. It's torment. Every cell in my body is electrified, arching in response to his touch.

His fingers thread through the hair shielding my entrance, pushing into the cleft between my thighs.

"Since the first moment I saw you, I wanted to own your pleasure," he whispers.

Unable to respond, I bite my bottom lip and arch my back. All I want is his cock inside me again. But he's the one in control, and I have a feeling he's trying to torture me.

If that's his plan, then he's succeeding admirably.

"Open your legs," he orders.

I spread my thighs, giving him better access to my entrance. He takes it greedily, pushing one finger, then two, into my channel.

"Christ, you are so wet," he moans. "And so goddamn tight."

Then I feel his lips on me, kissing his way down my stomach, over my hip, before burying his head between my thighs. I don't even have time to protest before his tongue snakes out to lick me. The sensation is so intense, I almost buck off the bed in response.

His fingertips dig into my hips, pinning me to the bed as he continues to lick my sex. He's a master at this—his tongue swirling around my clit before pushing back into my channel.

Every muscle in my body is pulled tight, like the string of a bow. Any moment, I'm going to break. The tension building inside me is too much, too intense. I can't…

His heady moan vibrates against me, and it's more than I can take. I shatter, my climax washing over me like a tidal wave. Hot, delicious pleasure pulses through my veins. I'm gasping and moaning, my head thrown back, my spine arched. And still, his tongue is working my clit, relentlessly drawing out every last shudder from my body.

When I finally float back down to earth, he's lying next to me, his lean, powerful body stretched out on the bed beside me. There's a wistful look in his eyes, something almost boyishly charming, and I smile up at him.

"What? Why are you looking at me like that?" I ask.

He's drawing little circles on my belly with his fingertip, causing goosebumps to spread across my skin. For the first time since I've known him, he looks relaxed, unguarded.

"You make the most delicious sounds when you come," he answers.

"You are very good at making me come," I laugh.

"What about David?" He's looking down at his finger as it trails a path across my stomach to my hip, studiously avoiding my gaze. There's an edge of jealousy in his tone.

I stiffen, completely thrown by his sudden shift in topic. "What about him?"

"You're still seeing him."

I swallow, deciding not to mention that I did in fact just see him half an hour before, at the elevator bank. And we're getting together for dinner tonight. *Here.* Nope that wouldn't be good to mention.

"He's never made you come like that. Has he?"

I swallow. David has never made me come at all, but I'm not going to tell Ash that.

He reaches up and grasps my chin, angling my face to his, forcing me to meet his gaze. "Has he?"

Without saying a word, I just shake my head.

"How do you even know about him?"

He waits a long moment before replying. "Your phone. He texted and called you several times last night. You'll need to tell him about me."

My cheeks flush when I remember David's texts. He has no idea where I am or what I'm doing. That I've had sex with another man twice since our last date. Last night. But something in me rises, defiant. This doesn't mean anything. It's just mindless, animal pleasure.

I turn to Ash. "*Why* would I tell him about you?"

His gorgeous features harden as if they're carved in granite, and I see determination and something else—possessiveness?—solidify in those midnight eyes. "You'll tell him about me and you'll end it with him because I don't like competition." Then, his grip on my chin tightens slightly before he adds in a voice with dark undertones. "And I will *not* share."

I blink, licking my lips and staring back at him, hoping to cover my shock as my mind races to come up with the appropriate reply.

But I already know he's not going to back down.

CHAPTER 7
PURE SIN

I STARE AT ASH, TRYING TO FIGURE OUT MY RESPONSE TO HIS challenge, his demand that I cut things off with David. Does Ash think he owns me because we've had sex twice in less than twelve hours? And does this mean anything beyond mindless enjoyment?

There's no way it could. We haven't even known each other a full day.

And I've invested too much time and energy into David and my plans for the future. David is the sprawling home with the white picket fence, the two point five kids, the classy society life.

But Ash?

Ash is pure sin. He isn't a future. Even if the sex is mind-blowing.

He is the present. The now. But no further.

"I won't share you, Lexi," he repeats, staring into my eyes as if detecting the nature of my resistance.

I swallow, still considering. Ash does seem like the type of man who knows exactly what he wants and will do whatever it takes to get it.

"Do you want my cock, Lexi? That same cock that made you scream with pleasure last night? When you thought it was David on top of you, fucking you, making you moan 'til you were hoarse?"

I blink and sit up, staring back at him defiantly. "There's more to life than just sex."

He gets a shrewd glint in his eye as he stands from the bed. He's still wearing his pajama bottoms, but I can see the raging hard-on beneath the thin material. He's huge, and I remember the feel of him inside me, stretching me. Suddenly, I'm flush with arousal again.

He approaches me. "I think you need to be educated about what you really want."

I swallow, looking up at him, and our gazes lock for a long, silent moment. But before I can respond, my stomach growls—*loudly*. Like, embarrassingly so.

And I'm reminded that I was so panicked about getting my phone back this morning that I rushed out the door without grabbing anything to eat.

I'd had no idea this morning would entail me having the hottest sex of my life *again*. I'm quickly becoming addicted to Ash's talented mouth, drool-worthy body and devilishly good looks.

Without another word, Ash breaks the stare and moves around the bed to the landline on the nightstand.

"Room service, please. The usual."

I take that opportunity to stand up and go looking for my dress and panties in the other room. They're in a small puddle, just where I'd left them when he'd commanded me to strip naked.

Just as I'm straightening from picking them up off the floor, I'm aware of his presence behind me. *Directly* behind me. Before

I can turn around, he cinches a powerful arm around my waist and pulls me fast against him and the hard, fat bulge of his cock.

"We're not through here," he mutters through his teeth in an authoritative tone.

"I'm getting dressed."

He laughs dryly as he buries his nose in my hair, inhaling deeply. How it's possible, I have no idea, but his already huge cock surges against my hip. "You came last night. Twice. And once this morning. I came inside you last night, but I think that count is a little unfair, isn't it?"

His other hand slides up to hold my throat as he kisses along the back of my neck. "Mmm. That one taste of you, that one, hot fuck was far from enough. Do you want more? Do you want this?" He rubs his cock against me again, and my inner core melts into liquid desire.

I moan as his mouth connects to the most sensitive parts of my neck.

"Show me how much you want my cock again, Lexi. Show me while on your knees."

He turns me in his arms, and I can barely stand, so quickly has he reduced me into a bubbling pool of need. I need the feel of his cock thrusting inside of me again, making me scream, making me come.

He gently pulls my clothing out of my hands and presses down on my shoulder, guiding me down onto my knees. And as if in a trance, I sink to the plush carpet. Without hesitation, I reach for his waistband but he pushes my hand away.

"No, no. That's not how things will be between us. I command, and you obey."

I frown, still staring at the tented material right in front of my face.

"Last night you thought the cock inside you, the one that felt so good—you thought it was his, didn't you?"

Without a word, I nod lightly, not a little ashamed about the fact that I'd made the mistake of crawling into the wrong bed with the wrong man. But I *am* ashamed that I enjoyed it so much that I can't stop thinking about it. That even after I'd realized it wasn't David, I'd screamed and writhed and fallen apart beneath him, begging for more.

"I think you need to make it up to me…"

"How–how?"

"By doing everything I say. Let me own you." He sets aside my dress on the nearby armchair, but he's holding my panties up so I can see them. "Put your hands behind your head."

I blink, confused, but my hesitation only seems to anger him. With a hiss of breath, he grabs my chin and forces my gaze up to his. "*Now.* I say it, you do it. Just like that. No hesitation. No questioning."

With a quick intake of breath, I comply, putting my hands behind my head. Before releasing my chin, he caresses my lips with his thumb. "That's a good girl."

Then, he uses my own panties to tie my wrists together behind my head. He does it quickly, confidently, as if he knows just how to do it. As if he'd done it many times before.

A sick feeling congeals in my belly, but I have no time to question it because Ash is now divesting himself of his pajama bottoms and the boxers underneath, kicking them aside.

And there it is, his glorious cock. I take it in for the very first time despite the fact that we had sex last night. It's long and girthy with a very slight, almost elegant curve to it. And it is very, *very* erect. To the point where it almost looks painful. I don't have tons of experience—only three lovers before this—but it's far bigger than any other organ I've laid eyes on.

"I'm going to enjoy your mouth, Lexi. The feel of you sucking me in deep, the feel of your tongue caressing me. Will you enjoy it, too?"

I nod.

He grasps himself and angles it toward my mouth. "Open for me, Princess. Take me deep and swallow me."

I lean forward, accepting the challenge, though thrown by the fact that my hands are tied behind my head. He steadies me, a hand on my shoulder, first, before it comes to rest behind my head, his fingers twining with mine.

Tentatively, I taste him, rolling my tongue over the tip of his huge cock, and he lets out a long, pent breath. He tastes salty, earthy. I relish the feeling of him filling me up as I slide my mouth along his cock. He doesn't move, letting me take him in at my own pace.

"Fuck, Princess. That mouth is sinful. *Jesus.*" His voice is hoarse, and I can tell he's unbelievably turned on. I slide my mouth deeper onto his cock until I feel the tip of him hit the back of my mouth, pushing firmly against my throat. My eyes widen as I note there's a lot more of him to go yet.

Deepening the suction, I pull my head backward, rolling my tongue as I go. His growl of pleasure gratifies me to my core, and I'm quite proud of myself. With daring and a need to make this the best head of his life, I slide forward again quickly, feeling him enter my throat.

He throws his head back and gasps, and his hand tightens over mine. A few more strokes like this continue, and I'm suddenly no longer in control. His hand on the back of my head is directing our pace and his hips are thrusting forward. Quickly, quickly, then slow. Then he holds me still while he instructs me to suckle him, caress him with my tongue.

My jaw and neck are starting to ache, but his obvious ecstasy is driving me to ignore those discomforts. Not only is he beautiful and a skillful lover, but he's very demonstrative and appreciative of the pleasure I'm giving him. Telling me, between gasps and grunts that I'm beautiful and fucking amazing.

"Yes, yes, Princess. Like that. Such a good girl. Such a fucking naughty, sinful little princess." He's pushing on the back of my head and thrust in so deep I can feel my throat stretch to accommodate him.

Then, he stills and I feel the girth of his cock widen and harden impossibly. With a loud groan, he releases himself into me, pulsing his semen down my throat. Over and over again. I wait and suck him dry, and then I swallow him greedily, just as he asked me to.

He holds me still until his orgasm fades and then releases me. I pull back, gasping for breath almost as hard as he is. Not only am I fully aroused again, but I've been holding my breath for a little while.

He quickly unties my wrists from behind my head and pulls me up against him, holding me tight and kissing the top of my head.

"Your mouth is fucking amazing," he says in a low voice.

I tilt my head up, relishing the feel of our naked bodies pressed together. "Amazing head in return for amazing head sounds like a good deal to me," I reply.

He pushes a loose strand of my hair back from my face and tucks it behind my ear, dark gaze locking with mine. "Beautiful, beautiful princess. I'm not done with you yet, today. Not by a long shot."

I swallow, acknowledging the flutter in my stomach. Anticipation, arousal. And not a little fear. Because even now. *Even now*, I have no intention of canceling that date with David tonight.

No matter how many orgasms this man wrings out of me. No matter how much he owns my body today. He could very easily stake his claim and own me. And I'm in danger of letting him do it. Our gazes are locked, and I can feel the force of our wills rising to battle until…

We both jump when there's a sharp knock at the door, pulling us out of our own little world. I let go a sigh of relief when he breaks that stare and reaches for his pajama bottoms.

I grab my dress and go to the bedroom to hide my nakedness until room service leaves. But before shutting the bedroom door, I turn to watch Ash take the steps up from the sunken living room. His defined muscles glide smoothly under lightly tanned skin. God, he's gorgeous.

And dangerous.

And not for me. Not for long, anyway.

CHAPTER 8
HUNGRY EYES

INSIDE THE BATHROOM, I HURRIEDLY PULL MY DRESS ON, ALL the while listening for the bellboy to leave. For several minutes, all I hear is the clinking of china and the low murmur of Ash's deep voice. I can't hear what he's saying, but it doesn't really matter—his baritone twists through my veins like warm Irish whiskey. Finally, *finally,* the bellboy leaves, the door shutting firmly behind him.

Alone again. I still haven't decided whether or not I'm staying for a bite or moving on and getting on with my day. I have a feeling Ash will decide for us both.

I open the bathroom door and walk barefoot into the living area. Breakfast is laid out on the elegant round dining table. It looks like a feast for half a dozen people—waffles, crepes, fruit, scones, muffins—every possible carb one could imagine.

Ash is drinking a glass of orange juice when I emerge from the bedroom. He's looking hot as fuck, of course. God, how does he manage to look scrumptious while doing something as mundane as drinking orange juice?

Setting the glass down, he rises from his chair and strides over to me with flattened lips, eyes narrowed. I've displeased him, and my heart races, wondering what it could be that I've done. Taking my low neckline between his fingers, he tugs lightly. "Take this off," he says sternly.

I frown and stare up at him. I know he'd mentioned "not being done with me today," but could that possibly be true? The thought sends a cold thrill vibrating through me straight down to my core to settle in and seethe with arousal.

When I don't immediately comply with his command, he lifts a disapproving brow. "Do it. *Now*, Lexi."

With those words, something inside me clicks into place, and I have this sudden need to please him. It's so weird. I don't even know this guy. We just met last night for god's sake. How could I know him? And yet, I want to make him happy, to please him. I crave his approval.

I shimmy out of the dress quickly, but I don't stop there. Slowly, I reach around and unhook my bra, sliding it off my arms. My nipples bead under his scrutiny, and he notices, licking his lips. Last to go are the panties, which drop to the floor without ceremony. I smile at the thought that this man has literally made my panties drop.

A smile spreads across his sexy lips. "Good girl," he says approvingly. "Don't ever hide yourself from me."

A wave of deep satisfaction washes over me, and I can't help but smile at his praise. I've pleased him, and it's a little frightening how good it makes me feel.

Without a word, I glance pointedly at his pajama bottoms and raise a brow.

"If I take these off, I'll have you up against the wall in two seconds flat," he says.

I shrug. He makes that sound like a bad thing.

Honestly, after sucking him off, I could use a rough, up-against-the wall, good, hard fucking. My body is still buzzing from earlier, and despite being hungry, I could absolutely go another round.

With a sly smile, he slides a finger down my arm, then hooks my fingers with his, and pulls me over to the table. He plucks a raspberry off one of the plates. "Open."

I open my mouth, and he places the tart berry on my tongue. I suck on his finger as it slides from my lips. He growls.

"I'm going to feed you," he says, "and then I'm going to pull you down, push my hard cock into that sweet pussy and ride you hard until you weep."

I swallow and nod, a bit taken back by his blunt honesty. I've never had a man talk to me so crudely. David, certainly, never has. I never thought I'd like it. But as the words tumble from his mouth, a thread of heat slithers through me. My core is wet, aching, already hungry for him to carry through on that promise.

Lowering me into one of the plush dining chairs, he places two raspberries in his own mouth. Bracing a hand on either armrest, caging me in, he leans forward. His hot mouth covers mine, and his tongue pushes into my mouth, the berries with it.

"Mmm." They are sweet with just a hint of tartness. I lick my lips when he pulls away.

He takes a butter knife and spreads marmalade across a piece of toast, then holds it to my lips. I take a bite, and then he takes a bite. It's sourdough—my favorite—and combined with the sweet tang of marmalade, it tastes heavenly.

"I find I'm quite hungry this morning," he murmurs. "Starving, in fact."

Setting the toast aside, he takes the little marmalade jar in his hand and dips his finger into the amber-colored jam and spreads it across my left nipple. Then he leans forward and follows that action by sweeping up the sticky substance with his tongue.

I moan, arching up into him. Sweet Jesus, his smooth, velvety tongue feels so good against my sensitive skin I don't want it to stop. So when his lips leave me, I clamp my mouth shut to silence the whimper bubbling up in my throat.

"Close your eyes," he commands.

"Why?"

He laughs faintly. "Because I told you to. That is always reason enough. Don't forget." He leans over me and kisses my left eyelid. "Now close"—he kisses my other eyelid—"your eyes."

I smile at his tenderness and close my eyes. He's such a serious guy that when I get these little glimpses of softness, I can't help but feel like it's just for me—a little bit of himself that he keeps hidden from the rest of the world.

"And you will keep them closed until I tell you to open them." He places my hands on the armrests and spreads my legs as far as they will go. "Stay exactly as you are. You will not move."

I nod, my entire body pulled tight in anticipation. My core is slick, already hungry for his cock. After a minute, I feel him spread something cool and slippery across my skin. The sweet smell of vanilla gives it away. Whipped cream. With his long fingers, he spreads the sticky cream over my breasts, my ribs, working his way down my body until I feel his hand between my thighs. He pushes a finger into me.

"Christ, you are so fucking wet, Lexi. So ready for my cock." I can hear the smile in his voice, and it makes me want to open my eyes. But I don't. I'm afraid he'll stop if I do, so I just bite my lip and squeeze my eyes tighter. He pushes another finger into me, stretching my channel, making me gasp.

My clit is pulsing, and each breath is sawing out of my lungs like I've just run a marathon. If he doesn't fuck me soon, the desperation will kill me. I'm certain of it. Never before have I felt pleasure and torment like this, and I'm near to bursting.

Clutching the armrests, I struggle to remain still. But everything inside me is dying to arch up and grind against his hand. A whimper escapes my throat.

"Shhh," he soothes. And then I feel his lips on me again, sucking the cream off my tight nipple. "You taste like heaven," he groans against my skin. "So fucking sweet."

I groan in response, tilting my head back as he moves to the other nipple, sucking, nipping gently with his teeth. I try to focus on something other than my building orgasm, but I can't. The feeling of his lips on me, the sharp, searing pain of his teeth biting into my flesh is more than I can take.

Holy shit. I'm going to come.

"Ash," I pant. "*Please....*"

He doesn't answer my pleas. Instead, he licks his way down my torso, swirling his tongue around my belly button before wending his way down to my swollen, aching core.

With his hand, he spreads a healthy dollop of whipped cream on my clit, and then presses his lips against me, slowly, languidly sucking the cream off.

It's more than I can take.

With one hard flick from the blade of his tongue, hot pulsing pleasure jolts through me. I'm engulfed in sensation, writhing beneath him, a thready cry erupting from my throat. Ripples of delicious heat course through my body as he continues to suck and lick and fuck me with his tongue.

And still he doesn't release me. Instead, he pushes one finger into my channel, then another, and another, until I'm stretched impossibly wide. His thumb gently caresses my clit, swirling over the swollen nub until that crest starts building again within me. So tender from the last orgasm, it's almost painful.

"No, Ash, I can't..."

I want to move my hips, buck against him. But I don't dare.

"Yes. You can," he growls. "Once more. Then I'll fuck you."

The promise of his cock buried deep inside me is enough to send me over the edge again. With my head thrown back, and my nails digging into the armrests, I surrender to it. Wave after wave of intense pleasure crashes over me, pulling me under, leaving me panting and breathless. I fall back, listless, against the cushioned chair back.

It's a full minute before I can collect myself. He pulls away, removing his hand from me. My eyes flutter open just in time to see him walk out of the bedroom. The faucet in the bathroom runs for a minute, before he returns with a white washcloth in his hand.

He moves toward me with the languid self-confidence of a man who knows power and control. And knows that he's already succeeded in dominating me.

His eyes narrow as he approaches me. "You've disobeyed me. I haven't given you permission to open your eyes."

I swallow and tilt my chin up, looking him square in the eyes. "What are you going to do about it?"

One side of his beautiful mouth tilts upward in a half-smile. "There's only one way to deal with disobedience, Lexi. You'll soon learn it well. *Punishment.*"

CHAPTER 9
DEN OF INIQUITY

*T*HERE'S ONLY ONE WAY TO DEAL WITH DISOBEDIENCE, LEXI... *Punishment.*

My breath catches in my throat, and a strange and new sort of excitement trickles through me. My skin begins to prickle.

Tossing the washcloth onto the table, he reaches down and curls a strong hand around my forearm, wrenching me up so that we're standing toe-to-toe. My body is still sticky, half-smeared in whipped cream, but he doesn't seem to care. Spinning me around, he bends me over the table and forces me down, pressing my front against the cold polished surface of the table.

He smooths his hand over my naked ass in gentle circles. "What did I tell you about opening your eyes?"

"To not do it," I answer.

His hand leaves my ass and then comes back down with a furious *slap* that jolts through my entire body. The sharp, biting sting takes my breath away, and I gasp. But entwined with the pain is the hot rush of pleasure.

His hand comes down again, and I bite my bottom lip to keep from crying out. For some reason, I don't want to give him the satisfaction of knowing it hurts. Or maybe I'm just afraid he'll stop.

After several more strikes, when it's all over, my skin is hot, tingling. Gently, his hand brushes over my ass again, feather-light and soothing.

"Wait here," he murmurs. I'm all but literally glued to the surface of this table, not going anywhere.

Ash walks into the bathroom. Now it's the tub faucet running, the tub being filled. It takes several minutes, but he finally returns to me. Slowly he peels me off the surface of the table and scoops me into his powerful arms, carrying me into the bathroom.

"I *can* walk, you know."

Laughing quietly, he lowers me into the giant, sunken, oval-shaped tub. The water is warmed to the perfect temperature and rose-scented. It feels heavenly against my skin. How long has it been since I've taken a bath? I can't even remember the last time. I'm normally so busy with school that a quick shower is all I have time for, honestly.

"Lean back," he instructs, taking a bar of soap off the chrome bathtub caddy.

I settle back against the tub, wincing a little as my back makes contact with the cold porcelain. He dips the soap into the water, and I suck in a breath when he drags it up my body slowly, washing away the whipped cream and sticky residue.

As Ash slides the soap along the contours of my body, I can see every muscle in his shoulders is tense, coiled tight.

"What are you thinking about?" I ask.

"I'm thinking how much I want to lick every inch of this delectable skin. How I want to taste every dip and valley. How badly I want to sink my teeth into this tight nipple."

"Mmmm." As his words wash over me, they are like a drug, intoxicating me. My own hands travel to my breasts. I pinch both nipples between my fingertips and moan. But it's more than just a show to tantalize him. And though this feels good, it wouldn't feel nearly as good as his teeth would feel.

"Christ almighty," he grinds out under his breath, Ash reaches down to wrench me out of the water abruptly. Cold air washes over my damp skin. He tugs a thick white towel off the wall hook and wraps me inside it immediately. I mourn the loss of a long soak on the tug, but this feeling of being manhandled—literally— is arousing me more than anything else. His movements are clipped, focused, as though he's working hard to hold himself back.

As soon as I'm dry, he sweeps me up again and carries me to the bed, tossing me roughly on the mattress. With a fierce look in his eyes, he drops his pajama pants and underwear to the floor in one swift motion. His completely naked body is beautiful, his long, thick cock jutting out and upward. Ready.

Holy shit. Just seeing the swollen purple tip makes me wet. *Again.*

Ash moves forward and lowers himself onto the bed, his body now hovering over mine. Then, he kisses me, his tongue sweeping into my mouth possessively. He tastes like the raspberries we just ate—sweet with just a hint of tartness.

He pushes my towel open so that I'm exposed to him, then lays on me, our skin meshing together. With his knees, he spreads me wide, the head of his cock nudging my entrance. I hardly have time to brace myself before he pushes all the way into me, balls deep, and I let out a cry of shock.

"Oh, God," I breathe.

"Fuck, Lexi," he growls against the curve of my neck. "You're so fucking tight. So hot."

His fingertips dig into my hips as he pushes his hips in quick, sharp thrusts, delving deep. The sensation of him filling me feels so fucking good, I can't even breathe each time he goes in. For long, silent minutes, he pumps me hard, relentless with each forceful thrust. Like he can't get enough, and the more he pushes, the more desperate he gets. Everything in me throbs when his pelvis strokes my clit.

I can no longer hold back, letting myself moan out my pleasure. My back arches up, as once again, my greedy body is yearning for yet another release. I whimper beneath him, pleasure slamming into me with every frenzied thrust. It's too much, and I break apart beneath him, ecstasy flooding me as he continues to thrust, over and over again, his moans hoarse and his words dirty, telling me how good I feel. How I was made just for his pleasure. How much he can't get enough of my hot pussy.

"Oh, fuck, Lexi," he growls. "*Fuck!*"

With one final thrust, he stiffens and I feel his cock pulse inside me, my channel clenching around his length. We feel like one being, fused together in our ecstasy. It's perfect. In that single moment, everything is perfect between us.

For long, quiet moments, he lies like that, on top of me, nestled between my thighs, his body completely relaxed. Then, he pulls out of me and rolls to the side, tugging me into his arms. Still, we lay in silence, with me tucked against him, my head resting on his chest. The slow, steady rhythm of his heartbeat is comforting. Lying here with him makes me feel safe. Protected.

Who is this guy? I mean, really? I'm curious about him outside the bedroom. Where is he from? What are his hobbies? Does he like pickles? I have so many questions.

I tilt my head up and look at him. "So, um, are you here in California on a visit?"

"No," he says as his fingertip idly traces swirls across my shoulder blade. "I moved here five years ago."

Untangling myself from his arms, I sit up and glance down at him. "So you live at Exeter House full time?"

"I have a home in the Pacific Palisades, but I come here when I need to focus on work."

Wow. Rich people problems. Must be so hard to focus while wandering about in a sprawling mansion that overlooks the ocean. I don't have any actual idea what his house looks like, but all those houses in Pacific Palisades are the same—huge, gorgeous and worth mountains of dough.

"So, um, what do you do for a living?" I ask.

His mouth twists into a frown, and his brow furrows. He is clearly displeased and not even bothering to hide it. You'd have thought I'd just asked him to confess his darkest sins.

"I'm a consultant," he answers tersely.

"Oh." I watch him closely. "Like cyber security or something?"

I know that can't be it. He looks more like a lawyer, or a doctor, not a guy who sits in front of a computer all day. There's just a restless energy about him that makes it hard to believe he'd ever sit still for more than three minutes.

With a heavy sigh, he pulls away and sits on the edge of the mattress, pulling his hands over his face in frustration. He curses under his breath.

My jaw drops. Huh. Things just got really uncomfortable, really quick. Why doesn't he want me to know what he does for a living? I'm confused. Should I have *not* asked? Not shown any interest in him beyond what his cock and mouth and hands can do for me?

It's such a basic question, and it's not like we ever agreed to keep personal details out of...whatever this is between us. We never agreed to *anything*, actually.

"I can't—" He shakes his head, cutting his words off.

He can't *what?*

I stare at his muscled back as he dips his head and rakes both hands through his hair. I itch to lean forward and wrap my arms around him, but something in his posture holds me back.

Something has shifted between us, and I'm not sure what it is.

I inch off the bed, head into the living room and fish my bra and panties off the floor before slipping them on. He doesn't follow me, doesn't ask me what I'm doing. Doesn't try to stop me.

I pull my dress on—for the second time—and then head back into the bedroom, and awkwardly step into my shoes. Then I gather my purse and phone—and yes, I'm double-checking everything to make sure I don't leave anything behind this time.

Then, I clear my throat and turn to him. He's still sitting on the edge of the bed, engulfed in tormented silence—though *why* he's tormented is a mystery. The question gnaws at me, but I'm not brave enough to ask him.

"I, um...have a lunch thing," I say.

That seems to snap him out of whatever daze he's in. Rising to his feet, he saunters over to me, still completely naked. My eyes rove down his chiseled torso to the dark curls nestling his cock. He's so fucking beautiful, and just like that, I forget what I was doing. My purse hangs limply in my hand as I watch him prowl closer.

He stops in front of me and brushes a thumb across my cheek. "You don't have a lunch thing," he says.

I lift a brow. "You don't know that."

He's right, I *don't* have lunch plans—I just need an excuse to dip out of here. This has already gone on too long. This was fun, but it was a fling. Nothing more. There's no future in it at all. And, quite frankly, this conversation is a potent reminder that I need to focus on the person that matters—David.

Ash's thumb gently caresses my cheek. "You blush when you lie." His hand falls to the base of my throat. "And your pulse races. It's an easy tell."

I blink, shocked he would pick up on such minute details. He's like a human lie detector. "Those are also classic signs of desire," I say, "and with you standing naked in front of me, is it any wonder why my cheeks are flushed and my heart is racing?"

He flashes me a sexy half-smile, his hand never leaving my neck. "You will return tonight? I have a meeting, but I'll be home by eight."

"I can't." I shake my head. "I have plans." And this time, I'm telling the truth. I told David I'd meet him tonight, and there's no way I'm breaking the date. Even for Ash.

His hand falls to his side and his eyes narrow. "With whom?"

I can't keep the sharpness out of my tone. I lift my chin to him. "Does it matter?"

"Yes. Yes, it does." A tick starts in his jaw, and his every muscle is pulled tight as he waits for my answer.

But what can I say? I release a heavy breath and move to push past him. He grabs my wrist and pulls me back around so I'm facing him.

"I wasn't lying when I said I don't share, Lexi. Who are you meeting tonight?"

"A friend." Which is true. Semi-true, anyway.

"David," he counters.

I twist my wrist out of his grip and walk from the bedroom into the living room. Just as I open the door to walk out of the suite, he reaches over my shoulder and uses his weight to force the door closed.

"Return to me tonight, Lexi." He's commanding me again.

But it's more than a command. It's also a plea. And the truth is, I *want* to see him again. Seeing him again is a bad idea, but I'm drawn to this man in a way I've never been drawn to anyone before. Why, I don't know. He's dangerous—I can feel it. I just don't know if I can stay away.

But I have to try.

I worry my bottom lip between my teeth and glance down at my feet. "I'll try," I lie. "That's all I can give you."

His hand falls away, and I don't hesitate to wrench the door open and step out into the empty hallway. For half a second, I hold my breath, waiting for him to drag me back into his den of iniquity. But he doesn't, and I don't dare look back.

"*Tonight*, Princess," is all I hear him say before the door clicks shut behind me.

CHAPTER 10
BEAUTIFUL DARKNESS

THAT AFTERNOON, I'M SITTING CROSS-LEGGED ON THE living room floor at Hill House, where I live with five other Caltech students. I'm eating chicken lo mein with Gwen while we watch a true crime show on streaming TV. The moment I returned home from my escapades with the too-sexy-for-his-own-good Ash, Gwen demanded I tell all—every sordid detail about my morning.

I sip my green tea thoughtfully. "It was *so weird*, though. The second I asked him what he did for a living, he clammed up. His entire demeanor changed."

Gwen looks at me like I'm an alien. "Haven't you looked him up?"

I blink at her.

"Oh, my God, Lex! You haven't Googled the guy you're fucking?" She pulls her phone out of her pocket, her thumbs poised to begin typing. "What's his name?"

"Ash Grayson. I have no idea if Ash is short for something. Ashland? Ashford?"

Her thumbs fly across her phone screen. She pauses, frowns, then scrolls. Scrolls again, and again. "That's weird. I get hits on other people, but I don't think any of them is him. Someone prominent, who's rich enough to be a partner at Exeter House would have hits all over the place. But I can't find anything on this guy," she says. "Does he go by any other name?"

I shrug dramatically. "How would I know? I literally just met him. I don't even know how he takes his coffee."

Gwen purses her lips. "Maybe he paid someone to scrub his information from the internet?"

I pick up a fried wonton and pop it into my mouth. "He does seem strangely private."

Gwen holds up a finger as though she's just had an epiphany. "Maybe he has a wife and a gaggle of kids or something, and he stays at Exeter House to, you know, pick up women?"

I glare at Gwen. "There's no way Ash has kids," I say. "Or a wife, for that matter."

"How can you be so sure?"

Actually, I'm not sure at all. There's so much I don't know about the man. Still, it annoys me when she's right, so I just shrug. "It's a gut feeling."

"Just be careful, Lexi. You don't have the best track record with guys. I mean, look at David. He's *totally* leading you on, and you don't even see it."

"Not true." I roll my eyes. "Besides, David is only *one* guy. One guy does not make a 'track record.'"

She hits me with a side-glance. "What about that guy at the gym with the balloon fetish?"

"Fine, *two* guys. But I never actually dated the balloon guy."

Gwen reaches over with her chopsticks and steals some of my lo mein. "So are you seeing Ash again?" she asks between mouthfuls.

"He asked me to go back and see him tonight." More like he commanded it, but I don't feel like elaborating on that right now.

Gwen winks and grins playfully. "For another epic fuck-a-thon?"

"It wasn't a fuck-a-thon." I pause when Gwen lifts a brow. "Okay, maybe it was," I admit. "But it doesn't matter. I'm *not* seeing him again."

Ash is no good for me—I'm smart enough to realize that. He's tall, gorgeous and an absolute devil in bed. He's someone my mother would go for, which should be reason enough for me to stay away.

"You're overthinking this, girl. So he doesn't want to tell you what he does for a living. Who cares? It's not like you're going to marry the guy. He's a fling. That's it. And after putting up with that jerk David, God knows you deserve a little casual fun. Just don't get too attached…"

I lean back against the couch and narrow my eyes at her. "You should talk. You haven't been out to a club since you broke up with what's-his-name two months ago."

"Sorin."

"Oh, right! Roarin' Sorin," I laugh.

One of our roommates, Cassie, gave Sorin the nickname due to his habit of roaring when he climaxed. Our paper-thin walls made it impossible to tune out. So Cassie and I did what anyone else would do—we sat in the living room while they went at it and mocked the guy mercilessly. It was our first real bonding experience as roomies.

Gwen throws a fortune cookie at me. "Oh, my God. You are so bad." She straightens. "For your information, I'm still a virgin. Technically. But that doesn't mean I'm a complete prude. In fact, I'm going out tomorrow night—to a *new* fetish club."

"*What?* Holy shit. A *fetish* club? Gwen, I had no idea you were kinky!"

She held out her hand placatingly. "Yeah, okay, don't get too excited. It's for a new article I'm writing. The magazine wants edgier topics."

"Edgier than 'Ten Ways to Sexier Thighs?'" I laugh.

Gwen recently scored a job as a writer at a local glamour magazine and associated website. She's at the bottom of the pole and desperate to prove herself as a serious writer, but she's got the smarts and enthusiasm to do it.

"Yeah, yeah, real funny," she says. "*You're* coming with me."

"What?" I bring my hands up defensively and shake my head. "Oh, no, no. I can't. Fetish clubs aren't my thing." I have to laugh at myself. I've actually never been to anything like a fetish club.

But I can't help but remember when Ash slapped my ass this morning. I can still feel the sting of pain and pleasure that rushed through my body. I liked the pain and I wanted more of it. Does that make me a freak?

Gwen leans forward and pushes out a pouty bottom lip, breaking my train of thought. "Come on, Lex. Friends don't let friends go to freaky sex clubs alone."

My hands fall to my lap, and I push out a defeated breath. She's totally got me there.

***

Later that night, I walk into the restaurant and spot David right away. He looks sharp in a crisp white shirt and a gray tailored suit, his blond hair neatly combed back away from his face in a posh *GQ* kind of way. He looks like he could walk into a gala, or step onto a yacht, and be completely at ease.

My heart skips a beat just seeing him, and I breeze past the hostess, heading straight for his table. As soon as he sees me, he stands and reaches for my hand. I slip my fingers into his large hand, and he pulls me into a quick, awkward hug.

Awkward, because I just spent half the day fucking another guy.

"Hey," I say, kissing him on the cheek. "Thank you for meeting me here."

"Yeah, I'm a little surprised you didn't want to meet at Isca," he says with a smile.

"Just figured we could do something different," I answer quickly.

It's a lie. I'd asked him to meet me here, because it's two blocks away from Exeter House, and I don't want to risk running into Ash, which very likely could have happened at Isca. If he sees me with David…there's no telling what he'll do, or what he'll say, and I can't take that chance. This whole situation is difficult enough to navigate.

David holds the chair out for me and I slip into it. He unbuttons his jacket and lowers himself into the chair across from me.

"I ordered you some wine," he says. "I hope you don't mind. I know Merlot is your favorite."

"Thank you," I say, taking a sip. It's exquisite. "How was your day?"

He flashes me that charming smile. "I've been watching the clock all day. I couldn't wait to see you."

Heat rushes to my cheeks, and I smile tightly. "I've…um, missed you, too."

He reaches out and takes my hand. "You weren't texting me back, so I thought you might have been upset with me for last night."

Guilt swamps me instantly. I hate having to lie. It makes me feel…gross. But there's no way around it. It's either lie about Ash, or reveal the truth, which would cost me everything I've worked so hard to build with David over the last several months.

I swallow. "I, uh, lost my phone for about half a day. I was going crazy without it."

"Ah," he says, and I can't tell if he believes me or not. "Where'd you end up finding it?"

In Ash's penthouse. "In my room," I say tightly. "It had slipped between my desk and my bed."

"I'm glad you found it." He squeezes my hand. "Thank you for being so cool about last night. I didn't mean to be gone so long. I got waylaid by Don Hunter." He smiles, and I can see the excitement in his face. "He said he'd recommend me for membership at Exeter House. Isn't that great? If I can get one more rec, then that's all I need."

"That's great, babe. Really cool." I untangle my hand from his and take a healthy gulp of wine while wondering if Ash has the power to block David's request. "Who's the other member you're going to ask?"

He takes a sip of his wine. "That's what I wanted to talk to you about. What do you think about setting up a double date with Maddie and Evan? He's one of the co-founders. With *his* endorsement…" He sits back in his chair and lifts his hand. "Game over. They'd have to let me in."

I nod and purse my lips. It's not the first time he's asked to meet my friends. But there's a reason we haven't gone on any double dates.

Hmm. I hold up my finger as if something has just occurred to me. "You know, that would be a great idea, except my friends aren't exactly thrilled with…us as a couple. I mean, you're *great*," I rush to clarify, "but they feel like we should be further along in our relationship."

His brows furrow, and he nods slowly, like he's absorbing my words. "Further along?" he repeats. "Interesting."

"Yeah," I say, taking a long sip of wine. "I mean, we haven't even slept together yet."

He leans across the table, one perfectly groomed brow lifted conspiratorially. "We can rectify that."

I sit back in my chair and bite my bottom lip. Here it is. Everything I've wanted for *months*. I should be excited. I should be over the moon. But his delivery is strangely disconnected. *Transactional.*

"Yeah, maybe." I nod. "We'll see."

Just days ago I'd literally jump at the opportunity to sleep with David. In fact, last night I had done just that. But now, I find myself hesitating. Why? It's not because of Ash, is it? He explored, mapped and staked his claim of my body in ways I never knew possible, bringing me to explosive orgasm after explosive orgasm. But that's all it was—mind-blowing physical, *animal* pleasure. Nothing more. Right?

David's gaze falls to my nearly empty wine glass. "You need more wine." He glances back up, over my shoulder. "Where's that waitress?"

I wave him off. "It's okay. One glass is plenty."

David smiles, exposing a row of perfect white teeth. "Nonsense. I'll go hunt her down."

"No, no," I say. "I don't want to lose you again."

Standing, he laughs and kisses me on the forehead. "I'll be right back."

Thankfully, he's true to his word. Several minutes later, he returns with two full glasses of red wine and sets one down in front of me. A third glass arrives with our entrees.

The room is spinning. I think the third glass may have been too much. I'm not usually such a lightweight, but I didn't eat much of my lo mein lunch earlier and haven't eaten more than three bites of my dinner yet either.

I grab a slice of bread from the basket at the center of the table, shoving half of it into my mouth. I need carbs. Maybe the bread will sop up some of the wine that's sloshing around in my stomach.

I'm mid-chew when David takes my hand again. The warmth of his palm envelopes my cold fingertips. "Lexi, I didn't just come here tonight to apologize for last night," he says. "I came here to ask a very important question. It's ironic that your friends were thinking we should be further along because I think so too. But I want it all. I want to marry you."

I glance down at our hands and then back up at him, confused. "I'm sorry, *what?*"

His smile widens. "I want you to be my wife, Lexi."

My heart jumps into my throat. We've dated for several months and he'd never once mentioned marriage. We'd never even really had the exclusivity talk either, though I'd assumed that we were exclusive to one another.

And now he's popped the question and my only reaction is confusion. I'd hoped for this outcome for weeks. Prayed for it, actually. And I never pray.

Now…I'm not so sure what I want. This is all happening so fast. How is it possible to go from zero to full speed in the span of *one* evening? I don't even know. My head is swimming, the room around me tilting and swaying.

"Excuse me," I say awkwardly, pulling my hand out of his grasp. "I'll be right back."

I stand up, a bit wobbly and go in search of the bathroom. The dark restaurant is a little difficult to navigate, but I manage to find a hallway that looks promising. Just as I round the corner, a strong hand reaches out from behind me and grabs my elbow. I stop and whip around to face David.

Except, it's not David..

"*Ash*," I breathe. I blink several times, convinced I'm seeing things. I'd deliberately chosen this restaurant to *avoid* running into him, and now here he is with his hand tightly gripping my elbow. I whisper at him harshly. "What are you doing here?"

His eyes narrow. "I was planning on asking you the same thing."

I huff and yank my arm out of his grasp, nearly toppling backward. He catches me around the waist and pulls me against him. My head swims. The room is spinning, and I'm starting to feel seek. And Ash…he smells delicious.

I place a hand on his chest to steady myself. "You shouldn't be here. I'm on a date."

Beneath my hands, I feel his muscles tighten. "How much have you had to drink?"

I search my memory. "Um…two glasses of wine. No wait, three." I pull away from him, but he still has his arm around my waist. Either to keep me close or keep me from toppling over, I'm not sure which. "Thank you for your concern, but I'm fine."

A slew of expletives fall from his mouth in that sexy English accent. He's so beautiful when he's angry. I should tell him that, but for some reason, I don't think he'll appreciate the compliment. He's definitely on edge.

"You make everything sound so sophisticated. Even cursing." Now *that's* a compliment I'm sure he'll like, except he isn't even paying attention. He's holding me with one hand while he texts with the other. He looks concerned. Or deep in thought. "Can you please let me go? My date is probably wondering where I am."

"I just texted your date. You're not feeling well, and you're coming home with me."

Annoyance spreads through me. I'm not ready to leave. David is waiting for my answer to his question—which is…um…I can't quite remember.

I blink at Ash for a few seconds before I realize the phone he's holding is mine. I recognize the distinct pink and blue Cinderella case I'd spent months hunting down on eBay. Reaching up, I take a swipe at the phone several times before finally snatching it out of his hand—and only because he allows me to. I have a feeling nothing happens in Ash's universe without his explicit permission. I am clearly no exception.

"Ash, is everything okay?" It's a woman's voice.

Ash turns his head toward her, giving me the opportunity to pull away. Without his support, though, I overcompensate and trip over my heels, falling backward into the wall. A queasy sensation coils in my stomach, and suddenly I'm finding it difficult to breathe.

I clutch my stomach—I'm definitely going to be sick. "I really don't feel well."

Ash turns back to me, concern etched into his features. "I know, Princess. I'm going to get you home safe."

"Who the hell is this?" I hear the woman ask, her voice tight and high-pitched, like she's on the brink of class-five tantrum.

I open my mouth to respond, but I can't push the words past my lips. I'm so tired, and my limbs suddenly feel heavy, like they're weighted down with lead.

"Lexi, look at me." It's Ash's voice. Apparently he's completely ignoring the woman firing questions at him and loudly huffing.

My eyelids flutter open, and I look up into his eyes. They're a rich brown. A shade or two darker and they'd be black. I marvel at the flecks of gold in his irises, and the way they play off the dim overhead lighting. He's so damn handsome—a perfectly sculpted work of art.

That beautiful face is the last thing I see before darkness closes in and swallows me whole.

Chapter 11
Princess's Day Out

WARMTH IS THE FIRST THING I BECOME AWARE OF. Slowly, I blink open my eyes, and the only thing I see is darkness. The curtains are drawn, only allowing in a sliver of light—enough to see that the room surrounding me is unfamiliar. But not enough to aggravate the massive headache that is currently splitting my head.

Sitting up slowly, I blink and try to remember where I am, but I come up blank. The last thing I remember is seeing David from across the restaurant. Everything between then and now is completely empty, as though the last conscious hours of my life have been wiped clean from my memory, replaced by nausea, a dry throat and a killer headache.

Slipping out of the bed, I walk barefoot to the window, wearing only a man's white T-shirt—no bra, no underwear—and edge the curtain open. The gorgeous coastline of the Pacific ocean spreads out below me, like I'm perched on a cliff.

"Do you like the view?"

I whirl around to face the familiar male voice. "Ash," I breathe.

He's leaning against the door frame, wearing gray sweatpants and no shirt. My mind is immediately cast back to that day I showed up at Exeter House to get my phone—that day, he was dressed similarly, flashing that same devilish smile.

"Where are we?" I reach a hand up to rub my temples.

"Pacific Palisades. This is my house. I've got something for that headache."

"But…how did I get here?"

"I ran into you at the restaurant last night. You were unwell, so I brought you home." He moves from the doorway to what I can see is an enormous attached bathroom, disappearing in there.

Unwell? I shake my head. None of this is making sense. If I were sick, wouldn't David have taken me home?

When he returns shortly with a cup of water and a bottle of aspirin, I ask him directly, "And David?"

He shrugs, handing me the cup and opening the bottle to pull out a couple tablets for me. "I texted him from your phone. You told him you were ill. He thinks you took a cab home."

"Shit." I sip at the water, then gratefully accept the tablets he offers me, washing them down with the rest of the water in the cup. I'm completely parched and feel like shit.

"That will have you feeling better in a little while. But you should have more water. You're likely dehydrated. You wouldn't drink any water when I brought you home last night."

I sigh. "Gwen is probably freaking out."

He sets the bottle on the nightstand and rakes a hand through his hair, making it stand on end. Somehow, it just manages to make him look sexier. "I texted her, too."

Wait, what?

I cock a suspicious eyebrow. "My phone is locked. How did you know the passcode to unlock it?"

"Your code is your birthday, 1022. Not very secure."

Wow, so much for fucking privacy. I might be more angry if Ash hadn't rescued me from the restaurant and whisked me away to this paradise.

Something he said strikes me. "Wait, how do you know my birth date?"

"You've mentioned it," he replies evenly, without hesitation.

Granted, there's a huge gap in my memory from last night, but I'm relatively certain I've never mentioned my birthday to him. Suspicion starts to trickle in. There's something going on—something he's not telling me.

"I'm going to ask you something, and I want you to be completely honest with me," I say, drawing out the word completely.

He nods expectantly.

"How the hell do you know so much about me?"

He shrugs. "I only know what you've told me, Princess."

"I never mentioned my last name or my birthday to you."

One side of his mouth lifts in a half-smile. "Are you so sure about that? You have to admit, the last two days have passed in a blur. The most pleasant sort of blur, to be sure, but a blur regardless."

I open my mouth to protest, but doubt slowly starts to trickle in. Whenever I'm around Ash, I'm driven crazy with need, and my mind seems to go blank. Is it possible I forgot mentioning those things?

It's not the only question I have. As much as I hate to admit it, another question has been weighing on me since my conversation with Gwen.

I lift my chin and look him in the eye. "Are you married?"

He laughs under his breath and shakes his head. "*God*, no. I don't hate myself that much."

Relief washes over me. "Good." I pause. "Wait, what does that mean?"

"Some people have no business getting married."

"People like you," I finish for him.

"Yes, people like me."

"Why?"

He rubs his neck, like this topic is making him uncomfortable. "Because I'm fucked up." I part my lips to ask another question, but before I can get the words out, he interrupts me. "Now, love. I think you need some more water and a hot shower. Something to eat. I have a surprise for you. One I think you'll enjoy. We're going to be taking a little overnight trip together."

I frown. *Overnight?* I don't have any of my things with me. Just whatever I was wearing last night, wherever that is. "But—"

As if hearing my thoughts, he replies. "I sent your clothes from last night to the laundry and had my assistant buy you some things for an overnight stay. It's all packed and ready in my car." He checks his watch, eyebrows bobbing up. "We should get going, though. Traffic won't be so bad going that way for a while yet, but we don't want to chance it."

"*That* way? What way?"

He reaches up and chucks my cheek with a sly smile playing on his lips. "I told you. It's a surprise. Now get in the shower, we need a little breakfast before we're out the door. I'll leave you some clothes on the bed."

I watch him turn and leave with complete confusion. What the what? I blink, trying to remember what day it was.

Monday…I'll be missing class, today and tomorrow. I grab my phone and send a quick text to my lab partner, asking him to take notes for me as I'm "sick."

Then I follow Ash's direction and hit the shower. When I emerge from the steamy heat, I feel like a new woman.

There's a brand-new toothbrush and hairbrush sitting on the counter. I blow my hair dry and pull it back into a high ponytail. Remembering that I'd brought makeup in my clutch with me last night, I apply a little mascara, blush and lip gloss, then move to the bed with the towel wrapped around me to see what clothes he's provided.

He's bought brand-new white sneakers, a pleated gray miniskirt and a T-shirt in my size. It's pale pink and fits me perfectly. There's a large glittery tiara splayed across the chest with the printed words *Treat me like a princess, 'cause I am one.* With delight, I laugh and hug myself. It couldn't be more perfect.

All this because of my Cinderella phone case? This man doesn't even know the half of my hardcore Disney fetish and yet he's already intuited a lot about me.

And we've known each other for just about thirty-six hours.

I blink, stunned at that thought, but have no time to contemplate it because he re-enters the room, this time fully dressed in jeans and a collared shirt instead of his incredibly sexy half-nakedness.

"Breakfast is served. Let's go, Princess." His eyes slide down my form, lingering on the expanse of bare legs and he nods approvingly. The underwear he gave me to wear under the short skirt is lacy, thin and barely there and I'm well aware of that as he looks at me. My nipples harden in response to his obvious attraction. Wherever he wants to take me today isn't going to be nearly as fun as what we did all morning yesterday.

I tentatively place my hand on the bed and give him a suggestive grin.

He licks his lips and pulls his eyes away from my chest to follow the gesture but sadly, shakes his head. "Oh no. If we do any of that, we won't be getting out of here 'til half the day is over."

I stick my lip out to fake pout, and he approaches, kisses the pouty lip before linking his fingers through mine and leading me through the palatial, immaculately decorated home into the massive granite and steel kitchen. He's made pancakes.

And they are to die for, light and fluffy and perfectly cooked, so I say nothing further about ditching the plan to get out of town in order to stay in bed and have more sex. Yet as I watch him across the table from me, eating his own breakfast and licking maple syrup off his fingers, I can't help but remember what that tongue did to me yesterday. I squeeze my thighs together and swallow…and shove more pancakes in my face.

By the time we're done, I'm too full to feel my headache or my sexual frustration. I am ready to slip back into a coma, which I do the minute we hit the freeway in his gorgeous red Ferrari.

I'm notorious for dropping off on car rides. Friends and previous boyfriends and family members have always teased me about it. I have no idea how long I'm out, but by the time I shake myself awake again, we're somewhere in Orange County, judging from the freeway signs.

I rub my eyes and stretch my arms over my head.

"Have a nice nap, Princess?"

I twist at my waist to crack my back. "Those perfect pancakes put me in a coma. It's all your fault."

His mouth thins. "You joke but…I'm pretty sure something else affected you last night and it wasn't either of our faults."

My eyebrows cinch together. "What do you mean? I had wine…"

He downshifts as traffic bunches up. We are almost to Anaheim, and I wonder how much farther we're going. San Diego? Mexico?

"Three glasses, you told me. Do you usually get that far gone on three glasses of wine?"

I shake my head. "Not normally, no."

"Were any of your drinks ever out of your sight last night? Even if for a minute?"

I frown. "No. Wait—yes. The waitress was ignoring us so David—"

"Left the table..?"

"Yes, and he returned with our drinks."

He shakes his head, grim-faced. "You never ever take a drink that has been out of your sight, Princess. *Ever.*"

I blow out a breath. "I know that but I trust—"

"Even with someone you trust. Even me. Besides, has that man given you a reason to trust him?"

I bite my lip and watch him fearfully as he keeps his eyes on the road. He hasn't once chastised me for going out on the date with David despite his repeatedly warning me not to the day before. I wonder if he's decided to take a different tack or…

Maybe he's trying to erode my attachment to David from the inside, by causing me to doubt him. In response to his insinuation, I just shrug. "I hardly ate anything yesterday. I went to that restaurant with an empty stomach."

His eyes narrow, but he doesn't look at me. I, on the other hand, can't keep my eyes off his beautiful hands, which grip the steering wheel so tightly his knuckles whiten. He clearly doesn't believe me.

But how could I possibly believe that David tried to roofie me…minutes after asking me to marry him? I frown, trying to sort through my hazy memory of what happened last night and the order in which it happened. Or had he asked me to marry him *after* I'd drunk the wine? I rub my forehead, right between my eyes just as he signals to exit the freeway onto Harbor Boulevard. My eyes alight on the huge green freeway panel: *Disneyland, next exit.*

No…he didn't. "You didn't! Are we…?"

Suddenly, a cocky grin dances on his sexy lips. "I thought you might enjoy a magical mini-break."

My jaw drops and I'm speechless as he drives us into the parking lot of my most favoritest place on earth. My studies had kept me away for over a year. I'd been practicing self-discipline until my thesis was finished, holding off a return visit as a reward to myself. But now, my whole being ached with a feeling of being *home.*

I can't keep the excitement out of my voice. "You are my favorite person right now."

A brow cocked. "I've been holding steady in that slot since making you come five times yesterday."

I laugh as he puts the car into park and turns off the ignition. The moment his attention is free, I practically jump on him. "Orgasms are very good, too."

Then I crawl into his lap and pull his head down to meet mine, opening my mouth for a passionate kiss. He indulges me for several long minutes, our mouths open to each other, lips sliding against each other, tongues tangling with one another. I feel his cock harden under my ass, and his grip on my waist tightens for a minute.

"Princess, your castle awaits," he breathes when he finally pulls his head away from mine.

Who am I to argue with that?

With hop and a thrill, I grip his hand tightly, and he leads me away from the trams to a meeting point. To my shock, we're greeted there by a Disney Cast Member. She's young, cute and perky in a matching plaid skirt and vest. "Hi, I'm Lonnie, your ambassador. You're Mr. Grayson…and Alexandra?"

"Lexi," Ash corrects. "And you may call me Ash."

She grins at Ash and cocks her head flirtatiously. "Ash and Lexi. Got it. I'm your guide for your visit today. Have you visited the Disneyland Resort before?"

Ash places a possessive hand on my lower back and smiles. "I've been two or three times, but I suspect the young lady, here, is an expert."

I laugh. "I used to live here when I was an undergraduate at UCI. But I haven't been back since leaving to go to grad school."

Lonnie's brows raise, impressed or maybe surprised that I might be smart enough or old enough to be in grad school. Hopefully it's the latter.

"Lexi is a computer science grad student at Caltech."

Lonnie's eyes widen. "Wow. Well, we know who the smart one is here!"

Lonnie then leads us on a whirlwind tour through the park, filling us full of little-known factoids about Disney and his proudest creation and even leading us through "backstage" employee areas to avoid the crowds. And line-waiting...what line-waiting? With a wave of her magical hand, we skip the line at nearly every attraction and ride without a wait.

If she wasn't so obviously flirting with my date, I'd think Lonnie was perfect. But since Ash is so incredibly hot, even a perfect angel couldn't help but have wicked thoughts about him, so I'm willing to excuse her that. For his part, Ash either doesn't notice or doesn't care about her attention. His gaze is almost always fixated on me.

One thing that's hard to put up with, however, is how we're seldom left alone to just be ourselves. On some of the closer rides—like the boat ride through the Pirates of the Caribbean, I manage to slide my hand onto his thigh, to his crotch, rubbing until it's hard not to notice his obvious arousal.

Lonnie can have Jack Sparrow. My man is infinitely sexier. But Jack is a very close second.

By the time we get ourselves to my favorite ride, The Haunted Mansion, the tension between us is high. We've been standing close and rubbing up against each other almost constantly, and I can hardly focus on anything else. In fact, the minute we wander into the darkened stretching room at the beginning of the attraction, he turns his body into me and slides his hands under my miniskirt, cupping the globes of my ass in his large hands. I half-wonder if this is why he chose this skirt for me. Easy access.

"I'm soooo thirsty," I tell him as we wander down the portrait gallery, artificial thunder and lightning striking just beyond the large, manor house windows. Lonnie leads us through the tightly packed line of people, and directly to our own "doom buggy." It's a small, cup-shaped vehicle that curves around us on every side, designed to make every guest feel that they are the only ones wandering the spooky mansion.

For us, it's just what the doctor ordered. Privacy and darkness at last… His lips are on mine the minute our buggy takes off, and seconds after that, his hands are freely roaming under my skirt and my barely there panties.

Maybe it's because he's the sexiest man I've ever been with by far or maybe it's because he already knows me so well, but my legs fall open, ready to let those hands do whatever they want to me. Ready to ignore the fun and gloom of my favorite park attraction to give into another powerful attraction. And to feed the hunger that's been gnawing at me all day.

When he slides his fingers under the lace crotch of my panties, I know I'm in for the ride of my life…

CHAPTER 12
THE HORNIEST PLACE ON EARTH

I'M SITTING IN THE DARKNESS OF MY FAVORITE ATTRACTION at my favorite amusement park. Beside me, the bulk and heat of Ash's body looms over me as we roll along in our private vehicle, experiencing the sights and sounds of a haunted mansion and the 999 happy haunts who "live" here. Music and sounds swirl around us. Ghosts jump up from behind gravestones in time with the music…but neither of us is paying any attention to any of that.

Ash's mouth is on mine, his tongue thrust deep into my mouth, moving in time with the fingers that are stroking my wetness, sliding into me. I've got a leg draped over his thigh and he's using it to hold my legs open. His fingers glide smoothly over my clit to his commanding rhythm, and I'm panting into his mouth as he drinks me up. He's playing me as easily as a virtuoso strumming a guitar, and every slide of those fingers pulls everything in my body, from the base of my belly to the tips of my breasts to the tingling at the back of my neck. I'm drunk on him and nearing climax faster than I ever thought possible.

When he pulls his mouth away from mine, he puts it next to my ear and whispers all the dirty things he wants to do to me—

and make me do to him—later. He wants me on my knees, taking his cock down my throat, he wants me to drink his cum and beg for more. He wants to hear me scream so loud I won't have a voice for days afterward.

When I let out a loudish moan, he quiets me, and I press my mouth to his shoulder while his litany continues. He wants to tie me up and make red marks with the ropes all over my beautiful skin. He wants to put me over his knee and spank me 'til my ass is warm and throbbing. He wants to force me to come over and over again even when I'm begging him to stop. He wants to dominate me and own my pleasure. He wants me to call him *sir*.

Everything he's saying to me is ratcheting up my arousal tenfold. Wherever we spend the night tonight, I'm sure there won't be much sleeping involved. I moan again, muffling it so hard in his shoulder that I'm sure the pressure will bruise him. But this shoulder is honed with thick muscle. My back arches as the heat arcs through my body like lightning. Ash's other hand comes up to tweak my nipple through the thin material of my shirt, and suddenly, my body is jerking and convulsing with an orgasm.

I blink, seeing glittery lights behind my eyes that have nothing to do with the splendors of the animatronics and special effects all around me. Ash draws out my pleasure, rubbing me until the last bit of tension and ecstasy is wrung from my tired muscles. Then he kisses me on the forehead and pulls his hands away...

Giving me just seconds to make myself decent before our doom buggy hits the conveyor belt and we are supposed to get off. *The ride of my life, indeed...*but it was just a precursor to what's coming once we're alone tonight. Because I have every intention of reciprocating and giving him the ride of his life.

Fresh off of that hot orgasm, I stumble up the escalator to the exit, leaning heavily on him. But even now, my body burns with fresh arousal in mere anticipation of all the things we're going to do to each other tonight.

Damn, any man hot enough to make me forget I'm in the happiest place on earth is definitely a keeper. *For now*, anyway.

But I can't help but force myself to remember what he said this morning, about marriage and a family being a fate worse than death—about how he was too fucked up for the very thing I'd been spending the past few years planning for myself.

I shake my head and shrug it off. Today is all about the fantasy. He's made that very clear, and I'm more than happy to indulge myself. And I'm all for appreciating the significant effort it must have taken for him to plan this magical day.

From there, things do not stop. As the afternoon grows later, Lonnie guides us toward the backstage employees area and we stop at a nondescript building. With her trademark wide smile, she says, "This is our cast member locker and gym area. But we're taking the back entrance. There's a private shower and changing area waiting for each of you."

My eyebrows bob up, and I shoot Ash a speculative look. What does he have up his sleeve now? But he says nothing, avoiding my gaze and obviously playing dumb so I can't get anything out of him.

Inside is a large sitting room with makeup tables and wall-to-wall lighted mirrors. Adjacent, there are changing booths and showers in the room beyond. But I'm the only one here. Lonnie hands me several shopping bags from nearby shops on the resort.

Talk about getting totally and utterly spoiled on a day when I was already being spoiled. I feel like I've hit the lottery.

And when I pull out what's inside, I gasp so loud, I'm sure even my roommates up in Pasadena can hear me. Out comes silky layers of pale-blue fabric with a silvery sheen over the top. It's a designer cocktail dress with a transparent tulle overlay atop a scooped neck, A-line, and a full knee-length, swishy skirt. In a rush to put it on, I rip off my T-shirt and miniskirt and am about to slip the dress over my head when I notice a lingerie bag as part of the bundle.

Digging into that bag, I pull out a pale-blue lacy thong—barely a scrap of fabric—and matching see-through lace bra. I grab the small toiletry kit that came inside yet *another* bag and rush to the shower for a quick rinse before slipping on the gorgeous underwear and finally, the beautiful dress. When I call Lonnie in to help me do up the buttons, she gasps. "You look so glam! Don't forget the shoes."

The last bag contains a shoebox of silver and crystal-covered strappy heels with a matching clutch. After I apply some light makeup and fix my hair, I toss the comb and cosmetics into the clutch purse.

"You look amazing." She smiles.

I twirl in front of the full-length mirror, inspecting the look, feeling just like Cinderella with Lonnie as my approving fairy godmother. My heart speeds up at the thought of Ash's reaction to seeing me…and what he'll think later when he takes the dress off of me.

Lonnie disposes of the empty bags and throws the clothes I wore today inside another bag that has something else in it.

When I toss her a speculative gaze she giggles. "I was told to save this bag for later."

I frown in puzzlement. Later? What's happening later? Besides all our clothes coming off at whatever hotel we'll be staying at?

Lonnie then looks at her watch and almost jumps in shock, pale-blue eyes widening. "Ooh, we've gotta go! You don't want to be late for *this* dinner."

I shake my head and make my way out to the hallway when I spy my delectable date standing, waiting for us. He's utterly breath-taking, his imposing height and physique exquisitely clothed in a bespoke black suit, shiny black shoes and tie, and a crisp white dress shirt. Simple, stark, elegant and oh-so-masculine. My heartbeat races, and the expression on his face is even more of a turn-on.

He looks utterly enchanted by what he sees. He studies me like a feral lion might study a gazelle on the Serengeti. A tingle of anticipation rains over my skin, and arousal weighs low in my belly. What kind of night of passion is all of this leading up to?

If I pinch myself, will I wake up from this dream? There's only one way to avoid waking up—I won't be pinching myself!

"You take my breath away, Princess."

I beam at him and do a slow twirl to give him the full effect, arms outward as if I really am Cinderella, newly arrived at the Prince's Ball. Only when I complete the circle do I realize that he's holding a long, flat jewelry box in his hand. He steps up when I stop, and I stare at it.

Then he opens it up. "For the princess..." A thin silver and diamond circlet styled like fantastical leaves glimmers up at me from the dark-blue velvet. A modern sort of tiara to rest in my dark hair, almost like a hair band. Lonnie steps up to help me adjust it and then snaps a quick pic with her camera so I can see how it looks.

"I'll wait for you two love birds outside, but don't take too long. We can't be late!"

Once she's out, he closes on me and dips his head to kiss me, but I turn my head away quickly. "Lipstick. You're one unbelievably handsome devil, and I don't want to ruin the effect."

Without missing a hitch, he lands a long, lingering kiss on my neck instead. I suck in a breath the moment his mouth connects, my skin tingling with sensation. My heart is already racing.

"That beautiful neck is far too bare." He opens the jewelry case again and pulls out something else—a silver chain. A necklace with an old-fashioned skeleton key pendant with a diamond at the head. He asks me to turn around and then slowly brushes my hair away from my shoulders to put it on me.

The mere tickle of his warm breath on the back of my neck, makes me shake with need. Unfortunately, he makes no move to touch me beyond the firm hand he places on my back as we turn to leave the building.

Lonnie leads us right back into the park, back to where we were earlier, near the scene of that hot orgasm. But we don't stop at the Haunted Mansion; instead, we head straight to New Orleans Square, where the buildings are inspired by the architecture of the French Quarter in that famous Louisiana city.

I swallow, anticipating a nice dinner at the Blue Bayou, but we pass that entrance, too. I frown, turning to Ash with the question openly on my face.

He smiles but says nothing until, a few paces beyond the restaurant doors, he stops at a nondescript blue door that has a large placemat in front of it. In the center is a stylized number 33. He rings the ornate doorbell.

He didn't. He couldn't... He...

"Club 33? Holy shit! I never even dreamed of setting foot inside." He looks quite satisfied that I've recognized the significance of this. Club 33 is the most exclusive club in all the Disney Resorts. Yearly membership starts at five figures, which doesn't even include the fifty-thousand-dollar initiation fee. Becoming a member is the ultimate Disney fan's dream.

We're greeted by a smiling cast member who escorts us into a gorgeous courtyard beyond. "Mr. Grayson, Miss Anderson, you're right on time! Welcome to Club 33."

The courtyard has plants everywhere, decorative tiled floor and blue sky above us in a private enclave. There's a beautiful winding staircase that leads up to the entrance of the restaurant. My heart is in my throat. I can't believe any of this. It is a dream.

"Hello, Alice...welcome to Wonderland." Ash laughs as he takes in my reaction.

Subconsciously, I adjust my tiara and smile back at him, trying but failing to affect nonchalance. He takes me by the hand and leads me upstairs to an elegant restaurant all paneled in dark wood and decorated in creams, white and gold. We're seated at a secluded table all decorated with gold-rimmed white china that bears the Club 33 logo. I look down at it, blinking several times while I study it.

Over the next few hours, we're served an elegant meal—creamed salmon on creme fraiche, filet mignon on a bed of foie gras.

There's not much conversation, just a heavy sense of anticipation in the air. I feel so full of it, my throat tight, that I can hardly speak. As magical as this whole evening is, I can't wait until we're alone together and I can feel his weight on top of me, his hot skin sliding against mine. I can't wait until I can spread my legs for him and he can ease the ache and tension there.

I swallow and sip my wine, then I finger the beautiful necklace he placed on my neck earlier, stroking the pendant with my index finger. "What does the key represent?" I finally ask.

He stares back at me with that intent gaze, setting down his wine glass and sitting back in his chair. Then he gives a slight shrug. "It's whatever you'd like it to represent, Princess."

I bite my lip and hold that intense gaze that hasn't faltered from mine once. "But it does mean something, doesn't it?"

His eyes slowly drop to my cleavage, then linger on the pendant and slowly rise to meet my gaze once more. "It does."

And that's the entire answer. When I want to press for more, I'm cut off by the sommelier returning to fill our glasses again.

What a huge contrast this dinner is to the night before, sitting across the table from David, his self-interested diatribe, his out-of-the-blue marriage proposal.

I hold up my wine glass. "Going to be extra careful tonight."

His eyes narrow as he studies me, then he turns back to his plate and asks me casually. "What, ah…may I ask what happened at that dinner that had you running so urgently for the bathroom last night? You almost ran into my date."

My eyes twitch at the mention of his date, and I remember, vaguely, some woman shrieking, demanding to know who I was and why Ash was attending to me. Illogical jealousy streaks through me like a heated force I can't control. Ash and I had spent all morning in bed, exploring each other's bodies and taking pleasure from each other repeatedly and yet we'd happened to be at the same restaurant that night on dates with other people? How very strange.

I frown, thinking again about last night. What a difference between last night and this. I shrug in answer to Ash's question. "He was going on about getting membership into Exeter House. Says he just needs another reference to get in. He wanted me to introduce him to Evan Kohl..."

His expression doesn't change as he chews his bite and watches me, as if urging me to continue without exactly asking me.

"You, uh, you're not going to interfere with that, are you? If he gets approval?"

A brow quirks. "It doesn't work like that...but would you be angry if I did?"

I bite my lip, considering my feelings. It had been annoying, lately, the way David had been fixating on getting into Exeter. It was all he talked about for the past few weeks.

"I'd just...feel guilty. If it was my mentioning it to you that would prevent him from getting what he wants so much."

Ash smirks in response. "Oh, I have every intention of preventing him from getting what he wants. That just doesn't necessarily have anything to do with Exeter House, however." His heated look leaves me in no doubt that he's talking about me, not membership in Exeter House.

I swallow, suddenly thirsty, suddenly hoping we can skip dessert and go on to enjoying each other's bodies like we did yesterday. Suddenly wanting his body for my dessert.

As if reading my mind, he reaches across the table for my hand, and I give it to him. I watch, hypnotized as those powerful fingers wrap around my palm, my wrist, and close firmly, holding me fast.

"You won't sleep with him. David. You won't give yourself to him."

I hesitate to answer, studying his beautiful, long-fingered hand twined around my own. That had been the plan the night before last...to go to David's bed. To move our relationship along.

He proposed to me, and I should be overjoyed in achieving that objective, but...I don't know, my emotions are a cluster fuck right now. I don't know what to feel, or what to think.

All I know is that committing to Ash in any way, even by promising exclusivity, is a bad idea. If I allow the fantasy to bleed into reality, I just know he'll eviscerate my heart. My body is available to him, but me, my soul...that's something he absolutely can't have.

His hand tightens around mine, gripping my wrist like a manacle, and I look up into his intent stare, dark eyes burning into mine. I swallow, feeling my will falter in the face of that intensity.

"Promise me, Princess. You won't go to bed with him. You won't sleep with him. You won't let him have you in any of the ways I've had you and any of the ways I intend to have you."

I open my mouth to answer, to protest, but even before I can get that out, he tugs that hand he's gripping and I feel a small amount of pain from the pressure.

"Promise me, Princess. *Now.*"

CHAPTER 13
SEX AND FIREWORKS

*P*ROMISE ME, PRINCESS. NOW.

I swallow and glance down at the beautiful gold-plated china in front of me. He's demanding I promise that I'll never sleep with David, but why? Isn't Ash allergic to commitment? Sure seems like it. So why would he even want me to make a promise like that?

I glance back at Ash, meeting his intense gaze. "Ash, I just—" I clear my throat. "I don't know where any of this is going."

His grip on my hand tightens a fraction more, and his eyes narrow. "What are you asking?"

"Nothing," I say quickly. "I'm not asking anything. But what you want long-term and what I want long-term are two completely different things."

He releases my hand and sits back in his chair, brows drawn together like he's trying to figure me out. I can tell he's a man who usually gets what he wants, and I have a feeling he's going to push the issue. But before he can demand my promise again, Lonnie appears at his elbow. "Mr. Grayson," she says in a hushed, intimate tone, her hand on his forearm. I should be jealous, but he doesn't even spare her a second glance. "It's time."

"Thank you." He sets his napkin aside and stands, re-buttoning his jacket.

I look up at him. "Time for what?"

Ignoring my question, he walks around the table and pulls my chair out, then offers me his hand. "Shall we?"

I laugh a little. "I see what you're doing. You haven't answered my question."

"It's something you need to see for yourself." He flashes me a devastating smile, and heat immediately pools in my stomach. I'm sure whatever he has planned will be incredible, but honestly, all I want to do right now is peel that tailored suit off his six-foot frame and trace every inch of naked muscle with my tongue.

We step outside and take a short walk to the entrance of the Pirates of the Caribbean. The line is pretty long, but I know Lonnie will make sure we get onto the ride quickly. I bet we'll even get our own private boat.

"Another dark ride?" I lift my eyebrows suggestively. "Yes please, and thank you."

My body is still humming from the orgasm he gave me in the Haunted Mansion, and I can't help but wonder what he has planned for Pirates. Forcing me to pant and moan to the tune of *Yo ho, Yo ho, a pirate's life for me?*

But instead of leading us to the entrance of the ride, Lonnie leads us to circle around to the right, to a set of stairs going up. The second I see the red stylized *21 Royal* plaque at the base of the wrought-iron staircase, my heart stops.

I know exactly what this is.

"Ash, no." I squeak in disbelief. "You *didn't.*"

I pause mid-step, and he turns to look at me, our hands still linked. "21 Royal is all ours tonight," he says with a quirk of his lips. "Are you ready to make some magic?"

"Oh, my God, that was so lame," I laugh.

He lifts his brows and chuckles. "Oh, there's so much more where that came from," he says, tugging me up the curved staircase.

Lonnie meets us at the top of the stairs, and another cast member, James, introduces himself as the butler of 21 Royal. With a flourish, he opens the door to show us around the uber, ultra, *super* exclusive suite. It's the *only* place one can sleep over inside the park, and I don't even think it can be reserved. You'd have to know the president of the company, or something.

The suite is incredible, truly magical, with a large parlor, decorated in the classic Victorian style. The room is swathed in gold leaf and deep-blue velvet, and of course, there are touches of Disney magic everywhere. There's a grandfather clock that comes to life on the hour, triggering images and music from classic Disney films. On the mantel, there's a mechanical bird that sings and paintings on the walls that come to life. Best of all, there's a huge heavy wood canopy bed in the master bedroom. It's all *truly* extraordinary.

While I'm marveling at one of the watercolors in the hallway, the butler turns to Ash. "We have a number of after-hours experiences arranged for you and your guest, Mr. Grayson."

"Thank you, Charles," Ash says. "We will be retiring for the night."

The suggestion in Ash's tone sends a tingle down my spine. It's almost nine o'clock. Whatever Ash has planned, I know it's not sleep. And just the thought of him fucking me on that beautiful canopy bed sends a wave of heat straight to my core.

"Of course, sir. A concierge will be available all night for anything you may require." Then, with a smile, Charles ducks out of the suite and leaves us alone.

I'm still studying the painting when Ash walks up behind me and places his mouth against the column of my neck. The warmth of his lips makes my stomach flip, and I sink back against him, my body curving to fit against his strong frame.

"There's something I want to show you on the terrace," he whispers against my skin.

I shake my head and groan. "I'd rather explore the bedroom."

With a deep chuckle, he turns around and takes my hand, leading me through the parlor and out onto a beautiful private terrace that overlooks the Rivers of America.

I lean against the wrought-iron railing and look up at the night sky. It's a deep, royal blue tonight, which seems so fitting. Today, Ash truly spoiled me. He really made me feel like royalty. And now, here we are, in the most magical place of all.

He glances down at his watch, then back up at me. "Just in time."

I open my mouth to ask him what he means, but right on cue, music fills the park, and a thunderous boom sends several sparks screaming up into the night sky. A moment later, fireworks burst in the air, a rainbow of vibrant colors against the clear night sky.

"Oh, my God! We have a front-row view. This is amazing," I breathe.

On windless nights, they do a whole fireworks show with music. It's completely private and agonizingly romantic.

With the breath caught in my lungs, I glance over at Ash. He's not watching the fireworks, he's watching *me*. His lips are turned up in a devastatingly handsome smile that makes my stomach flutter.

I turn toward him. "Can I ask you something?"

"Yes."

"Why are you doing all this?" I ask, suddenly suspicious.

He shrugs one shoulder and glances down quickly, before looking back up at me with those sharp blue eyes. "You deserve it, Lexi."

"We just met. You hardly know me." I shake my head. "This can't be real. *You* can't be real. There has to be a catch." I narrow my eyes at him. "Are you a serial killer or something?"

Ash reaches out and tilts my chin up with the crook of his finger, his thumb brushing across my bottom lip. "I am very real, Princess, and it pleases me to see you happy. That's all you need to know."

I practically melt at his feet, right then and there. My God. This guy is rich, gorgeous, and it *pleases him* to see me happy. Is it actually possible for a guy to be this perfect? But, wait…did he just sidestep my serial killer question? "So, just to be clear, you *don't* kill people as a hobby?"

He laughs under his breath. "Not as a hobby, no."

I laugh, too. "Whew! Thank goodness. That could have been awkward."

As the show comes to its conclusion, fireworks exploding in the sky above us, Ash slips his arm around my waist and pulls me into a long, passionate kiss. This is *quite literally* the most sickeningly romantic thing that's ever happened to me. A kiss under a riot of fireworks with the hottest guy I've ever seen in my life. And he's not a serial killer.

Life doesn't get much better than this.

He slides his hand down my bare arm and hooks his fingers with mine, pulling me back into the privacy of the suite. Once we're inside, he hooks a thumb under the thin strap of my dress and pulls it down slowly, until it falls off my shoulder and exposes my lacy bra. Tugging the fabric of the bra aside, he growls when he catches sight of my beaded nipple.

"I've been craving you all day," he growls. Inching forward, he dips his head and takes my nipple between his lips, sucking hard, his teeth grazing my sensitive skin. My entire body comes alive, and I thread my fingers through his thick hair, tugging gently, urging him on.

"Oh, my God," I gasp. "That's…oh, God!"

When he pulls back, he says nothing, just picks me up and carries me to the master bathroom. Setting me down, he moves to fill the giant circular tub that's tucked into a blue-tiled alcove on the far side of the room. If a bathroom can be extravagant, this one definitely fits the bill. A beautiful stained-glass window, light from behind, glows just above the tub, and everything is equipped with gold-plated fixtures.

Once the tub is filled with water and soap bubbles, Ash approaches me. With a flick of his chin, he directs me to sit on the edge of the tub. He kneels, and as soon as I'm seated, he pulls my foot into his lap and begins unfastening my heels.

"Thank you for today," I say. "It's the sweetest thing anyone has done for me. *Ever*, actually."

My own mother never thought twice about me. She was too focused on her next relationship, on the next bad boy she could rope into marrying her. And once she'd managed to snag them, keeping them took every ounce of energy she had. An endeavor that always, inevitably failed. And me? I never factored into any of that at all. I was sidestepped. Ignored.

"Oh, the night isn't over, Princess. Not even close."

Once my heels are off, he sets them aside and tugs me up into a standing position. Then he undresses me, unbuttoning my silky dress, stripping off my lacy underwear, pulling my tiara from my hair. Then, I'm standing naked in front of him, wearing nothing but the necklace with the diamond key pendant.

His hungry gaze rakes over my body, and I shy away a little, covering myself self-consciously. We've had sex before, sure, but he's never seen me like this–standing in front of him, completely naked. I'm starkly aware of the extra fifteen pounds I'm carrying, the gentle curve of my hips, the little bulge of my stomach. Being studied by this gorgeous man is a whole new level of vulnerability that makes me want to crawl into a hole and hide.

Reaching out, he pulls my hands away from my breasts. "You are so fucking beautiful," he says, awe threaded into the deep timbre of his voice. "Don't ever hide yourself from me."

I reach out and tug at the lapel of his suit. "My turn."

With a half-smile, he shakes his head. "Into the tub."

I glance over my shoulder, then back at him. "Only if you join me."

He lifts a brow in silent challenge. I already know arguing with him will get me nowhere, so I do what I'm told and step into the tub, lowering myself into the warm water. Oh, my God, it feels so heavenly.

With a groan, I rest my head against the tub wall and close my eyes. I hear fabric rustling, but I keep my eyes closed. A couple of minutes later, Ash says, "Open your eyes."

When I open them, I suck in a sharp breath. Tiny lights sparkle overhead, inlaid into the dark blue tile surrounding the tub, giving the effect of twinkling stars in the night sky. There's even a hidden Mickey nestled amongst the "imagineered" constellations.

"It's amazing. How did you do that?" I ask.

"There's a switch in the bedroom," he responds, kneeling on the mat in front of the tub. At some point, he ditched his jacket, so now, his shirtsleeves are rolled up, just below his elbows, exposing his muscular forearms. And that's when I remember, seeing it again, the tattoo of a skeleton key on his forearm in black ink. Seeing it there, knowing it matches my necklace is so arousing for some explicable reason.

I want to ask him about it, but later. Right now, I want to enjoy this moment. I close my eyes again, and a second later, I feel his hands on me, a soapy washcloth moving up my body, over my stomach, and across my sensitive breasts.

His hand slips under the water. "Open your legs," he commands.

Without hesitation, I spread my legs, and his fingers slide down my body, past the curls at the apex of my thighs, and push into me—two or three at a time—filling me.

"Oh, fuck," I breathe, arching up into his hand.

The gentle pressure of his fingers gradually grows harder, faster with every masterful stroke, and if it's possible, his fingers seem to reach deeper inside me. I spread my legs wider and arch my hips upward, searching for the beautiful release. But he keeps it at bay, purposefully leading me right to the edge, then pulling back.

He's denying me on purpose. I can feel the restraint in every stroke. Slow, rhythmic movements. Gentle pressure. My body is wound so tight that I don't think I can take it much longer.

I arch into him again, my ass lifting off the floor of the tub. "Ash, please. My God."

"Tell me." That deep baritone reverberates through my bones. "Tell me what you want. Say it."

I swallow and squeeze my eyes shut. It's hard to think with his fingers inside me like this, stroking my clit with his thumb in soft, circular motions. "I want your cock inside me," I finally say.

"You want my cock, Lexi, or you *need* it?" His voice is infuriatingly calm. But behind that serene tone, I can hear the clawing desire in his voice, the barely there constraint that just adds to my desperation.

"I *need* it." I swallow again. "Please."

Before I can even process what's happening, I'm being lifted out of the water, and flung over the ledge of the tub. I glance over my shoulder and watch as Ash unzips his black slacks, just enough to pull out his rock-hard cock. He palms it, the weight of his shaft heavy in his hand.

With a slow, deliberate stroke, he glances down at me. "That's right, Princess. You *need* my cock and *only* my cock."

CHAPTER 14
NOT THAT SORT OF PRINCE CHARMING

I'M DRIPPING WET—IN MORE WAYS THAN ONE—AND BENT over the edge of the tub, and my entire body is wound tight with anticipation. With his polished shoe, Ash nudges my knee, spreading my legs wider.

I feel so vulnerable right now. If he hadn't just worked me up into a lather in the bathtub, I might just protest being flung over the tub with my ass in the air, but honestly, I'm wound so tight right now I just want the sweet relief of his cock inside me.

Resting my forehead on the smooth white porcelain, I wiggle my ass to convey my frustration.

"Patience," he growls, kneeling on the plush bathmat beneath me.

Reaching out, he palms the globes of my ass, his short nails digging into my skin. It takes everything in me not to wiggle again. He told me to be patient, and I know better than to disobey. He might punish me, or worse, refuse to touch me.

Spreading my ass cheeks, I suddenly feel his tongue on my pussy. One, long and languid stroke that sends pleasure sparking through my body. My toes curl, and I throw my head back. "Holy shit," I groan. "Oh, my God."

His tongue dips inside me, and he sucks gently. The gentle pressure on my clit is almost too much, and I clench my hands into fists. *Fuck.* I don't want to cry out, but holding back is taking every inch of self-restraint I have.

"I'm going to come inside this sweet pussy," he says against my folds. The deep rumble of his voice echoes through me, starting at my core, and radiating out to my limbs.

Oh, *yesss.*

I'm impaled on a bolt of white-hot lightning. I bite my lip as Ash lifts his head, and I feel the tip of his cock at my entrance. On instinct, my body jolts forward. With a deep growl, he digs his fingertips into my hips and pulls me back, entering me in one swift motion.

I gasp at the size of him. We've had sex a handful of times already, but I'm still getting used to his impressive length. Thankfully, I'm wet and ready, so he slides into me easily, all the way to the hilt. A long, bone-deep moan erupts from his throat, like he's been waiting for this moment all day.

"Fuck, Lexi," he grates out. "You were made to fit my cock. Feels so fucking good with you wrapped around me."

He takes a handful of my hair, and pulls my head back. The pleasure of his hard rod inside me, combined with the pain of him tugging on my hair is fucking intoxicating.

Drawing back slightly, he shifts his hips, and slams into me, again and again. I draw in a sharp breath in between the frenzied crashing of our bodies. At this angle, his huge cock feels even more overwhelming, reaching to the very depths of my core stretching me so wide as if just short of splitting me open.

"I own you, Lexi," he says. "You're *mine.* Say it."

He plunges in again with a sharp jolt. Once. Twice. But I don't say it. My mind is racing, fighting between intense arousal and trying to process the implications of what he's urging me to declare.

He blows out a hiss between his teeth when I hesitate a moment too long. His hand in my hair tightens to a painful level as he pulls out of me abruptly. When he releases his grip, I glance over my shoulder and see him standing.

"Wait, where are you going?" There's a whimper in my tone that I'm not proud of, but seriously, what the fuck?

Without a word, he picks me up, still wet from my bath, and slings me roughly over his shoulder, then slaps my ass—*hard*. I yelp as he carries me into the master bedroom and tosses me onto the canopy bed.

As soon as I hit the mattress, I roll onto my back. He glances down at me, his face drawn in anger, and I feel a flash of real, honest-to-God fear. What did I do wrong?

Shucking his clothing with clipped movements, he stands naked, his hard cock stretching toward me. I swallow, my mouth watering.

Every time I see him naked, I'm stricken by his harsh beauty. He's all hard lines. There's nothing soft, or vulnerable about him. He's all honed muscle. Fuck, even his thighs look like they could crush a grown man's skull. And his forearms—God, heat and hunger devour my core.

My eyes narrow on a mark on his forearm I hadn't seen or noticed before. A birthmark—no, a tattoo. It's a small key. A skeleton key.

But I have no time to ask him about it because he's unthreading his leather belt from the pants he was wearing while never taking his eyes off me. With that stern stare focused completely on me, he straightens to his full height and folds the belt in half, doubling it. My gaze fixes on it, the cold fear inside me escalating. Is he going to whip me with that?

"I-I'm—sorry," I choke out in between breathless gasps. I don't even know what I'm apologizing for. I just want us to start fucking again. I need his cock inside me, riding me forcefully until I come. I'm willing to say just about anything to get it. "It won't happen again."

He takes a step forward, and I swallow hard. Fuck, he's so imposing, and I'm feeling completely vulnerable like this, laid out before him as he hovers over me. *Damn.*

"On your stomach, ass up. *Now,*" he commands.

I hesitate. His intentions aren't entirely clear. Is he going to fuck me or punish me?

He lifts a brow in challenge. "Do I have to keep asking you twice?"

I don't dare question him, so without a word, I flip onto my stomach and raise my ass in the air. I feel so painfully exposed, the most intimate parts of my body on full display.

"You will be punished."

Before I can react—or even roll away—he places a strong, firm hand on my lower back, holding me in place.

I swallow. "For what?"

"For your hesitations. Not answering my question. Not rolling over immediately when I tell you to. I should *never* have to ask you twice to do what I ask or to answer me."

"I did as you asked," I protest. I've never been whipped before, but if I'm being honest with myself, I'm a little turned on by the idea.

"I own you. You are *mine*, Lexi. It's not a question, it's a statement. And when I tell you to repeat it, I expect you to do so without hesitation. When I tell you to roll over, ass up, you do it, immediately. No questions." His voice is calm and controlled. *Tightly* controlled. The pressure of his hand on my back increases as if he's anticipating me putting up a fight.

"Oh-okay," I say.

"*Yes, sir,*" he says in a tone that prompts me to repeat it.

"Y-yes, yes, sir."

"That's good." His hand on my back slides lower, smooths over my backside. "You learn quickly. And to make sure the lesson sinks in…three strikes on this pretty little ass."

Three strikes? That seems a bit over the top for such a small infraction.

"B-but—"

"*Please, sir,*" he grits out between clenched teeth. And before I can even argue, I feel the bite of the first lash at the full swing of his arm. The sharp, razor-like sting makes my eyes water, and I cry out.

He hesitates, waits for me to catch my breath. Knowing this might increase the punishment if I say nothing, I repeat dutifully in a hoarse voice. "Please, sir."

He doesn't draw the punishment out. Lashes two and three come in quick succession. By the time he's done, I'm biting down on my bottom lip, fisting the silky comforter, struggling to keep tears from falling down my cheeks. But mixed with the pain is the undeniable edge of pleasure, as well.

A moment later, I feel the tip of his cock positioned at my entrance. Instead of surging forward, he pauses. "You are mine, Lexi. Say it now. I will not ask again."

"Yes, I'm yours," I say in a rush.

Stillness. Silence.

"Sir," I add. "I am yours, *sir.*"

He enters me then, and I swear to God, it feels so good. His cock, once again, stretches me to capacity. His large hands clamp my hips, holding my pelvis fast against him as he slams into me with a grunt. My ass is still stinging, but the pleasure of him once again fucking me hard has me sinking into the mountain of throw pillows beneath my head.

The feeling of him inside me goes beyond the physical. I can feel him taking possession of me, staking his unrelenting claim. With each thrust, he's repeating that claim. *I own you. I own you. You are my possession.* It's a powerful drug, and I'm swept up in the intoxicating effect, under his power completely. I don't know how I'd ever be able to give it up.

He's far from gentle. His hold is hard, tight, almost bruising. His body rides me urgently. Each thrust is hard, almost violent, like he can't get deep enough inside me. His grunts of pleasure only spur my own moans in response.

He leans forward without breaking the rhythm of his thrusts. Once again, he threads his fingers through my hair and pulls my head back again.

He presses his mouth to my ear. "I'll use you for my pleasure, Lexi. As much as I want—however I need it. Your body is my *private* playground." He emphasizes the word *private*, growling the word into my ear, and I completely understand his meaning. David isn't allowed to touch me. *No man* is allowed to touch me.

I'm his and his alone.

His complete ownership of me, of my body, lights something inside my chest, a flame I'd worked so hard to suppress throughout my life. But I can't with Ash. I can't deny the white-hot passion between us, the flame that grew into a bonfire over the past couple of days. The symbiosis of his power to dominate me and my need to be dominated.

"Promise me *no* other man will touch you." He continues his unyielding pace, pounding into me, his cock reaching to my cervix, then pulling back, before surging forward to powerfully fill me once more.

I squeeze my eyes shut, consumed by the feel of him. "I promise," I murmur.

For the first time since he's started again, he halts his thrusting. With his cock buried deep inside me, his voice is quiet, dangerous. "I couldn't hear you."

"I promise, *sir*," I repeat, louder this time.

Releasing my hair, he nips at the shell of my ear. "Very good, Princess." I can hear the pleasure in his tone, and it makes my insides melt. My God. I live for this man's praise and assurance. What has he done to me?

He leans his full weight on my back but hasn't resumed moving, letting out a long breath, as if relishing the feel of our bodies hooked together. Then he reaches under me and touches my clit. I buck, unable to so much as move with his full weight pinning me down. The immediate shock of energy nearly launches me into the stratosphere.

Those long fingers stroke and stroke and stroke, and the deeply pleasurable sensation causes me to clamp down on him. He grunts as if relishing the feel of my muscles squeezing him. He still hasn't moved. I feel the heat of his ragged breath on the back of my neck. And yet, his fingers don't stop. Heat floods through my body, and I'm swamped with the need for him to fuck me even harder, faster.

Moaning, I press my cheek against the silky comforter, arching my back to get him to move again but he doesn't. He's coaxing me...closer and closer. I can't suck in enough oxygen, and my breath comes out in pants to match his.

"I love the feel of your tight little pussy squeezing me. Feels so fucking good, Princess. My sweet little tight princess. I want to feel you come on my cock."

That now-familiar pressure begins gathering in my center, brewing like a storm. His strokes are coming hard and fast now, his pelvis rocks gently against mine.

"I'm going to fill your pussy with my cum," he murmurs, his voice strained. "Would you like that, Lexi?"

The pressure of his fingers intensifies. "Yes, sir. Fill me, sir."

He's moving again, but slowly. His fingertips stroke my clit in short clockwise circles, in time with each measured thrust.

Soon, Ash's orgasm slams into him, and he growls my name. That's it. That's all I need. Something inside me shatters, and I completely come apart at the seams, pure pleasure rushing through my veins. I'm moaning and gasping, wave after wave of heat crashing over me, pulling me under, drowning me. I fist the comforter and lift my head, trying to catch my breath.

But he doesn't immediately roll off of me and I can feel him inside me. His hands slip up my sides, reach under me, cup my bare breasts. He kisses my neck, my ear.

"That was incredible, Princess. I could stay like this, with you forever," he breathes.

Uh, what? He's talking like some kind of dirty Prince Charming, come to whisk me away with promises of amazing sex ever after.

Long moments later, we're still breathing heavily when he finally pulls out of me and rolls aside. I collapse, rolling onto my back, panting. Every molecule in my body is vibrating, and I'm lightheaded, almost faint. It takes a full five minutes to come back to reality. I reach for him, but he's gone.

Minutes later, he returns with a warm washcloth.

"Spread your legs," he commands.

I'm too exhausted to fight him, or insist I do it myself, so I open my thighs obediently. He wipes me down gently, then takes the washcloth back into the bathroom. It's clear he'd already washed up while in the bathroom.

When he returns, he stops by the door. He's still naked, and I take a minute to appreciate his Adonis-like physique. He must be in the Exeter House gym all day, every day. Every muscle is honed to perfection and outlined under his taut skin.

"Watch this," he says with a smile. It's the first time I've seen a genuine, unguarded smile from him. A smile that reaches his eyes. And it melts my fucking heart.

Reaching out, he presses a button, and the entire room darkens. Thousands of stars are scattered across the ceiling, sparkling like diamonds, transforming the room into a nighttime paradise. But the most impressive effect is a painting above the bed that comes to life, revealing the mermaids from *Peter Pan* swimming in a sparkling cove.

"Oh, my God," I breathe. "Amazing."

With a low chuckle, he joins me on the bed, pulling me into his arms. We lie like that for...I don't know how long, curled up together. My head is on his chest. I'm warm, and I feel safe, listening to the slow, steady beat of his heart.

There's nowhere in the world I'd rather be than right here with Ash Grayson.

I twist my head to look up at him. "So, um, do you bring all of your girlfriends here?"

I don't know why I'm asking the question. The second the words slip past my lips, I regret them. What does it matter if he brings women here? I shouldn't care at all. But for some reason, I do.

"No," he says, reaching up to stroke my hair again. "I've never been in here before. This is only for you."

A sense of contentment drifts over me.

The last thing I remember him saying as I drift off into a pleasantly exhausted slumber is, "Sleep, my princess, but be forewarned, I won't stop at waking you in the night with just a kiss. I'm not that sort of Prince Charming."

Chapter 15
Too Good to Be True

Hours later, I come to consciousness slowly, languidly, the heat of arousal infusing every cell of my body. My body is a pool of melted liquid. My nipples are beaded to hard, aching points and my core is heavy, like molten metal.

As I slowly emerge through layers of sleep, I become aware of the source of this heavenly feeling. I'm flat on my back, my hands tied over my head to the bed frame and my thighs are spread as wide as they will go.

And between them, Ash's dark head hovers, lavishing my clit with attention. My eyes crack open in shock even as he presses his mouth harder against that bundle of nerves, and I'm launched immediately into toe-curling pleasure. Already so close to coming. I've only been awake less than a minute. When he begins to suck my clit, I can no longer contain the moans of deep pleasure, they rumble in my throat and escape my lips with animalistic wordlessness. I'm lost and feral in this cloud of ecstasy, enveloped and completely owned by the movements of his mouth, a slave to his whim.

The muscles in my leg tense and my back arches as I'm seconds away from coming when he stops and pulls away from me completely. I cry out, immediately shivering with need. I

133

strain against the tie he's used to keep my hands above my head. If they were free, I'd immediately be reaching to finish myself— I'm so close it might only take a stroke or two.

Instead, he comes to his knees, hovering above me, examining me. "My kiss has awakened Sleeping Beauty after all."

My eyes squeeze close as my back arches to him. "Please, finish me."

He reaches out and palms one of my nipples, and I gasp. He rolls the tip between thumb and forefinger. "Mmm. Did you really think I'd let you come before you'd earned it?"

"Ash!" I kick my leg, banging my heel against the mattress. "You woke me up. I deserve—"

"I'm the one who decides what you deserve, Princess. Don't ever forget that." His voice is stern and has an edge to it. With it, he demands my obedience and compliance without even having to utter those words.

His erection is painfully swollen and juts straight up. Where he's on his knees between my legs, he begins to slowly stroke himself, hovering mere inches above my pussy. I thrust my hips toward him, hoping he'll take the bait and push that hard cock inside me, fill me with what I need.

Instead, he puts a hand on my hip and pushes me flat against the mattress, then moves up my body, straddling me until his knees are beside my armpits and his huge cock fills my vision.

"I think it's my turn to enjoy the same attention I was just giving you." His eyes narrow, gazing down at me expectantly, and I open my mouth with no further prompting.

He lets out a long breath of expectation, then lowers himself, angling his hips so that his cock slides between my lips. With my hands tied to the headboard, I'm vulnerable and at his whim, unable to control the depth or speed of his thrusts into my mouth.

However, he starts slow, first pressing the tip and sighing with approval when I roll my tongue across the head of his pulsing erection. A growl forms in his throat, and almost immediately, he's deepening his thrusts, short and sharp, relentless.

Soon, he's got a grip on my jaw and he's thrusting deeply, then pulling out slowly. He groans with relish, telling me how good I feel, never breaking that primal rhythm, telling me he wants to own every part of me. Then, his cock swells huge in my mouth, and he thrusts it deep until it enters my throat. With a shout, he comes, spilling his seed down my throat. I suck him dry, and he gasps, the tension in his shoulders and his entire body dissipating with release.

Then, he's quickly unknotting the necktie he used to tie my hands. Not that kind of Prince Charming, indeed…

"I think my naughty little princess has more than earned an orgasm."

Oh, yes, please.

His hand strokes my clit as he lies beside me and takes first one and then the other of my nipples in his mouth, scraping them gently with the edge of his teeth. Pain and pleasure shoot down every nerve ending at once, and when I squirm, a heavy arm pins my body down as he continues to lavish his focused attention on my breasts, licking, sucking, tugging at them until they throb with pain and pleasure.

Meanwhile, his fingers slide across my wet folds and enter me as his thumb circles my clit. I'm vibrating with fresh need in less than a minute, and my body is tensing and contracting with ecstasy seconds after that. My eyes roll back into my head, back arching as I come violently, screaming his name.

He continues to stroke me and suckle my nipples until every last bit of my orgasm is wrung from me and the nerve endings are so sensitive they hurt. Then, he lifts his head and pulls me against him tightly, kissing my hair.

And the unmistakable feeling of his erection bumps my hip. I let out an exclamation, and he laughs. "I can't help it. When you moan like that, I don't care how exhausted I am, you're going to get me hard. Fuck, even looking at you sleeping made me hard as a rock. That's what started all this."

I turn and kiss his chest, pressing my cheek and our sweaty skin together. I can hear his heartbeat thrumming. Part of me wants to reach for his cock and start something again, but most of me is too exhausted to even think about it.

I wonder how many times he can fuck me in one night? One of these days, and soon, I want to find out.

But right now, I want to sleep.

We lie there in silence for several minutes when suddenly the peace and quiet is interrupted by buzzes from my phone. I have no idea what time it even is. Rolling over, I pluck it from the nightstand and glance at the time, 2 a.m. When I read the notification, I let out a groan.

"What is it?" Ash asks stiffly. I'm sure he thinks it's David.

"My mom," I answer, moving to reclaim my spot in the cradle of Ash's arms. "She just texted me. She's coming to town next week and wants to visit."

"Shouldn't that be a good thing?" he asks.

I scoff and set my phone aside. "I wish. She's probably just coming to tell me she's divorcing husband number five. It's always the same thing with her. She chases after the bad boy, marries him, then she's shocked when he inevitably fucks her over."

Ash strokes my hair. "Hmmm. What's that saying? 'Insanity is doing the same thing over and over again and expecting different results?'"

"Yes, that. Exactly."

"Who texts someone at 2 in the morning?"

"Oh, she does. The woman is up all night and sleeps through 'til the early afternoon." I readjust my position a little. "Anyway, I don't want to talk about her."

"Okay," he says easily.

"Distract me," I say. "Tell me something about yourself."

His hand stills, and I can sense the tension in him. "What do you want to know?"

I shrug. Honestly, anything at this point would be a plus. "How many siblings do you have? What's your family like? Your favorite color?"

With a deep breath, he seems resigned to my line of questioning. "One brother, younger by two years. My father was a shit parent, a shit husband. He was an angry drunk, and he often turned that anger toward my mother."

I swallow past the emotion that's bunched up in my throat. "My God, I'm so sorry."

"I just wanted to protect her," he says. "Even as a kid." He points to a long, thin scar on his forearm. "He gave this to me when I was eleven, trying to shield my mum from the knife he was threatening her with."

"Holy shit," I breathe. No wonder he craves control. His childhood was filled with pain and vulnerability.

"I hope she left him…"

There's a long stretch of silence, and when he finally speaks, he ignores my leading comment. "And my favorite color"—he takes my chin between his thumb and forefinger and angles my head up, so I'm looking up at him—"is emerald green. *This* color. The exact shade of your eyes."

I smile up at him, my heart thudding hard against my ribs. Fuck. He's really got me. Despite my better judgment, Ash Grayson has me firmly in his grasp.

Today was amazing, and I have to admit to feeling like Cinderella. Plucked from obscurity, seduced by Prince Charming. I only pray this prince isn't too good to be true.

I reach out and trace the small tattoo on his forearm, not far from the scar he's just shown me. "And this key? It looks just like the necklace I wore tonight. What does it mean?"

"Mmmm. I could tell you…but then I'd have to kill you. Or maybe fuck you senseless so you forget and don't ask me any more questions." As if threatening me with a loaded gun, he presses his still-hard cock against my hip.

I laugh, pulling back. "I never thought I'd say this, but you've completely exhausted me and I need some sleep."

"Mmm, sleep sounds good. Better if you do it wrapped in my arms, Princess."

With a rush of contentment and a feeling of complete security, I can't imagine anything better. So it happens just like that, me drifting off to sleep while wrapped inside his strong embrace.

At some point the next morning, I reach out and realize I'm completely alone in the bed. With a groan, I flip onto my back and blink my eyes open. Staring up at the blue pleated fabric of the canopy bed, I suddenly remember where I am—the Royal Suite at Disneyland. I still don't know how Ash pulled this off.

When I move to sit up, I instantly regret it. My thigh muscles burn from last night's sexcapades, and both my nipples feel raw and sensitive. But mixed with the pain is a delicious ache in my core that makes me feel thoroughly *owned* by Ash.

On the nightstand, there's a cup of coffee waiting for me and a pastry wrapped in a brown paper baggie. They must have come from the Starbucks on Main Street.

I remove the little lid stopper and take a sip. Mocha latte—my *favorite*—and miracle of miracles, it's still hot. Who knows how long it had been sitting there?

I lean back on the pillows and enjoy the heavenly coffee, wondering if Ash might just be *my* person. He's sexy as fuck, rich, dominant, thoughtful. He ticks all the boxes. Even a few boxes I didn't know existed until he came along.

And yet…there's something in my gut that's telling me to be careful. If watching my mom's fuck-ups has taught me anything, it's to never trust a bad boy. And Ash might just be the worst of them all. The jury is still out on that.

After a quick stop in the bathroom, I come back out and find a white oversize T-shirt folded neatly on the chaise lounge in the bedroom. I don't remember it being there last night, but then again, I was a little distracted. I unfold the shirt and snort at the logo. It says "I wanted the 'D'" with a stylized Disney "D."

"So inappropriate," I laugh to myself.

Ash will laugh when he sees me wearing it, so I slip the T-shirt on, grab my coffee and go in search of him. As I cross through the empty parlor to the short hallway, I hear his deep baritone drift in from the patio. The hallway is just a wall of windows, and I can see he's wearing a pair of Mickey Mouse pajama bottoms—the bottoms that match my T-shirt—and his cell phone is pressed to his ear. He's barefoot, pacing, and he looks deep in conversation.

Working while still on our Disney date? I'll have to punish him for that, methinks.

Cracking the patio door open, I move to step out and surprise him when something he says stops me cold.

"She's bloody useless," he growls into his phone, his back turned to me.

I suck in a sharp breath. Uh, what? *Who* is useless? I know it's none of my business, but I'm dying to get a little insight into Ash's life, even if it's his business life—whatever that business is. What makes someone useless in Ash Grayson's world? A lackadaisical assistant? A careless lackey?

"No, no, you're not hearing me. Lexi Anderson is nothing— she *means* nothing. It's not going to work." He's agitated, angry even, but it's clear he's trying to keep his voice low. "You know what, never mind, I'll talk to Katherine about this later."

What the *fuck*?

I swallow hard and close the door quietly. My cheeks heat with mortification as I head back to the bedroom. He thinks I'm *useless?* I mean *nothing* to him?

I don't even know how to process what I just heard, so I don't even try. All I want right now is to disappear. Finding my phone, I pull up my Uber app and schedule a car to come pick me up. Once that's done, I just focus on getting dressed, brushing my teeth and grabbing everything I brought with me yesterday— everything that's *mine.*

I'm just zipping my purse when Ash comes sauntering in from the patio, looking sexy as fuck. The Mickey Mouse pajama bottoms hang low on his lean hips, and his abs flex as he moves. His body is perfection, and he knows it. But his mouth is his real weapon. That smile. With the subtle twist of his lips, my insides melt into molten lava.

But that gorgeous smile fades when he sees I'm already dressed. "What are you doing?"

"I, uh, need to leave," I say stiffly. "I called an Uber. They'll be here in fifteen."

Don't cry. Don't cry. Do. Not. Cry.

His face is a mix of confusion and anger. "You called a car? Why? I'll take you home."

"*No*," I practically spit. "Thanks. I got it."

I move to brush past him, but he grabs my arm firmly without hurting me. He tugs me close, my breasts pressed against his naked chest.

"Lexi, what is this?" His face is so close to mine I can feel the heat of his breath on my cheek. His tone is smooth, and calm. "Where the fuck are you going?"

"I don't know why it matters to you. I'm useless, right? I'm *nothing* to you." I rip my arm out of his grip. "Fuck you, Ash Grayson."

I don't even wait for his response. Before he can stop me, I turn on my heel and rush out of the suite, tears stinging the backs of my eyes.

I should have known he was too good to be true. In real life, there are no Prince Charmings. There are only villains who wear false crowns.

CHAPTER 16
AN ADVENTURE?

"YOU KNOW WHAT? YOU PROBABLY HEARD IT OUT OF context. It probably has nothing to do with you at all."

Gwen is lying on my bed, sharing a carton of mint and chip ice cream with me. We're in our PJs watching old Doris Day movies. Gwen insists it will cheer me up. I'm not sure about that.

"It was absolutely as bad as I think it was," I say between spoonfuls of ice cream. "*Lexi Anderson means nothing. She's bloody useless.* He said that. He said my name. How else would I interpret that?"

She shrugs and considers for a moment, spoon poised in the air. "Well, like, who was he even talking to? What was the other side saying? You don't know any of that. Maybe there's an explanation."

"Um, yeah. He's an asshole who wines me, dines me, uses me for sex all night and then talks shit about me to some other woman in the morning," I say flatly.

Gwen's eyes light up like I've just wheeled in another gallon of slow-churned ice cream. "*Sex all night?* Jeez, I just realized I got zero deets from you. Tell me—"

I hold up my spoon like a weapon meant to fend her off. "Not in the mood to talk about it right now. He used me, let's focus on that."

Only I don't get the user-asshole vibe from Ash at all. He has more of an alpha, I-see-what-I-want–and-I-take-it type. And the extravagance of yesterday and the evening before our sexcapades had been limitless. I mean, the type of date a girl dreams about but never expects. He'd spent *thousands* on me and taken a considerable amount of time planning it, too.

I still have his damn necklace around my neck. I've been too tired to take it off, so I tucked it into the T-shirt of my jammies, determined to figure out the elaborate clasp later.

"All I'm saying is that you should give him a chance to explain. You stormed out of there before he could. What's the harm in a simple convo? If you're still not satisfied, *then* you can despise him. And I'll despise him with you." She points her spoon at me. "I'd just hate to see you walk away from something amazing."

I roll my eyes at her. "You just don't want me to accept David's marriage proposal."

Bit by bit, the events of the night that David proposed have slowly started to trickle back into my memory. I remember meeting David at the restaurant, sharing several drinks, and then the moment he asked me to marry him. But it's all hazy, foggy, as if it were a dream.

She smiles. "That too."

I toss my spoon onto the bed and roll onto my back, covering my eyes with the heels of my palms. "God, how did my love life get so complicated so quickly?"

Not long ago, I would have *killed* to hear the words "Will you marry me?" from David. It had all been a part of my plan. David was perfect husband material.

But now…with Ash in the picture, it's so much more complicated. And honestly, though I was furious with Ash, I still had no idea how I'd respond to David's proposal. It wasn't as easy as I'd envisioned.

"You know what you need to de-stress?" Gwen asks after swallowing another spoonful of ice cream. "A night on the town, an adventure. Exploring new things. Like…for example, a sex club."

I cover my eyes with my hands. "Oh, Jesus, not that again."

"It's for my article. You said you'd go with me," she whines.

"You're right. I did," I sigh. "But there's no chance that one of the other roomies will go with you instead?"

I've never been to a sex club, and I'm more than a little wary about this hare-brained scheme of hers.

But she gives me a look. The *you promised me* look.

To stall her, I let her know I need a nap. I actually am really exhausted.

And still sore from all the sex the night before. The memory of Ash's hands, his mouth, his body on mine has me shivering with the memory of him. And I just can't anymore.

But the moment Gwen leaves, muttering that she'll "ask around" to see if someone else can go, I don't lie down on my bed. Instead, I pull my phone off the charger and turn it on.

And it practically blows up with messages. There are four voicemails from Ash and nearly double the amount of texts from him. I delete the voicemails, unlistened to, ignoring Gwen's advice to "hear him out." I leave his text messages unread and instead key in on David's name. There's a red number three by his name.

Hey...been thinking about you since our date the other night. You've been quiet on all your social. I assume you're still not feeling well?

I swallow, thinking about Ash's suspicion that David roofied me, then sigh and shake my head. Probably another bullshit lie to get me to doubt David.

I'm really hoping you're feeling better by now. Starting to get worried I haven't heard back from you. I'm dying to see you, baby. Can we meet up? Even if to bring you chicken soup?

Awww. I bite my lip. What a sweetheart. My mouth tugs up at the corners, and I blink, warmed by his concern and his desire to see me. So different from Ash's arrogant two-faced behavior. David is so genuine and affectionate. Sweet. Attentive.

Dying to hear from you. No pressure on that certain question I asked, of course. I just need to hear your voice. I'm truly worried. Send me an emoji? Some sign of life? Don't make me come knock on your door because I just might do that tonight.

I laugh. After the pain from Ash's words, it's such a welcome relief to know that someone cares.

I swallow and text him back, deciding to keep it light.

I'm fine. So sorry. The phone's been off for over a day. I sigh. It's a lie but...maybe he'd feel less rejected that way?

The dots show up immediately, and I see that he's reading and responding to my text.

God, what a relief. You wouldn't believe what's been going through my mind.

I smile as I key in my reply. *So sorry you were worried about me.*

Come over tonight? Have dinner with me. Maybe watch a movie and just chill?

I blink. Netflix and chill…. Did he just proposition me? I'm about to agree to it when I hesitate, my thumb hovering over the screen.

Oh, sorry…I have plans. Gwen needs me to go with her to do some research for an article.

It was good for an excuse anyway, even if I really wasn't planning on going with Gwen. Especially if she could scare up a replacement. Though if I'm being honest, I am a little curious about this *club.*

I've never been to, nor did I even hear of, places like that before. Gwen promised to open me up to a whole different world.

Want company? I can come along…

I frown at the message. What would he do if I told him where Gwen wanted to take me tonight? Curious to see the reaction, I key in my reply quickly before I chicken out.

She's researching sex clubs and taking me to one. Some place in Westwood.

The dots show up again immediately. Go away, then show up again. This repeats three or four times before I set my phone aside and go to lie down, suddenly wanting that cat nap.

Just as I lie down, the phone rings. Assuming it's David, I scoop it up but make sure to check in case I accidentally answer a phone call to Ash. *Maybe I should just block the fucker.*

"I seriously thought that was a typo," he says the minute I answer. "A sex club?"

I sigh. "She's afraid to go alone and she says she has a great lead on an article."

"Okay, but is it that particular sex club or just any sex club? Because I know a classy place in Malibu I can get us into. And you're definitely going to want a bodyguard. I don't want to chance the men being all over you. And if they have eyes, they *will* be all over you."

I frown. "You go to sex clubs?"

"It's not a hobby of mine, no. But I've had a couple out-of-town clients ask me to show them the town, so to speak."

I arch an eyebrow. "My, my. You are full of surprises." Nevertheless, the corners of my mouth tug up in a smile.

"Just want to protect what's mine..." I blink, unsure how I feel about it. Being claimed as *mine* by two different men in as many days is as dizzying as it is exhilarating. With a pinch of overwhelming thrown in there for good measure.

I swallow. "I'll, uh, I'll check with Gwen."

"Yes, please don't go to some shady place, two women all by yourselves. If you want to explore, let me take you to this place in Malibu. I've only been a couple times, but it really is a sight for curious eyes. Classy but definitely of another world."

My eyebrows twitch up. Now I'm more than curious. I'm intrigued. And wondering what type of effect such a place would have on David. I swallow.

"Let me get back to you after I talk to Gwen."

"Okay, well, assuming it's okay with her, I'll have a car pick you both up at eight and take you there so I can meet you. I'm working over on this side of town today. If that's okay."

Repeating that I'd let him know, I click off but not before he tells me, very pointedly, that he loves me and can't wait to see me tonight.

Minutes later, I yank Gwen out of the hallway as she passes on her way to the bathroom. I less than gently pull her into my room.

"Ow! Jeez. Why so crabby?"

"Did you find someone to go with you?"

Her eyes widen. "Oh, you were serious that you didn't want to go? I thought you were just pretending to be a bad friend—you know, as a joke or something."

I heave out a sigh and roll my eyes. "I'll go, okay? But on one condition."

"And what's that?" she replies, eyes narrowing suspiciously.

Oh, she's not going to like this...but I don't care. She needs me more than I need her. "Well, I was just talking to David..."

"What, why? Weren't we writing him off?"

I scowl. "I was just talking to David," I repeat as if she hadn't said anything, "and he has a better place to take us."

Several emotions cross Gwen's face as she's apparently trying to figure out if I'm serious. "What place? Did he give you a name?"

I shrug. "He just said it was in Malibu and that it's classy."

"It's not his house, is it?"

I laugh. "No, he lives in Brentwood."

Her mouth quirks. "Okay, fine. But it better be good or we're going to the other place tomorrow night. *Without* him. Got it?"

I don't nod or agree to that. I've learned my lesson on committing to her schemes.

"I don't want to hang out at this place for hours, either," I say. "Promise me we'll leave the second you have enough material for your article."

"As long as your dude's place is sufficient for said material, I'm fine with that."

"Pinky promise?"

With a feigned heavy sigh, she rolls her eyes and holds out her pinky. I crook mine around it and she does likewise.

"Great," I say dryly. "Now what does one wear to a sex club?"

With David sending a car for us and promising to meet us there, and with Gwen promising we can leave the minute she has her story, I feel a little better. Hopefully we'll be in and out in less than an hour. Maybe afterward, David and I can have a long walk on the beach—and a serious talk.

And maybe, just maybe all of this will help me forget Ash.

It seems like a futile hope, but I can try. Once Gwen vanishes back to her room to dig through her own closet, I reach over to my phone and block Ash's number, leaving his text messages unread.

That will drive him crazy.

At 8 p.m. sharp, a town car pulls up and the driver rings the doorbell. Gwen and I are ready to go. I've opted for a little black cap-sleeved dress that hits just above the knees with matching black patent Louboutins. It says classy while still being simple. I'm hoping to be able to blend into the woodwork and be a proverbial fly on the wall, a curious observer.

The driver is silent, and beside me, Gwen stares out the window, practically vibrating with excitement as she keys some notes into her phone. At least I hope those are notes and not her live-tweeting the experience. Good God. That'd be a nightmare.

I'm distracted as the bright lights of Los Angeles whir by. We speed down the 10 freeway toward Malibu. Even with relatively light traffic later on a weeknight, it takes nearly an hour to get there.

But I'm not paying much attention to the drive. Instead, I'm thinking about Ash, goddamnit. I miss him already and it's been only twelve hours since I left him in Anaheim and hopped into an Uber.

My mind is jostled from my thoughts when I feel the car slow and I glance out of the window to see a familiar building, if a slightly different entrance to it. My stomach immediately drops as my eyes crawl upward to the sprawling, elegant twin towers conjoined by a walkway.

And our driver has pulled up to the decorative, covered porte-cochere of the driveway.

Unmistakably, it is Exeter House.

CHAPTER 17
THE FIELD TRIP

"**O**H, FUCK, NO," I SAY, SHAKING MY HEAD. "THIS CAN'T be right. Exeter House doesn't have a sex club."

I reach over and knock on the glass partition separating us from the driver. The window lowers.

"Ma'am?"

"Hi, yeah, I'm sorry, you've made a mistake. This is Exeter House. We're looking for a club. I think it's here in Malibu—" I dig my phone out of my purse. "You know what, I'll call David and ask him for the address."

"This is the place. Mr. Melnik gave me the address." He holds his phone up and shows me the text. Yup, he's right. This is the place. David even says in his text that it's connected to Exeter House.

The driver holds up two black, feathery masks. "He also said you need to wear these. Something about club policy."

With a squeal of excitement, Gwen snatches up the masks. "These are so pretty. I'm taking the one with pearls around the eyes." She hands me the other one—just a black velvet half-mask with long black feathers affixed to one side. Simple. Elegant. And it matches my plain black dress.

With the mask in my hand, I fall back against my seat. "This isn't what I signed up for. I'm not going in there."

"*What?* Why not? This has got to be the most exclusive sex club in the L.A. area hands down. We *have* to go in." Gwen is practically breathless at this point.

I shake my head again. "I can't run into Ash. If he finds me in there without him, he'll go into orbit."

Well, maybe. We're broken up. Or are we? He has to know that I'm upset about what he said on the phone. But does he know I never want to see his smug, unnaturally handsome face again? There's a chance that blocking his number didn't make that clear.

"Okay, I hear you," Gwen says, sobering. "But what are the chances he'll be in there today, right now? Besides, we have to wear masks. If by some chance he's in there, he'd never recognize you."

She may have a point about the masks. "Okay, but we leave *the second* you have enough material. One hour, tops."

Gwen's green eyes light up. "Deal."

Lovely.

I sigh, resigned to my fate. This isn't what I want to be doing with my Monday night—watch a bunch of weirdos bumping uglies in full view. And not just regular weirdos. Rich-as-fuck weirdos.

"You are literally the worst roommate ever," I say flatly as we get out of the car and tie on our masks.

"Just stop acting all squirrelly," she says. "Or the other guests will suspect something."

"Squirrelly?" I scoff. "I'm not acting squirrelly."

She flashes me side-eye.

"Fine," I say. "But who wouldn't get a little squirrelly about going to a fetish club? I mean…really." I glance at the glossy black double doors ahead of us, anxiety coiling in my stomach. "Let's just get this over with. I have some old *Friends* reruns waiting for me at home."

A hot cup of tea and *Friends* reruns are my go-to cure for just about anything. And right now, I need a cure for Ash. The man has seriously gotten under my skin and in my head. Even now as I'm about to walk into a damn sex club, all I can think about are his lips gliding across my skin, his hands gripping me tightly as I writhe beneath him. I'm so fucking hopeless.

"Should we wait for David?" Gwen asks.

I check my phone and scroll to an unread message I hadn't noticed before. Then I put it away, sighing. "He just texted me. Says he'll be a little late. But we're 'on the list' whatever that means and just to go on in." Weird…since he'd seemed so intent on being our protector tonight. Now he wants us to just go on in without him?

Just as Gwen and I approach the entrance, one of the doors opens abruptly, revealing a tall, incredibly beautiful woman with dark hair and brown eyes. She's wearing a gold, knee-length dress that hugs her curves to perfection. Wow.

Beside me, I hear Gwen suck in a breath. "Oh, uh, hi. We're…" There's a long, awkward stretch of silence as her words fall away.

"My name is Ms. Lawrence," she says stoically, her gaze falling to my necklace, lingering for several moments on the key pendant. "You must be Ms. Anderson. Will Mr. Grayson be joining you tonight?"

My heart leaps into my throat, and I instinctively reach up and cover the necklace Ash had given me, a key that matched the tattoo on his arm. I'd forgotten to take it off…or, if I'm being honest with myself, maybe I wasn't ready to take it off.

I guess I've been quiet too long, because Gwen reaches out and squeezes my arm, pulling me from my daze. "No," I say quickly. "I won't be with him tonight. This is Ms. Taylor. We should be on the list."

With a slight, almost imperceptible nod, Ms. Lawrence steps aside. "There are no phones allowed inside the club. Please check them in at the first room before the main entrance. Also, you must keep your masks on at all times," she says. "No blood play, and if you wish to make use of the fetish rooms, just give the concierge your names."

"Um. Okay, thanks," I say, swallowing. Blood play? Fetish rooms? What the fuck have we gotten ourselves into?

I glance at Gwen and suppress a grimace as I power my phone down, hoping David will have a way to find me whenever he gets here. Hopefully not long now. Then we do as asked and turn our phones in and are given tickets in order to claim them later.

Music pulses as we move through the doors and into the club. The entry area is a balcony that looks down onto a sea of writhing, masked, half-clothed bodies below, all dancing to the steady pulse of music in low, sensual lighting. As we head down the staircase to the main floor, a masked waitress hands us each a drink.

My anxiety is next-level, so I take a sip immediately. Vodka and cranberry. Nice.

Glancing around, I take in our surroundings. It's all polished gold chrome and gold-veined black marble. Strings of amber lights barely penetrate the darkness. Directly in front of the bar, there's a sunken lounge area with low tables, velvet couches, and a grand piano. The walls are lined with more private booths, many with their black curtains pulled closed to hide the occupants.

To our right is the dance floor, and it's filled to bursting with people. Holograms of scantily clad, writhing couples are projected on the walls. Half-dressed women undulate on elevated platforms that surround the dance floor, their hips swaying seductively to the pulsing rhythm.

Shit, this place just drips with sin and decadence.

I glance around, searching for…I don't know what. One thing is certain, I'm *not* looking for Ash Grayson. Honestly, even if he was here, Gwen is right, there's no way I'd be able to pick him out of the crowd. Everyone, including the staff, is masked, and the lights are so dim, it's hard to see anything in detail. Probably the very point.

Gwen clears her throat and pulls out a pen and small notepad from her clutch. "Good thing I brought this. I suspected they'd take our phones. Now that we're in, we just need to find someone who will talk to us."

I blink at her. "You aren't seriously going to *interview* these people, are you?"

She looks exasperated, but it's a little hard to tell under the mask. "Why else would we be here?"

"I don't know, to observe?" I offer, equally exasperated. We probably should have laid this out before we left the house. But here we are. "First things first, no taking notes at a sex club. That's just weird. And you said you want us to blend in." I take the pen and paper from her hands and set them aside. "Second, if we're going to get out of here in an hour, we need a strategy. You take the lounge area. And I'll take the fetish rooms." I have a feeling I'm going to regret volunteering to enter the darkest parts of the club, but it doesn't matter. I'm going to get Gwen the details for her article if it kills me—and it just might, especially if Ash gets wind of the fact that I'm here.

Gwen nods. "Okay, good plan." Then she pauses as though just realizing something. "Wait, we're separating?"

"Yes," I hiss loudly. "Just…keep your clothes on and you'll be fine. Meet back here in an hour."

Before Gwen can argue, I turn and make my way toward the staircase, dodging half-naked, gyrating bodies as I pass. No one even glances up at me, thank God.

At the top of the stairs, there's a large, muscular bouncer standing there, hands clasped in front of him, all business. "Members only," he grates out.

"I'm Lexi—" Before I can tell him to check with the concierge because my name is probably on the members-only list, his gaze falls to my necklace, and he stiffens.

"Of course, Ms. Anderson," he says, his gaze darting over my shoulder. Is he looking for Ash? If he is, then he's going to be disappointed. And I'm not offering an explanation for his absence. I don't owe this guy anything.

I wait a second, then lift my brow. "Well, can I pass?"

He looks a little hesitant to let me go, but he ultimately steps aside.

"Thanks," I snap and pass him.

Just like Exeter House, Obscura is dripping in wealth. The private area is gorgeous, this room decorated in muted creams and white with gold accents, sleek white and gold marble. Even an exotic fish tank, all in low lighting in the central lounge area. There are three hallways that stretch out in different directions.

Expensive pieces of artwork hang on the walls. Like I said, *dripping* in wealth.

Up here, the music isn't quite as loud, but I can still feel the slow, rhythmic melody vibrating through my body. People sit closely with drinks in hand or are already in the throes of foreplay on the couches, but there's nothing lewd, fortunately.

Sucking in a deep breath, I make my way down one of the dark hallways to a door at the very end. The door is slightly ajar, and I step inside. The room is small, nearly empty with a dark leather couch and a low wooden coffee table. There are no windows, except for one large pane of glass that takes up the entire west-facing wall. I step closer and realize with a jolt that it isn't a window that looks *out*—it's a window that looks *in*. It's a two-way mirror, designed to allow the occupants of this room to watch whatever is happening in the adjacent room.

And there's *a lot* happening next door.

At least a dozen different types of whips, paddles and riding crops hang neatly on the walls—and several contraptions that looked like medieval torture devices, complete with spikes and leather restraints.

Three women are kneeling in the center of the room, naked, their hands secured above their heads by heavy metal chains. They each have ball gags in their mouths with two men hovering over them. I can only see the men's backs, but both are wearing jeans—one is dark and swarthy with several long scars bisecting his back. The other guy has long dirty-blond hair, pulled back in a messy man-bun. They are both sexy as hell and wielding whips, circling the women.

Watching them, I feel my own body begin to respond—heat pulses through my veins, pooling between my thighs, making me ache. In another life, I could have been one of those women—on my knees, taking pleasure in the hot lash of the whip. But in my carefully constructed world, this kind of pleasure is shocking. Twisted.

The breath catches in my throat as the dark-haired man drags the tip of his whip down one of the women's backs, circling the globe of her ass. Then he pulls the whip back and strikes her. She arches her back, a look of pure ecstasy on her face.

Just watching them sends white-hot desire rushing through me. I can imagine Ash doing that to me—tying me up, spanking me. And as much as I hate to admit it—even to myself—the idea of giving him complete control, of surrendering to him, makes me wet.

I'm watching the scene play out, when I get the sense there's someone behind me. Before I can turn around, I feel a hand on my hip, fingertips digging into my skin through the thin fabric of my dress. Hot breath bathes the back of my neck, and I stiffen when a pair of warm lips press against my nape.

A familiar voice whispers in my ear. "Hello, Princess."

CHAPTER 18
CAUGHT

I WHIP AROUND, WRENCHING MYSELF OUT OF HIS GRASP. "Ash." Fuck, did I just conjure him out of thin air? "What are you doing here?"

He looks all-powerful in a tailored gray suit and a black domino mask. Every time I see him, I'm reminded just how beautiful he is—the strong line of his jaw, those full, perfect lips. But it's his confidence that gets me. He could walk into any room and be perfectly at ease. He owns every space he's in.

But what the fuck is he doing *here?* I should have trusted my instincts. Something deep in my gut told me he'd be here tonight. I don't know how he managed to find me, but Ash always seems to be everywhere at once. It's like he's fucking omniscient.

He doesn't answer my question, instead, he steps forward and takes my chin between his thumb and forefinger. "We have unfinished business, you and I."

I swallow and gaze up at him unflinchingly, the show beyond the window now forgotten. I need to show him my resolve. "We don't have any business together. Not anymore. Not after what I heard you say about me on the phone."

He closes his eyes briefly like he's trying to gather his patience. "You don't know what you heard."

Uh, *what?* Does he think I'm an idiot? "When I hear my name, followed by the words 'she's nothing,' the message is pretty damn clear." My voice is raised now, I can't help it. He's trying to fucking gaslight me. "A statement like that isn't open to interpretation."

"Whatever you *think* you know, Lexi, you don't," he says through his teeth, like he's barely in control of his anger. It must be hanging on by a thread. "You have no fucking idea what you've walked into."

I twist my chin out of his grip. "Then tell me."

His hand falls to his side, and he shakes his head. "It's too dangerous."

I lift my hands up, then let them fall to my sides. "Typical response. I ask for clarity, and all you give me are riddles." I move to push past him. "Honestly, I don't have time for this. David's on his way. He could already be here." I deliberately use David's name, because I know it will piss him off. Petty? Maybe. But pissing Ash off feels damn good. "He's probably looking for me right now. I need to go downstairs."

As I brush past him, he reaches out and grabs my wrist, tugging me so that I spin around, facing him. I hate to admit it, even to myself, but Ash has a pull on me that I can't escape. I'm trapped. Caught in his snare.

His perfectly shaped lips lift into a sardonic smile. "Your *boyfriend* isn't coming." He practically spits the word.

I pause and furrow my brow. "What? What do you mean? How do you—"

He doesn't even let me finish. "This is *my* world, Princess. My dark domain. You don't think I know everything that happens here? Ms. Lawrence told me you were here and that David had added your name to the list. He arrived ten minutes ago and I had him turned away at the gate. You're both lucky I wasn't out there to greet him personally."

I feel a moment of despair. David was my shield, the only defense I had against Ash. "Why? David hasn't done anything to you."

There's something in Ash's eyes—anger? Resolve? With his free hand, he reaches out and brushes a finger over the skeleton key pendant that's hanging around my neck. "Because he dared to try and claim what is *mine.*"

That was my first mistake—thinking I could walk in here and stay hidden from Ash. David is no match for Ash's power and control. A flimsy mask could never hide me from him. He's right, this is his world, and the power he has here seems infinite.

"I'm not yours," I say, but my voice sounds pathetically weak in my own ears.

"Oh, no?" He's still holding my wrist, and he pulls me toward him. I don't fight, because there's no point. His hand skims up my naked thigh and reaches the hem of my dress, then dips beneath. His finger moves to the inside of my upper thigh, to the heat of my center. "I'll show you just how much I own you, Lexi."

The sound of my name on his lips practically makes me whimper. His deep, languid baritone is an aphrodisiac. I could listen to him for hours, just saying my name, whispering dirty things in my ear. Fuck, I'm so weak.

"Open your legs," he commands.

When I don't immediately obey, he curls his hand around my upper arm and roughly pulls me over to the two-way window. In the room beyond, the two men and three women are still there, though one of the couples is now fucking.

Oh.

As the scene in front of me plays out, a renewed surge of desire rushes through me. Heat pulses in my center, making it ache. My nipples tighten, and my breasts feel heavy. I pull my gaze away from the entwined couple, attempting to ignore my body's intense reaction. I don't want to give Ash the satisfaction of knowing it turns me on.

"You want this, Princess. I see the way your eyes light up when you watch him punishing her," he says roughly in my ear. "You can't hide this part of yourself from me."

I just stare at the people on the other side of the glass, wondering what it would feel like to be owned and cherished and commanded like that. "You don't know me at all," I say, but even as the words tumble from my mouth, I know it's a lie. We just met, and yet, somehow, he seems to know me better than I know myself.

"Look at me," he commands.

I swallow and turn around.

"You ran out of the Royal Suite without allowing me to explain. And now I find you at a fetish club," he says. "That's very disobedient."

He cocks his chin in a devilishly handsome way, and I just want to lift up on my tiptoes and press my lips to his—then strip every piece of clothing off his body and beg him to fuck me. I don't, though. Instead, I tilt my chin up and glare at him. "I can do whatever the hell I want." My fists close at my sides.

His dark eyes collide with mine. "I told you that David is dangerous."

"I'm not your problem anymore, Ash," I say tightly. "We're done."

That phrase, *we're done*, snaps something in him, obviously, because he advances on me, pressing my back harder against the cold glass. The heat from his body pulses through me, and I suck in a trembling breath. "*Ash...*"

Dipping his head, he pulls the lobe of my ear into his mouth. "We're not even close to done, Lexi," he whispers in my ear. "Tell me you don't want my cock inside you right now." In one fluid motion, he flips me back around, so my front is pushed against the window again, my hands braced on either side of my head. His hand slips beneath my skirt and finds the lacy edge of my panties. "Tell me you don't want me to fuck this sweet little pussy."

"I..." I try to tell him I want him to leave, but his fingers find my wet channel and push inside, filling me. "Oh, God," I breathe.

I should tell him I don't want this. He fucked up and needs to stay away from me. But I can't. I need this. I need to feel his hands on me, possessing me. I *want* it.

With his knee, he guides my legs farther apart, giving him better access. His fingers pump in and out of me in a steady, powerful rhythm. I can't take it. It's too much. His thumb swirls around my clit, applying just the right amount of friction and pressure.

"Do you see how good I feel inside you, Lexi?" When I don't answer, he pauses. It's just a split second, but panic wells up inside me. "Answer me," he growls.

I manage to push out one word, "Yes."

On the other side of the window, I can see the women, still on their knees, their backsides pink from the whip. With every flick of the whip against their skin, they cry out and then immediately beg for more. "Do you want to be spanked,

Princess? Is that what you want?" Ash must be following my line of sight. I don't answer, too engulfed in sensation to form a coherent thought.

He pulls his hand away and takes a step back. I whimper.

"Take off your panties."

Still braced against the window, I try to catch my breath. My entire body is humming with tension, desperate for release. Slowly, I tug my lacy black panties down and step out of them, then flick them aside.

He sits on the edge of the low table and pulls me down so I'm kneeling beside him. He puts me over his lap, facedown, and pulls the hem of my dress up, exposing my backside.

White-hot anticipation pulses through me. My entire body is lit like a flame, and I feel like I'm going to explode.

"You know you shouldn't be here," he says. "You're *mine*, Lexi. Shall I remind you?"

I draw in a sharp breath at his words, raw need clawing at me from the inside.

Smoothing his hand over my ass, he lifts his hand and brings it back down with a heavy *whack*. A jolt vibrates through my body, and I gasp, squeezing my eyes shut. The pain is sharp and prickly. Another whack, then another, and another. Tears form in my eyes as all of my emotional barriers begin falling away, one by one.

"God, I love this hot, tight ass," he growls. "Your body was made for me to fuck."

His words wash over me, pushing me to new heights of pleasure. I imagine him inside me, hard as stone, and I swear to God, that image is enough to make me come. I'm on the brink already.

The door opens and several people filter in, laughing, kissing, and falling all over one another. Ash doesn't even flinch. Another *whack.* Then another.

"Oh, will you spank me next?" one of the women coos.

My jaw clenches. Every instinct in me wants to shove her away, out of the room. It's on the tip of my tongue to say, "He's mine," but I'm too overwhelmed by sensation to utter a single syllable.

Suddenly, Ash rises to his feet, pulling me along with him. I can see the women now—one has long blond hair, and the other has a short pixie cut. And they're both gorgeous with curvy, hourglass figures and red pouty lips. The pixie has breasts that are way too perky to be real.

A man is kissing the back of the blond woman's neck, but she's too focused on Ash to care. With greedy hands, she starts clawing at his suit jacket, smoothing her hands over his back even as his full attention is focused on me.

With a low, guttural growl, he unzips his pants and pulls out his cock. My gaze flicks to the swollen head, and I swallow. A bead of pre-cum wets the tip, and I nearly groan.

The pixie licks her lips and moves forward, running her hands over his shoulders. I want to scream, to claw her eyes out, but I'm rooted to the spot by Ash's hard stare. He doesn't react to the women at all. His singular focus is on me. And only me.

CHAPTER 19
LIKE A MAN POSSESSED

ALL OF ASH'S ATTENTION IS TURNED TO ME, AND IT looks like he wants to devour me. Maybe he does. *I hope he does.* Watching the women being punished in the other room has my body vibrating with need, and God, I pray he puts me out of my misery.

The crotch of his trousers is gaping open, his swollen cock on full display. With his gaze burning into me, he takes himself in hand and slowly begins to stroke. His strong hand moves from base to tip, and I'm completely transfixed. I remember how the swollen head felt between my lips, and my mouth starts to water.

Still slowly stroking his cock, he steps forward, and on instinct, I retreat, pressing my back against the cold glass. His gaze is dark, like he's staring into the deepest parts of me.

"You've been so fucking disobedient," he grates out, continuing his advance.

I swallow. I can't retreat any farther. He has me trapped. "I'm sorry...sir."

"Are you?" he asks.

I nod, my whole body on fire. I hate to admit it, but the thought of Ash punishing me is a little thrilling. Does that make me fucked up? I don't even want to analyze that right now.

With a devilish smile, he releases his cock and presses his hips against me, trapping me against the window. Roughly, he pulls the neckline of my dress down, revealing my bra—and then, he pulls that down, too, exposing both breasts. His tongue swirls around my left nipple, taking it into his mouth, biting down. I jerk in reaction and it ignites every cell in my body. My sex is already throbbing, wet and ready for him.

Holy shit.

Releasing my breast, he pulls me into a kiss. As he sucks on my tongue, I thread my hands through his thick hair, my body vibrating with need. Vaguely, I hear a voice from somewhere behind Ash, and I'm reminded that people are watching us, commenting on our bodies, asking to join our tryst. But all I can do is focus on is Ash and the white-hot arousal burning in my veins.

He devours me, his tongue twisting with mine, and it makes my head spin. He tastes like mint and sin, and honestly, I could drink him in forever.

With our lips still connected, he takes my breast in his large palm, his thumb brushing across my sensitive nipple. I break the kiss and tilt my head back, my eyes fluttering closed. When I glance up, into his eyes, I see a vulnerability in him that I'm not prepared for. Could this beautiful, self-confident man actually be catching feelings? I don't even know how to feel about that.

"You are so fucking ripe for me," he says, his breath hot against my skin, bringing me back to the moment. He takes my nipple in his mouth again, biting down, sending another bolt of pain straight through me.

"Oh," I gasp. The pain feels so fucking good, I can hardly take it.

Arching my back, I squirm a little, and his hands find my hips. He applies pressure, holding me still. "Tell me what you want," he grates out.

I glance up at him. "You." His beautiful dark brow lifts in question, and I'm forced to elaborate. "I want you inside me," I say.

"Good girl," he says, his voice rough with need. "Now tell me who you belong to."

I lift my chin. "I belong to you," I say, brushing my lips against his.

I feel his lips lift into a smile, and my whole body purrs just knowing I've pleased him. He frees my hips and lifts a hand, threading his fingers through my hair as he cups the back of my neck. He pulls me into another hot kiss.

On a sigh, I open my mouth and let him in, yielding to the force of his kiss. Our tongues war and twine, as I pull in the air from his mouth. His free hand slips between us and finds my wet center, then his finger slips past my folds and plunges into me.

I moan into his mouth, the sensation of his finger both foreign and electrifying. The heel of his palm is pressed against my clit, sending hot waves of need pulsing through my body. My channel clenches around his finger as he pushes in deeper.

I break the kiss abruptly. "Oh, my God," I breathe.

Murmurs surround us, and again, I'm made aware of our audience. One woman, the pixie, is staring at us while pleasuring herself. The blond is watching the scene behind us through the window as a man fucks her from behind. On the other side of the glass, I can hear the women being whipped and spanked, and it stokes my already raging need.

Normally, I'd be mortified to be fucking in front of strangers. But there's a twisted part of me that relishes in it. A part of me that's claiming him, just as much as he's claiming me, and I want all these women to see it. He's mine. Just look how desperate he is to taste me.

When I glance back up at him, something flares in his eyes, a dark intensity. Curling his arms around my waist, he pulls me up roughly, and I encircle my legs around his hips, the glass at my back. I can feel the ridge of his erection against my hot center, and I'm fucking desperate for him to be inside me. I rock my hips forward, which elicits a deep rumble from his chest. Then he kisses me again, hard and frantic, like a man who's been to the brink and back. There's a desperate edge to his kiss. He's devouring me, his tongue flicking into my mouth, taking control.

With our lips still connected, his hands shift to the globes of my ass, and he lifts me up slightly, then lowers me back down slowly until the tip of his cock is pressed against my entrance. My breath hitches. He lowers me that final inch, and his cock impales me—filling me completely, and we moan in unison.

The sensation is glorious. Breaking the kiss, I close my eyes and throw my head back as he moves within me. He fucks me with deep, focused thrusts, his pelvis rubbing against my clit. He knows just how to move, just what my body needs. The feel of him inside me is nothing I've ever experienced before. He's so big, he fills me to the point of pain—the tip of his cock slamming forcefully against my cervix.

But it's the pain I love. It's the pain I crave.

His lips fasten to my neck and he bites down hard, making me gasp, driving my need for more. My body clenches around him tightly, and I let out a little gasp. I wish I could stay like this forever, connected to Ash, filled by him.

"Christ, you are so bloody tight. You feel so fucking good," he rasps, surging upward. His gaze collides with mine as he thrusts again and again. He drives into me hard, like a man possessed, and I gasp with every forceful surge.

My muscles tighten in expectation, and I bite back a loud moan. I want to scream. I want to call out with all of the passion bubbling up inside me.

Another moan escapes my lips as he drives harder and faster. My body clenches tightly around his cock, as he pushes into me so deeply, I feel like I'm going to break apart. I tilt my hips to accept him, moving slightly to meet his fevered thrusts. The pleasure is more intense than anything I've ever felt.

"God, I'm going to come. I'm going to come in your pussy," he says through clenched teeth.

That familiar pressure begins building inside me. I'm only a few strokes away from shattering. And I want it. I'm so fucking hungry for it.

"Yes," I rasp. "Come inside me. Fill me."

That's all it takes. Somehow, he pushes up farther inside me and it breaks me. I suck in a sharp breath, my head spinning, as he pushes and pushes, fucking me as deep as he can. My entire body lurches as a jolt of white-hot energy zips through me. My heart is beating so hard, so fast, I wonder if I might pass out. The potent drug of pleasure pulses through me, like liquid ecstasy zinging through my veins.

With a deep guttural growl, he surges up into me, even deeper, forcing me to take every swollen inch of him.

"Fuck, Lexi," he says through clenched teeth. "Fuck!"

He keeps pushing, driving into me. He closes his eyes and tilts his head back. His fingertips dig into my ass, holding me tightly in place. And then I feel his cock pulse inside me. My channel clenches around him, and that's it, I surrender myself to it. I thread my fingers through his thick hair, as another wave of ecstasy engulfs me, pulling me under. Hot, undulating heat rushes through my veins as another intense climax crashes over me, leaving me dizzy and breathless.

I don't know when it ends. I feel like I've just had an out-of-body experience, when I finally come back to myself. I blink up at Ash. He's staring down at me with the most confused look on his face—like he's seen a ghost and doesn't know how to process it. But a second later, that look is gone, and I'm left wondering if I imagined it.

We stay like that for…God, I don't know how long. Minutes, maybe. Still connected, the breath sawing from our lungs. My body is still humming when he pulls out of me and lowers me to my feet. A couple voices behind him murmur about how hot we were, but I'm not listening. To me, they're already gone.

Ash reaches for a nearby handful of tissues and cleans us both off, then tucks himself back into his slacks, and straightens my dress. The pixie is now fawning over him, begging for a ride on his "huge cock," but he shrugs her away without a word and takes my hand. He pulls me out of the room and into the hallway where we are alone, for the moment.

He looks shaken and distracted, and I wonder why? What we just shared was fucking amazing, and I'm already hungry for more.

But, instead of taking me to another room, he tugs me toward the main staircase, leading down to the public part of the club.

I pull against him. "Wait, where are we going?"

"I'm taking you home," he says brusquely.

What the fuck? He just took me to the heights of pleasure, and now he wants me to go home?

"Why?" I ask.

He turns, and takes my chin between his fingers, his grip painful. There's a flash of anger in his eyes, and it's directed at me. "Because I fucking said so."

CHAPTER 20
DAZED AND CONFUSED

BECAUSE I SAID SO.

His words echo through my mind, and I instantly rebel, jerking my chin out of his grip. He wants me to leave? *Fine.* I shouldn't have come here, anyway. I shouldn't have let him fuck me like that—especially with an audience. None of this should have happened—because it doesn't change anything. Ash Grayson is still a bad bet.

And the faster I get home, the faster I can forget this ever happened. But as much as I want to get the fuck out of Dodge, I need to find Gwen first. There's no way I'm ditching her in a sex club.

"I came with my roommate," I say. "And I'm not leaving without her."

Ash curses under his breath. "Do you know where she is?"

I shrug. "Downstairs, somewhere around the dance floor."

With a stiff nod, he takes my hand and pulls me down the hallway, past several rooms. Earlier, I hadn't had time to explore, and now, I'm so curious. Many of the rooms look themed, richly decorated in velvet and furs. Some look more like modernized medieval dungeons, fitted with every whip and paddle imaginable. There are women inside the rooms moaning in ecstasy, and I can't help it, my gaze lingers. I crave the lash of the

177

whip. To feel the sharp sting as the thin strip of leather licks my skin as the pleasure and pain that explodes in my veins.

But Ash isn't giving me an opportunity to watch. He tugs me down the main staircase and over to the dance floor. "What does she look like?"

"Petite. Shoulder length blond hair, green eyes."

The club is still crowded, and my gaze travels over the sea of bodies, moving across every masked face. Gwen's mask has a long feather on it, so she should be relatively easy to spot. The light is dim and pulsing, but not so dim that I can't see clearly. And my heart sinks…she's not here.

"Do you see her?" Ash asks.

"No. Maybe she's in the bathroom?"

Ash follows me to the bar area and down a short hallway. He waits outside as I dip into the ladies' room. It's incredibly fancy, complete with its own attendant, plush carpets, sofas, and sleek vanities lining the far wall. Beyond that are the stalls, but unlike your run-of-the-mill bathroom stall, these doors are floor-to-ceiling, no gaps. Fuck.

"Gwen?" I call out. No answer. "Gwen, are you in here?"

Several women sitting at the vanities turn to look at me.

"I'm looking for my friend. A petite blonde?" I offer, panic edging into my voice.

One of the women shakes her head, then they go back to chatting, completely dismissing me. *Great.*

I return to the hallway, where Ash is leaning against the wall, arms crossed over his broad chest. Fuck, he's handsome. Now's not the time to admire him, but *dayum.*

"She's not in there," I tell him.

Ash curses, then grabs my hand again, holding it tightly as he leads me past the bar, to the entrance area, where Ms. Lawrence is standing. Her gaze briefly shifts to me, and I think I see a satisfied glint in her eye behind her cat mask. I know she's the one who told Ash I was here. *Snitch.* But can I blame her? She was just doing her job. A little too well, if you ask me, but whatever.

She smiles at Ash. "How may I be of service?"

"Miss Anderson is looking for her companion, the woman she came in with. Have you seen her?"

Ms. Lawrence's jaw slackens, in alarm maybe? She leans in and whispers something in Ash's ear. I can see the features on Ash's face shift from mildly annoyed to deeply concerned, and it kicks my own anxiety into high gear.

He glances at me. "Come with me. *Stay close.*"

I follow him across the club, back up the same staircase we just came down, and down the hall. Only this time we go in the opposite direction of the viewing room where Ash just fucked me. There's a concierge here, too, blocking entry.

"We're going in," Ash says to the concierge.

The man's gaze flicks over Ash, and he nods, letting us pass.

"Where are you taking me?" I ask, trying to keep up with him. "Gwen isn't up here. She wouldn't be able to come up here since she isn't a member."

Besides, we agreed that she'd stay downstairs and interview people. There's no way she'd just wander off and not tell me— especially considering we don't have our phones. She knows I'd have trouble finding her.

"The Devil can tempt *anyone*," Ash grates out cryptically.

Before I can ask him what he means by that, we stop before a black door at the very end of the hallway. He tries turning the knob, but it's locked, so he knocks once.

I can hear moaning on the other side of the door, but no one answers.

"Where are we?" I ask, glancing around. The hallway on this side of the club is quieter, with fewer people milling around, randomly fucking in dark corners. The music from downstairs is muted, but the base thumps against the walls like a heartbeat.

"These are the exclusive, VIP rooms." He knocks again, this time more forcefully.

"Are the VIP areas different than the members-only areas?" I ask.

"Yes," he says, distracted. "There are members-only areas, and then there's this area. It's open only to the Exeter House founders and their guests."

The founders. Does that mean Ash is a *founder* of Exeter House? How did I not know that? *Wow.* No wonder he has so much power here.

"Dom, open up."

Dom? He's on a first-name basis with the Devil? And what the hell does any of this have to do with Gwen?

My question is answered before I even have to ask. The door swings open to reveal a very tall, ridiculously handsome man with dark hair and pale gray eyes—a mythic god or perhaps a demon, since he's wearing a red devil mask. It covers his face past his nose, leaving just his sensual mouth revealed. The top of the mask is crowned with long black horns, and the brows are furrowed into a wicked grimace. He wears a white button-down shirt, open at his strong throat with sleeves rolled up to his elbows, and black trousers that make him look oddly sophisticated for a devil.

Beyond his tall frame, I see Gwen standing in the middle of the room, fingers pressed to her lips, a stricken look on her face. Behind her are both men and women, tied up with thick rope, intricately knotted. One woman has her arms tied tightly behind her back with a ball gag in her mouth, and another is tied to a table with ropes keeping her legs spread wide open while a man fucks her with a large dildo.

I push past Ash and move toward Gwen.

"Gwen, are you okay? Why aren't you downstairs?" I ask, grabbing her shoulders.

Why is she up here, alone with a guy she doesn't even know? Well, I'm assuming she doesn't know him, but I'm not actually sure about that. I glance at the masked devil again. I'd think she'd mention knowing such a gorgeous specimen at some point.

She blinks at me, a dazed look on her face. A few seconds tick by, and she finally shakes her head as though shaking something off. "Sorry, I'm fine. We should go. I have everything I need."

I glance around. "What is all this?"

"It's called shibari," the Devil—*Dom*—says with an accented voice, sidling up to me. His gaze rakes over my body slowly, from head to foot, and one side of his lip curls up in a wicked smile. "Want to try it, kitten? I have some rope—"

Before I can even answer, I hear Ash growl from clear across the room. In three long strides, he's in Dom's face, shoving his shoulder. "*You* stay the fuck away from her," he says, drawing out every word slowly, deliberately. There's lethal tension in his tone.

My heart leaps into my throat. It's clear these two know each other well, and Ash isn't a fan. Maybe this guy propositioned me deliberately to get under Ash's skin. If that was the plan, it worked like a charm. Just the suggestion of another man touching me has Ash enraged. But Dom—whoever he is—is playing with fire. I hope he's smart enough to know that.

The Devil laughs and lifts his hands up in surrender. "*Whoa.* Sorry, brother. Didn't see the necklace. She's all yours. Got it." His accent is measured, clipped and very upper-class British.

Ash throws Dom one last, scornful look, then curls his large hand around my wrist—his grip tight, like he's afraid I'll be snatched away. "I'm taking you two home," he tells me.

I shake my head and tug my wrist out of his hand. I don't need anything from Ash. "We'll call a car," I firmly state.

Taking Gwen's hand, I brush past Ash as we walk through the door. Just as I pass, he grabs my elbow and pulls me to a stop. There's a depth of emotion in his eyes that forces the breath out of my lungs.

"We're not done." His voice is low, for my ears alone.

I swallow as those three words wend their way through me, sending a burst of heat straight to my core. There's something about Ash. He has the ability to read me in a way no one else can. But he's not good for me. A man like Ash Grayson will *never* be good for me. My mom taught me that hard lesson with her poor choices. I've learned from her mistakes.

"Yes," I say, reaching deep down, calling on all of the strength I don't feel. "We are. We're done."

CHAPTER 21
INTO THE LION'S DEN

ASH STEPS UP TO ME. HE'S NEARLY SIX INCHES TALLER than me, so he looms over my smaller frame. "Don't test me, Lexi." The words emerge as a deep, threatening rumble from his chest. "I don't play games."

Games? What the fuck? Does he think I'm deliberately toying with him? I shake myself mentally. It's not even worth getting into with him. I can't get sucked back into his chaos.

"Gwen and I are leaving," I bite back in response.

I thread Gwen's fingers through mine, and we wend our way through the labyrinth of hallways and stairs, and people fucking, until we reach the front entrance of Obscura. Ash has followed us the entire way, of course. Probably to make sure no one touches me on the way out.

Ms. Lawrence spots us and approaches. She has a fake but elegant smile spread across her face, which is only accentuated by her cat mask. "Miss Anderson, leaving so soon?"

Ash comes up from behind and answers for me. "Please retrieve their phones. And call a car for Miss Anderson's companion."

Why is he calling the car for Gwen only? Ugh, whatever. We're going to the same house, so it doesn't really matter whose name it's under. Gwen and I hand over our claim tickets.

"Absolutely," Ms. Lawrence chimes before heading over to the phone check room. She returns with our devices, and I immediately power mine back on. The second it comes to life, it starts pinging like a fucking pinball machine. A flurry of texts and missed calls flash across my screen, all from David, telling me what happened, and asking me to call him.

Shit.

I type out a quick response.

Got your messages. Heading home for the night. I'll call you in the morning.

Then, I shut my phone back off. I'll do damage control with David after I've dealt with the Ash situation. I can only handle one hot mess at a time.

As Gwen and I move out to the porte-cochere to wait for the car, Ash tugs on my elbow, spinning me around to face him. I see heat in his eyes, and it makes me gulp.

"You're not leaving," he says, determination dripping in his tone.

"What?" I yank my elbow out of his grip and scowl. "Weren't you just trying to send me home a half hour ago? I'm *obeying* your edict. That should make you happy."

"We have things to discuss," he says in a dark voice.

"We don't have *anything* to discuss," I spit back. "Not a damn thing."

A hard look flashes across his face. "You're playing with fire, Princess."

I lean in and try my hardest to infuse my voice with strength. "Then, I guess it's a good thing I crave the heat."

Anger flares in his eyes, and I instantly regret my cheeky response. What was I thinking? Saying "no" to Ash Grayson is tantamount to throwing down the gauntlet. There's no way he's letting me walk out of here now.

Maybe it's better to get it over with, anyway—have a chat and end this for good.

I push out a breath. "Fine. I'll come with you." I point my finger at him. "But *only* to talk. Nothing else."

A self-satisfied smile spreads across his stupid, handsome face, and I swear, I've never wanted to deck someone so badly in my life. My hands ball into fists at my side, and I squeeze so tight, my nails nearly break the skin on my palms. "I'll go tell Gwen," I push out in frustration.

Ash nods once, like a king giving his leave.

I curse at him under my breath, then turn to Gwen, who's standing a short distance away. She glances up from her phone as I walk up.

"Hey, I'm going to stay with Ash for a while," I say. "We have a few things to get straight."

She laughs under her breath. "Yeah, I figured. Looks like you two have quite a few things to work out."

"Are you okay with going home on your own? I can totally ditch—"

She stops me with a wave of her hand. "No, No. It's fine. Really. It'll give me time to think. The story I'm working on just got a whole lot bigger. Like, *huge*."

"Oh, wow, okay. So, um, what happened in that room?" I ask, raising my eyebrows suggestively.

She pulls her mask off and looks away. She's not meeting my eyes, which immediately makes me suspicious. "Nothing happened."

I shift on my feet. "That didn't look like nothing, Gwen."

She smiles sheepishly. "He's…interesting."

"Okay, but *who* is he?"

Identities are kept strictly confidential inside Obscura—hence the masks—but if someone wants to share their name, they can. Maybe he gave her some kind of clue about his identity.

She shrugs. "I don't know. I only have guesses, and not good ones at this point. I need to cross-check a few details."

I flash her a warning look. "Just be careful. It looks like that dude is into some dark shit."

Not that I can talk. Ash can also get pretty dark and twisted, and lately, I've reveled in it. But that's all about to change. From now on, I'm on the straight and narrow. Pearls. Vanilla ice cream. White picket fences. All the boring I can handle.

"Yeah, that's the weird thing. Domino—that's his pseudonym by the way—he wasn't participating. Not that *I* could see, anyway. I was down by the bar when he approached me and we talked. Then, he offered to show me around. I think he was…I don't know, sizing me up? Gauging my reaction, maybe?"

Huh. Gauging her reaction for what? Why?

I wave my hand dismissively. "Well, whatever. You'll never have to see him again."

Gwen glances over my shoulder to Ash, who is standing just a few feet away. "And what about you? Where'd you two end up?"

"I got my own private tour," I say. I'm not quite ready to admit I let Ash fuck me in front of a group of people, but by the look she's giving me, she already knows *something* happened.

She shakes her head. "Wow, no wonder you're hooked. I forgot how fucking gorgeous your guy is. What the hell is he doing here, anyway?"

"I think Ms. Lawrence called him when we arrived," I say, deliberately not mentioning the necklace. I don't need her questioning the whole "ownership" thing.

Gwen pushes out a breath. "David won't be happy we left before he even got here."

I scrunch my nose because I know what I'm about to say is going to sound a little crazy. "Yeah, uh…Ash had David turned away at the gate."

"Wow," Gwen says. "Talk about possessive. And now you're going up to this guy's penthouse?"

"Yeah," I say a bit sheepishly. "But we're just *talking*."

What happened with Ash tonight was a mistake, a spur-of-the-moment thing. It doesn't change what he did or how tragically fucked up he is. I just need to remember that.

Gwen smiles knowingly. "I don't believe you."

Yeah, well, that makes two of us.

Her car pulls up to the curb, and the driver gets out, coming around to open the door. "Miss Taylor?"

We exchange a quick hug, and I promise to text her later.

Ash is waiting for me near the entrance, watching me patiently as I walk back to him. A dark smile spreads across his face, and I wonder for the zillionth time if going up to his penthouse is a good idea. No, it's not. It's definitely a bad idea.

But I know he'll never give me a moment's peace until he has closure.

Stepping forward, he slips his strong arm around my waist as he guides me back into the club. But this time, we deviate to the left, up and up a set of stairs that ends at a glossy black door. There's a keypad on the wall to the right of the door, and Ash quickly punches in a code. The metal lock clicks as it slides free, and Ash opens the door, holding it to let me pass first. I walk through, into a short hallway. At the end, there's another glossy black door and another keypad. Ash keys in the code again and opens the door. On the other side is a familiar marble floor. That's pretty cool. It's a private door that leads from Obscura to one of the lower floors in Exeter House.

Ash takes his mask off and pulls me through the labyrinth that is Exeter House until we end up at an elevator that whisks us up to his penthouse. Oddly, I'm a little relieved when we walk through his door. I tug my mask off and kick my heels aside. God, my feet are killing me. I never wear heels, and now I remember why.

When I turn around, Ash is pouring me a glass of something from what looks like a wine bottle. He walks over and hands it to me, but I wave it away.

"I'm not drinking tonight," I say. This is going to be hard enough. I don't need anything clouding my judgment.

He lifts a brow. "It's water from Sweden. It's the best."

I take the glass and smell the clear liquid. Yep, just water. I take a sip, then walk to the sofa and lower myself down onto the stiff cushions. I set my water on the coffee table in front of me. "Okay, I'm here," I say. "What do you want to discuss? And make it quick, I have a *Friends* episode at home locked and loaded."

He's standing at the bar across the room, pouring himself a glass of whiskey. He puts it all back in one gulp, then sets his glass back down and walks over to the sofa. But he doesn't sit. He's standing with his feet shoulder length apart, arms crossed over his broad chest.

I pull a throw pillow into my lap and tuck my feet underneath me, waiting.

"What we have, Lexi, is extraordinary—"

"No," I interrupt, sitting up. "You don't get to do that. You don't get to say we have something extraordinary when you're not even telling me what's really going on."

His eyes narrow, and he stands there for a long second, like he's deciding how much to tell me. Finally, he pushes out a harsh breath and lowers himself into the leather chair across from me. He leans forward, forearms resting on his thighs. "Fine. What do you want to know?"

"The phone call," I say immediately. "Who were you talking to, and why did you say those things about me?"

He lowers his head and curses under his breath like this is the last conversation he wants to have. Well, too fucking bad. "Very well." He glances back up at me, his dark gaze colliding with mine. "I own a cyber-security company, and we've been tracking David."

That throws me. "David? *What*? Why?"

He shakes his head, and I can see a muscle twitch in his jaw. "When you heard me on the phone, I was speaking to someone who thinks you know more than you're telling me."

I scoff at that. "Know more about *what*, exactly? David isn't doing anything."

David is so boring and normal, there's no way he's doing anything close to illegal. Actually, his boringness is the most attractive thing about him. He's kind and safe. Exactly what I need.

Ash shakes his head. "You heard me telling them to leave you out of it."

My thoughts are cast back to that phone conversation. *She's bloody useless. Lexi Anderson is nothing.* Okay, his words might make sense under that context. Except…one thing. "What is it you think David is involved in?"

Ash pushes up from his seat and walks over to me, kneeling so we're eye-level. "I would tell you if I could." He reaches out and brushes a stray hair away from my face. "But I'm handling it, Princess. In the meantime, you have to stay away from David. He's dangerous. Trust me."

I honestly don't know what to believe now. But I press my lips together and nod slowly. Trust is a big ask, but he seems genuine, so I'm willing to let this David thing go…for now. I'll get to the bottom of it all tomorrow.

His finger traces the line of my jaw until it reaches my chin. He takes it in a painful grip, tilting my head down slightly to look at him. He leans in, his lips just a hair's breadth from mine. "Now, Princess. Let's talk about your punishment."

CHAPTER 22
NO BOUNDARIES. NO JUDGMENT

*N*ow, PRINCESS. LET'S DISCUSS YOUR PUNISHMENT.

I swallow. "Punishment for *what?*"

He releases my chin, and rises to his feet, standing over me. When he speaks, his tone is deadly serious. "You were meeting another man at a sex club, Lexi. That kind of disobedience can't go unanswered."

My tongue darts out to lick my bottom lip. "We went to the sex club to get intel for Gwen's article. David suggested Obscura, and he was coming to *protect* us. Not to, uh…" How do I word this? "…take advantage of the situation."

Ash tsks and shakes his head slowly. "No man but *me* will ever protect you."

My grand plan to come up here and tell him what's what is disintegrating right before my eyes. And I should have known it would. *No one* tells Ash Grayson how it's going to be. He makes the decision, then just…commands the world to rotate to his dictates. And from what I've seen, the world is only too happy to be commanded by him—myself included.

I hear a chime, and Ash pulls his phone out from his trouser pocket. He reads whatever text message has popped up, smiling down at his phone. Then, he types something out before slipping it back into his pocket.

Who was that text message from? And why that enigmatic smile?

I don't have time to contemplate the answer, because he reaches down and curls his strong hand around my elbow, pulling me up so that I'm standing in front of him. My bare feet awkwardly step on his polished shoes. He stares at me with an intensity that I swear I can actually feel. Even relaxed, he's a powerful, intimidating presence.

Desire slams into me and suddenly the air is too thick to draw into my lungs. I stare at his lips and I ache, actually *ache*, to feel them on my skin. I crave the feel of his teeth biting me, the sharp sting of his hand connecting with my bare ass...

"You dare to disobey me," he says, his tone dark and sexy—that delicious accent rolling off his tongue.

His mouth moves to my neck, and he sucks gently, his lips soft against my skin. I tilt my head and sink into him, totally helpless against the pull he has on me.

"You taste like sunshine," he murmurs against my skin.

Already, I'm on edge. My panties are damp, and my breasts are heavy, aching for the sharp bite of his teeth.

"What do you want, Lexi?"

I swallow, remembering the women on the other side of the glass at Obscura. The women who were tied up, vulnerable, the whip licking at their flesh.

"Tell me," he says quietly. "No boundaries. No judgment."

"Pain," I say, surprising myself. I've never admitted that to anyone. Not even to myself. I take a deep breath. "I want to feel a whip against my skin."

He sucks in a breath as if that information excites him. "Good girl." With a hand at my chin, he tilts my head back, forcing me to look into his eyes. "You're a fucking dream, Lexi, do you know that?"

Relief washes over me. Part of me feared he would tell me that I'm sick, twisted. I've never even told Gwen about the dark, erotic fantasies that sometimes claw to the surface. What kind of person *asks* for pain? Craves it, even? But there's no judgment in Ash's eyes. Only desire.

Dipping his head, he brushes his lips across my collarbone and up the column of my neck, causing little shivers to skip along my spine.

"I want to bring all of your fantasies to life, Lexi," he murmurs against my skin. "I want to know what turns you on, what makes you wet, what makes you scream..."

"Yes," I breathe, tilting my head, giving him better access to my neck. He rewards me by nipping at my skin, then sucking again gently.

"I want to make you come so hard, you forget about every other man."

Yeah, I'm already on the way there. Any other man would pale in comparison to Ash—and that's a frightening thought. How could I ever hope to move on when every cell in my body craves only him?

Finally, his lips find mine and he captures my mouth in a kiss. His tongue parts my lips, then sweeps inside, curling around mine. There's a delicious push and pull, our tongues sliding against each other's in a languid, erotic rhythm. I don't have the strength to push him away. I'm too revved up, too intoxicated by the taste of him to even think clearly.

When he pulls away, I'm still panting, desire humming through my veins. I feel weak, lightheaded, and I'm sagging against him.

"Now, for your atonement." He takes my hand and guides me around the coffee table to the white sheepskin rug in the middle of the floor. "Down on your knees."

I swallow and lower myself onto the carpet. My heart slams against my ribs as he circles me, stalking like a predator. I sway a little and close my eyes briefly to try and get a handle on my racing heart. It's both excitement and fear rolled up into what feels like an incoming panic attack. With a few deep breaths, I'm able to calm my nerves and open my eyes.

Ash's dark gaze meets mine. "Place your hands behind your back."

I hesitate. "Ash, what are you—"

He cuts off my words by placing his fingers beneath my chin and tilting my head up. He loves doing that. "You will not speak unless I give you permission," he growls. "Do you understand?"

"Yes, sir."

"Ah-ah," he chides.

Right. No speaking. I swallow again and nod once.

"There's an exception. I'm going to give you a word—a safe word. If at any point you want to stop this, you will say *nein*, the German word for *no*. Do you understand?"

I nod again, fear tripping through me.

Why the hell do I need a *safe* word? What's he going to do to me? The darkest parts of me want to find out, but the more sensible parts of me want to know exactly what he is about to do. I struggle to keep from asking, but I manage to bite back the words.

"Good girl." His hand falls from my chin and he takes a step back. "Now, I want to feel that pretty little mouth wrapped around my cock."

My gaze drops to his crotch. I can see his erection straining against the fabric of his trousers and my mouth waters. I lick my bottom lip. Slowly, he unbuttons his suit pants and unzips, pulling them down slightly, revealing his hard, swollen length. The purple head stretches toward me, and my core instantly floods with heat.

Obediently, I lean forward and run my tongue up the length of him, from base to tip, before taking all of him into my mouth. We groan in unison. He's so big and my mouth stretches to encompass him.

He threads his long fingers through my hair, pulling me closer as he thrusts into my mouth. I use my tongue to stroke the underside of his cock, then pull back to swirl my tongue around the sensitive tip. He bucks his hips and releases a growl that vibrates through me.

As I suck and lick and stroke his cock with my tongue, a shudder of pleasure rolls through his body. He bucks his hips, thrusting deep into my mouth and throat. When I take in his full length, he lets out a strangled moan.

I tease him, setting the pace, taking him to the very edge, then pulling him back again. His breathing becomes more strained, his grip is tighter on my hair, gently guiding his cock even deeper, entering my throat.

"Fuck, you feel so good," he says through clenched teeth. "I'm going to come."

I don't let up. Sucking hard, I groan as he pistons forcefully in and out of my mouth, mimicking the rhythm of sex. Then, with one last forceful thrust, he pours himself into me.

I swallow his come, drinking him in. He lets out a low, guttural growl, and it makes me feel powerful. His pleasure is mine. At this moment, I'm the one in control and the feeling is intoxicating.

After several long moments where he savors the feel of my mouth around his still-hard cock, he pulls away and tucks it back into his pants. I lick my lips and wait in silence, as I've been commanded, for my next set of instructions. They don't come fast enough. Anticipation shivers through my veins.

Reaching down, he brushes a finger down my cheek. "So fucking beautiful," he says under his breath, almost to himself. "But you've been stubborn. You've been disobedient." He pauses. "Bend over the coffee table."

I glance at him, then over at the low, wood coffee table, before doing as he asks. I stand and walk the short distance to the table, then kneel. A second later, I feel his hand on the back of my head, pressing me down gently until my cheek is pressed against the smooth, cold surface of the table.

My heart beats heavily in my chest as I wait for Ash's next move. The wait is agonizing. All I can hear is my own shallow breathing. Ash leaves the room, then returns a second later. Finally, he kneels behind me and lifts up the hem of my dress, exposing my panties. He pulls them down to my thighs and brushes something over my ass. The soft leather thong of a whip, I guess.

I draw in a shaky breath seconds before the whip leaves me and comes back down, hard. I gasp as the jolt vibrates through my entire body. I bite my lip to keep from crying out.

The whip comes down again, and again, harder with each powerful strike. My skin feels hot, tingly, pain slicing through me. I'm not sure I can take much more. With another hard snap against my ass, I gasp and my eyes tear up—but I'm facing away from him, and I pray he can't see me. For some reason, I want to prove to him, and myself, that I can take this. That I can take even more than what he's given.

After only five strikes, he stops, rubbing his hand gently over my hot, throbbing skin. He kisses the globes of my ass. His lips feel cool against my heated flesh, and I can't help it, I release a quiet moan.

"You like that, do you?" he murmurs. "Good. Now let's see how well you obey."

CHAPTER 23
THE TIES THAT BIND

PULLING UP MY PANTIES OVER MY NOW VERY SORE ASS, Ash sweeps me into his arms. I tuck my head against his chest, my backside still stinging from his assault just seconds ago.

Deep inside, a warm, contented feeling unfurls inside me. I feel safe. Ridiculous, I know, after everything that's happened between Ash and me. But I can't shake the feeling as he carries me into the bedroom and sets me down on my feet beside his bed.

It's dark. An iridescent glowing reflection of the moon shimmers off the black ocean just beyond the floor-to-ceiling windows. But I can see him clearly as he brushes a strap off my shoulder, then the other.

"Turn around," he commands.

I do as he says, and he unzips my dress, letting it fall to the floor at my feet. My bra and panties are next, flicked aside casually. Cold air slips over my skin, making me shiver and my nipples bead tightly.

"On the bed," he orders.

I climb onto his bed and lie on my back, the fabric of his dark blue duvet chafing my sensitive backside. He dips into his closet for a second. I hear drawers opening and closing before he emerges with an amber-colored bottle and a length of thin silk rope in his hands.

Briefly, I wonder what the hell I've gotten myself into. Is he going to tie me up? I'm not sure how I feel about that—fear, excitement, and anticipation all tumble through me at once—so I just press my lips together and try to focus on steadying my breathing.

Setting the rope aside, he climbs onto the bed and straddles me, then opens the bottle and pours honey-colored oil onto my body. The smell of coconut swirls around me, and suddenly his hands are all over me, rubbing the oil into my skin—massaging it into my thighs, my stomach, my breasts...

His hands feel glorious on my body, smoothing over my skin. Never before has a man treated me in such a reverent manner, and the feeling is unreal. His thumbs brush over my nipples and they throb in response. My body is alive for him, tingling with anticipation.

With every movement, the muscles in his arms flex. I watch him, desperate for him to strip his clothes off. I want to trace every taut sinew, but I don't dare try. His features are stern and focused, and I'm afraid any initiative on my part would give him reason to stop or punish me for disobedience. So I remain still, soaking in the feel of his hands smoothly gliding over me.

"When I learned David was joining you at Obscura, I wanted to take him by the throat and squeeze, watching the life drain out of him. Never before have I been enraged to the point of such fantasies of violence." He pinches both my nipples between his fingers and I squirm in response. "You've displeased me, Lexi. You will never put me in that position again."

I give him one decisive nod of agreement.

Another sharp pinch, and I suck in a breath. The pleasure and pain are almost too much. "Say the words, Lexie. I'm giving you permission to speak."

"I…will never put you in that position again," I stutter.

His hands slip down to my center, parting my sex, and he pushes one finger inside me. "You don't sound sure." He pushes another finger inside me, then another, stretching me wide. "Tell me, Lexi, do you want to see me angry?"

Oh, sweet Jesus. How can he expect me to think while he's finger-fucking me? His long fingers glide in and out of me in a slow, torturous rhythm. Already, that familiar tension begins to build in my veins.

"Do you, Lexi?"

I shake my head, no.

"Say it."

"No," I moan. "I don't want you angry."

It's taking everything for me to focus, let alone speak. I'm *already* close. So damn close.

"You are mine, Lexi." With his free hand, he touches the necklace around my neck. "That's what this means."

"Yes," I pant, my hips writhing beneath his expert hands. "Yours."

"And you will not permit anyone to touch what is mine."

"*Yes*," I hiss, my entire body clenching tight.

"Good girl," he says, his voice rough and sexy.

Then he pulls away, and I cry out, suddenly empty.

"Wait, no. Please," I breathe.

I'm burning, white-hot desire licking at me from the inside out. Desperate for release, I reach up and try to pull him back to me.

He stares down at me, eyes hard and as cold as marble. "You've disobeyed me again. I didn't give you permission to speak."

In one fluid motion, he flips me over, exposing my backside. Without warning, his hand comes down on my ass—hard. I cry out. The pleasure and pain rock through me, and I arch my back. The feeling is so damn intoxicating. I just want more.

Then, he takes the rope in his hand. "Now, I'm going to tie you up. Would you like that, Lexi? Would you like to be left vulnerable, completely at my mercy?"

I lick my lips and nod.

Having my freedom stripped away sounds frightening, but also…thrilling. Ash makes me feel safe and protected. I know he won't truly hurt me.

He pulls my wrists together behind my back, and with the rope, he wraps it around a few times before knotting them together. He then proceeds to thread the rope around my waist, knotting it occasionally, until my arms and hands are completely immobile. The patterns the knots make resemble a little bit how the women were tied up in Obscura, in the room with Gwen and Domino. What had he called it? Shibari…or something like that.

The way Ash has tied me is uncomfortable, but not a quite painful. Though I've been rendered completely helpless. There's no way I could get out of this, even if I wanted to.

When he's done tying my arms, he rises from the bed and disappears back into the closet again. When he reappears, he has a long strip of black silky fabric in his hands.

He holds it up to me. "I'm going to put this over your eyes."

I nod and lift my head, allowing him to tie the blindfold. The world is obscured from my vision. My wrists are tied behind my back. I've never felt so vulnerable, so helpless, in my life. Fear slithers through me, and for the first time since starting this, I consider using the safe word.

But before I can open my mouth, he grabs my hips and pulls me upward until I'm up on my knees, ass in the air, my face still pressed against the mattress. Cold air brushes over my skin, making me shiver. He takes the tail of the rope he used to tie up my wrists and begins tying up my ankles, then shoves a pillow in the space between my stomach and my legs, giving me support.

A low, guttural growl issues from his throat. "Such a beautiful ass." He spreads my cheeks, and I feel the long sweep of his tongue along my entrance. "Mmmmm, you're so wet for me. You taste sweet, like honey. I could eat you out all night." His tone is rough, erotic, and filled with hunger.

A mechanical chime rings out. The doorbell. The sound echoes off the walls of the penthouse, and my heart stops.

He plants a kiss on my ass, then slaps it lightly—too lightly. "I won't be a minute. Stay quiet and don't move." He draws out the last two words slowly, and then he's off the bed and down the hall.

I can hear him open the door followed by the sound of voices. Two voices, actually. Ash's unmistakable baritone, and the lilting tone of a woman.

A *woman?* Seriously? Is that who he was texting earlier?

There's a part of me that wants to climb off the bed and storm out there—if I weren't naked, tied up, and blindfolded, I may have done just that. Instead, I just clench my teeth and wait for Ash to usher the woman out.

Several minutes tick by before I realize that's not going to happen. I can hear the woman laughing in the other room, followed by Ash's low, seductive voice. I can't hear the exact words, but his tone is easy, relaxed.

Anger burns in my chest. Is he out there flirting with *another woman* while I'm naked and tied up on his bed? *Seriously?*

After what seems like forever, I hear someone walk into the room. I can only pray it's Ash. He'd forbidden me to speak, and I don't dare disobey. I don't *want* to disobey. Something deep inside me still wants to please him.

But that doesn't mean I'm not pissed.

"Give me a minute to get dressed," Ash calls out to the woman.

His voice is casual and cool as he disappears into the closet—I'm only assuming that, because I still can't see a damn thing. I hear the opening and closing of drawers and the rustling of fabric.

Any minute, he's going to explain what the fuck is going on.

The minutes tick by slowly.

Any minute now...

"Are you ready?"

I stiffen when I hear the woman's voice just feet away from me. She must be standing in the doorway.

"Oh, my—what do we have here? Another one of your little playthings?"

Another one of his little playthings? Who the hell is this woman?

"Amusing, Rebekah," he says flatly. "Go wait for me in the foyer."

She blows out a breath. "You're no fun."

Seconds later, I feel his hand smoothing over the globes of my ass. I want to slap him away—the fucking bastard—but I'm tied up and any attempt to fight him would just be clumsy and awkward. So I remain perfectly still, biding my time until he leaves so I can get the fuck out of here.

The warmth of his breath brushes across my cheek. "You are not to move. If you're good, I'll ride you hard and fill your greedy little cunt with my come when I get back. You'd like that, wouldn't you? My cock buried deep in that tight, sweet pussy." He presses a kiss to my forehead and brushes the hair away from my face. "Be a good girl."

CHAPTER 24
A Room Full of Secrets

WHEN I HEAR THE FRONT DOOR CLOSE AFTER ASH and Rebekah, I immediately set to work trying to get my arms loose. I focus on my wrists first, twisting them to try and loosen the knots. But they're tied too tightly, and with every movement, they cinch even tighter.

That *fucking* bastard.

A half hour later, my arms are burning, and I swear my hands are going numb. Maybe it's just the fear, which is slowly starting to wend its way through my bloodstream. How long is he going to leave me like this? Hours? Days? I want to cry, but I'm too pissed off.

When he gets back, I'm going to kill him. I'll knee him in the nuts, bash something over his head. Seriously. Ash is so dead.

After trying unsuccessfully to free myself, I decide I'm just making it worse and stop. I lay across the bed, my arms burning from the strain of being tied behind my back for so long. I close my eyes behind a blindfold I can't seem to shake. I try to force myself to relax. I've never meditated in my life, but I've done yoga and that's sort of the same thing, right?

Focusing on my breathing, I command my muscles to relax. The burning lessens a little, and the knot of fear in my stomach melts into simmering anger.

An hour—or what feels like it, anyway—has slowly ticked by. In the distance, I hear the front door of the penthouse open and slam closed. Seconds later, heavy footsteps head toward the bedroom. *It's Ash.* But I'm only sure of that when I hear him walk into the room and curse under his breath. The mattress dips under his weight as he begins tugging at my restraints—pulling them loose one by one.

As soon as the rope is loosened enough for me to move, I pull my arms free, and wrench the blindfold off my face.

"You fucking bastard," I spit as I turn toward him and slap his beautiful face—*hard*. His head whips to the side, and I pull my hand back to shake off the sting. "You left me here while you went out on a date with another fucking woman?"

I raise my hand to strike him again, but this time he sees it coming. He grabs my wrist, stopping my hand just inches from his face. Something dark and dangerous flashes in his eyes.

"I told you *explicitly* not to move." With his free hand, he grabs the coconut oil off the nightstand. "*Christ*, Lexi. You've injured yourself."

I glance down at my wrists. They're chaffed, close to bleeding. They sting, but I'm too angry to care. With my unrestrained hand, I grab a throw blanket from the bottom of the bed and wrap it around my naked body.

Dropping my wrist, he unscrews the cap and pours a quarter-sized dollop of oil into his palm. He takes my wrist again and rubs the oil into it, massaging away the pain. He does the same for the other wrist, extending his touch all the way up my arm, soothing the places where the rope pulled and scraped my skin.

"Who is Rebekah? Are you having sex with her?" I ask, my eyes narrowed, watching as he tends to my injuries. The answer is pretty obvious, but I want to hear the words—I *need* to hear the words so I can leave once and for all and never look back.

He glances down at me, and when his eyes meet mine, my heart stutters. He's so fucking beautiful, and he's awoken the darkest parts of me. It's really too bad he's a cheating bastard.

"I've known Rebekah a long time."

For some reason, that simple statement sends a stab of pain straight through me. He's known her a long time, which means she takes priority over me. They have history. We don't. That's not what he says, but he doesn't have to. I know that's what he means.

"Yeah, and…? That doesn't answer my question. Did you have sex with her?"

He pushes out a breath. "Do you want the truth?"

Is he kidding?

"I wouldn't be asking if I wanted you to lie," I bite back.

There's a challenge in his eyes. I can see it. God knows why, but he's testing me.

"No," he says finally—and I feel like a weight has been lifted off me. "We work together. I have no interest in *fucking* her."

Do I believe him? I pause. Maybe. His tone is sincere, and he holds my gaze. But I still have questions.

"Okay, why was she here so late? Where did you two go? These aren't exactly office hours."

He closes his eyes briefly, and I swear I hear him counting to ten under his breath. He opens his eyes again and pins me with one of his commanding stares. "You don't ask questions, and I don't explain myself. Before I left, I told you not to move and you did." His eyes narrow. "I won't ignore such willful disobedience."

Even as hate slithers through my veins, excitement trips through me. Man, I'm so fucked up. The idea of being punished by this man is thrilling, and my treacherous body reacts instantly—my nipples tightening, my core aching...

He reaches out and pulls the throw blanket down, exposing my breasts. I don't stop him. God, knows I should, but there's a part of me that wants this.

"W-what are you going to do?"

He leans forward, pressing in on me until my back is flat against the mattress, his large body hovering over me. "I'm going to punish you." The darkness in his voice makes my heart stutter to a halt.

Without a word, he rises, unbuckles his belt, and unzips his pants, pulling out his swollen cock. He strokes it from tip to base, his gaze never leaving mine. The sight of him stroking himself is so hot, I wonder if I'll come just from looking at him.

"Spread your legs," he demands.

I inch my feet farther apart until I'm spread wide, open for him. Leaning forward, he takes me by the hips and pulls me to the edge of the mattress. Need claws at me, and my body floods with heat. He's already fucked me once tonight, and I can't help but want more. I'm like an addict, hungry for that next hit.

"This is all I've thought about while I was out with Rebekah, *this* is all I could focus on," he mummers. "Being inside you again, moving deep inside your pussy."

His cock nudges my entrance before he pushes fully into me. I gasp at his abrupt intrusion—it literally takes my breath away. He pistons into me, thrusting forcefully, his fingertips digging into my hips as he fucks me. It's not kind or gentle, and he doesn't take the time to ease me into it. It's fast and violent, and everything I need right now.

Once again, my body starts that climb toward climax, every muscle tightening in anticipation. But just as it feels like the dam is going to break, he pulls out of me. I whimper at the loss of him—actually *whimper*. I've never whimpered in my life. But I can't help it. My body is on fire and he's the only one that can give me what I need.

He straightens, grabs a tissue off the nightstand, cleans himself up, then zips up his pants. I reach up and try to pull him back to me. "Ash, *please*."

"Please what, Lexi? What do you want?"

"You," I manage to say. "I want you."

Lifting a brow, he studies me. "I will not reward disobedience."

This is my punishment for moving when he told me not to.

But I'm so revved up, I can't stand it. In desperation, I reach down and rub my own clit, my fingers circling the sensitive nub. My free hand finds my nipple, and I pinch. Oh, *yes*. Pain spikes through me, sending pleasure straight through me.

He steps forward and pulls my hand away, his grip on my wrist forceful, bordering on painful. His eyes darken, and I can tell that he's turned on.

I lift my gaze to meet his. "I want you to taste me," I say. For the first time in my life, I'm telling someone exactly what I want—without shame—and it feels amazing.

Flashing me a devilish smile, he prowls down my body until his mouth finds my slick entrance. His tongue thrust into me, licking, sucking, swirling around my clit. I'm already on the edge, and my entire body feels like a live wire, sparking under his expert tongue. I writhe as an orgasm crashes over me, sucking me under. For several minutes, I'm completely lost to the sensation of my body spasming in acute pleasure.

As I slowly float back down to earth, I notice him staring at me. Propped up on one elbow, looking relaxed. It's the first time I've ever seen him completely at ease, and the sight throws me a little.

"It's a little unfair that I'm naked and you're not," I say, fingering the top button of his shirt.

He brushes his thumb across my bottom lip, his gaze following the movement. "What is it about you, Lexi, that makes me want to break all of my own rules? I'm absolutely addicted to you."

The feeling is totally mutual, but I don't tell him that. He doesn't need to know how completely intoxicated he makes me feel.

I unbutton his shirt and push the fabric off his shoulders, my hands brushing over his muscles. I push him onto his back and straddle him, unhooking his belt. His cock is hard, straining against his zipper. Talk about greedy for it... The only thing separating us is the fabric of his trousers—which I plan to strip away as quickly as I can.

"What the fuck are you doing to me?" he asks, his hands skimming up my rib cage and cupping my breasts. He squeezes gently.

"I'm not doing anything," I say truthfully.

In one fluid motion, he flips me over so I'm on the bottom, his large body pressed between my thighs. I grind against him, rubbing my clit against the hard ridge of his erection through his pants.

"Ash," I groan. "*Please.*"

"What do you need, Lexi? Don't ever be afraid to tell me."

Writhing beneath him, I claw at his back through the fabric of his shirt. "I need *you.*"

Unbuttoning his fly, he reaches into his pants and pulls his cock out. The hot flesh is pressed against my core, the tip teasing my entrance.

"If you want my cock, you need to beg for it, Princess."

Greedily, I arch up into him, my body so hungry for new release, I think I might actually go insane.

"God, Ash. Please." I pant. "*Please.*"

The tip of his cock pushes into me, just an inch or two. It's not enough. "Please what, Lexi? I need to hear you beg for it. Beg me, Princess."

Every boundary between us shatters in that moment. I'm driven mad with wanting, and I'd do anything, tell him anything, to satisfy the hunger that is gnawing at me from the inside.

"I want you to fuck me, Ash. *Please.* I need your cock inside me. I'm begging you."

Rewarding my confession, he slams into me forcefully, and I gasp, my head thrown back in ecstasy. His rock-hard length is so deep inside my channel I don't know where he begins and I end. He thrusts his hips, once, twice, and I'm completely lost, frantic. Desperate.

"Look at me." Taking my chin, he forces me to meet his gaze. "I want you to look into my eyes as I pump my cum into you. I want you to remember who owns your body."

His words send me over the edge and another orgasm slams into me, stealing the breath from my lungs. My eyes are locked on his as I come harder than I've ever come before. Violent, shuttering spasms tear through my body, and I scream out in ecstasy, completely lost to sensation.

"Oh, God, Lexi," he moans, his eyes locked on mine as he pushes into me, each thrust deeper, more forceful than the last. "Fuck, yes. Oh, *fuck*."

His cock swells larger, grows harder inside me as he continues to slam into me repeatedly. Until, with one final thrust, he growls my name and pumps himself into me. I lock my ankles behind his hips and pull him tight against me as he shutters, his climax twisting through him.

When it's over, Ash rests his forehead against mine, his breathing ragged and shallow. "Three orgasms in as many hours. Fuck. I don't think I'll ever get enough of you, Lexi. The way you make me feel…it scares the shit out of me."

God. How does he do it? With just a few simple words, my anger is completely forgotten. I'm shattered. Destroyed. *Completely his.*

"I know exactly how you feel," I whisper. "You are my drug."

For long minutes, we remain that way—connected, our hearts beating in unison until finally he rolls to the side and faces me. "Are you hungry?" he asks.

I purse my lips, thinking. "A little."

"How does an omelet sound?" he asks. Then, before I can answer, he adds, "It's the only thing I can make."

I laugh. "Well, then, an omelet it is. While you're cooking, I think I'm going to take a shower."

"Sounds good."

He places a kiss on my forehead, then gets up and walks into his huge closet. When he re-emerges, he's wearing a pair of pajama bottoms and nothing else. My gaze trips over his muscular form. *Dayum.* Every time I see him, I'm amazed at just how perfect he is. How can one man be so many things all at once? Smart, infuriating, commanding, sexy as fuck, kind, wealthy...? Being in Ash Grayson's orbit is both thrilling and overwhelming.

Ash leaves the bedroom, and I roll off the bed and walk into his closet. When I walk in, I inhale. It smells like him, mint and sage and something uniquely Ash. I glance around. It's twice as large as my bedroom, all mahogany with a marble-topped island in the middle, and racks and *racks* of suits in colors ranging from black to navy to several shades of gray. If he owns a pair of jeans, they must be in one of the drawers. And on the left, there's an entire wall of shoes. Holy shit. He has more shoes than any woman I've ever met, and I live with a houseful of women, so that's saying something.

I open one of the drawers and find a pair of his boxers and a plain white undershirt. I pull them both on. The shirt is huge on me, but it looks kinda cute. My bare feet sink into his plush carpet as I head toward the bathroom. I really *should* take a shower, but I decide to wait until after we eat so Ash can join me. A joint shower sounds so much more fun than showering alone.

I pad out of the bedroom, and I'm halfway down a short hallway when a closed door catches my eye. All the other doors along the hallway are open, giving me a glimpse of what's inside. A bathroom, another bedroom...but this door is conspicuously closed, and I can't help but wonder what lies beyond the frosted glass door.

I only hesitate a second before placing my hand on the handle and pushing the door open softly. I step into the room and switch on the light. What I see makes me draw in a sharp breath.

There are at least thirty photos pinned to the wall, all taken in a variety of settings. Coffee shops, street corners. And every photo features one specific person.

Me.

CHAPTER 25
FIRE AND ASH

I'M IN ASH'S OFFICE, BLINKING IN CONFUSION AT THE pictures of me, all in various settings—the coffee shop, outside Hill House, walking to class. And they're covering his entire wall. Like wallpaper. All it's lacking to look like one of those lunatic conspiracy maps is a bit of red string. Or if it's an obsessive's altar, a few lit candles and flower offerings.

What the fuck?

Confused, I glance down at the papers stacked neatly on his desk. Among them is a document with my name on it. I pick it up and read carefully, anger slowly spreading through me. My entire life is laid out in excruciating detail, from my favorite color to my dress size.

Fury pulses through me as I turn on my heel, storm out of the office and into the kitchen where Ash is making our omelets. The smell of onion and eggs fills the air, making my stomach grumble, but I shove the feeling away.

Ash glances up at me. "That was fast."

I hold up the report with my name on it. "What's this?" I demand.

"What is what?" He dices up some peppers and tosses them into the saucepan with the eggs.

I lick my lips. I've connected the dots and somewhere deep down, I already know what this is, but I need to hear it from him. I need to hear him *say* the words.

I can't keep the fury out of my tone. "The document detailing my every move since fucking childhood!"

He freezes for a moment and tension arcs through the air between us. Then, he turns off the stove, wipes his hands on a white towel, and tosses it over his shoulder. Hands braced on the counter, he dips his head, then glances up at me with those dark, fathomless eyes. "That door was locked."

"Obviously," I say slowly, "it wasn't."

"Sit down," he says firmly, his eyes darting away, refusing to meet mine. "You need to eat."

Typical. A non-answer answer. Everything I've been holding back since this morning—the fear, the frustration, the confusion, snaps in that moment.

"I don't need to fucking eat," I scream. "I need to know why my face is plastered all over your wall."

He moves around the marble island and reaches out for me, but I shove his arms away. "Lexi." There's a pleading in his voice that guts me, but I just shake my head. This is seriously fucked up.

"Tell me it isn't true," I say. "That you didn't hire someone to follow me."

But he can't. I know he can't. I can see it on his face, in the way he dips his head and rubs his neck. He can't even look at me.

I just stand there for a second, blinking like an idiot, shaking my head. Waiting for his denial. Waiting for him to say *something,* anything. He pushes out a breath and walks over to me. "Sit down," he commands.

"I told you, I don't want—"

"Sit. Down," he says again firmly and calmly. "And I'll tell you what this is about."

I clamp my mouth shut and sit at the round breakfast table in his huge kitchen, scowling. I should leave. I shouldn't be here. But I need to know why. I need to know what the fuck is happening.

"Okay," I say. "Tell me."

He pulls out a chair and sits across from me. "A few months ago, I was approached by some very powerful people within the government. They said they needed my expertise in cyber security to track someone extremely dangerous. My background and my status as an Exeter House founder made me the ideal asset."

"But why the interest in David?" I ask.

"David Melnik has connections to Russia, and he's looking to use Exeter House as a way to influence American politics," he says. "Initially…you were my…conduit to David."

"Your…*conduit*," I repeat.

He dips his head like I'm not going to like what he's about to say. "I slept with you to get to David."

I hear the words, but they don't make any sense. It's like I'm hearing him speak a foreign language. I blink at him. "What does that mean? You slept with me to get to David? That first night between us was a mistake, a misunderstanding." I was delivered a note that I *thought* was from David… "Or was it?"

I remember the scribbled words verbatim.

Apologies for tonight. Let me make it up to you.

Suite 403

I'm waiting…

"I wrote the note knowing you would think it was from David," he says flatly.

I launch to my feet, on the verge of tears. "You fucking asshole. You lied to me. You manipulated me into sleeping with you. Who does that?"

He stands, too, and for the first time since meeting him, I see real fear in his eyes. He pulls in a breath, then lets it out slowly. "I'm working for the CIA, Lexi. David is a dangerous man, and they asked me to get close to him, get as much evidence as I could. Then you came into the picture, and my feelings for you complicated things."

I narrow my eyes at him. "So, you're a spy?"

A muscle ticks in his jaw. "A consultant."

"Right." I nod slowly. "A *consultant*."

There's real sorrow in his eyes. "I'm sorry you had to get caught up in all this."

"You're *sorry?*" I repeat in disbelief. "Wow. I honestly don't even know what to say to that. You knew you were using me, and yet you still pulled me in deeper..."

Tears prick at the backs of my eyes, but I blink them away. I *will not* cry in front of him. I refuse to show Ash the damage he's inflicted.

He steps forward and grabs my arms. "Lexi, listen to me. That first night was contrived, yes, but every moment after that was me fucking falling for you. This, what we have, is real. More real than anything I've ever felt for anyone."

"So real that you *lied* to me? All this time?" Anger drips from every word.

"Princess..."

"No!" I pull myself out of his grip and shove the tip of my finger into his chest. "You don't get to call me that. You are so fucked up, Ash Grayson—if that's even your *real* name. Whoever you are, stay away from me."

I push past him and storm into the living room, scooping my phone off the sofa. Then I head to the bedroom and snatch my dress off the floor. He follows me, but I'm already stalking back down the hallway into the living room on my way to the foyer, where my heels are. I pick them up and shove them into the bundle of fabric in my arm. I'm ready to walk downstairs in my skivvies—or his—I don't even care right now. All I'm seeing is red. When I reach out to open the front door, his voice stops me.

"Lexi," he says, his tone pleading. "Let's talk about this."

I half-turn to look at him, my hand still on the doorknob. "Go fuck yourself. And you stay the *fuck* away from me." Then I open the door and flee.

∗∗∗

By the time I reach the house where my mom is staying in San Marino, the sun is just beginning to rise. After finding my way down to the lobby of Exeter House, I'd dipped into a bathroom, slipped my dress on. Instead of asking the front desk to call me a car to take me to Mom's house, I order an Uber instead.

I thought about going home to Hill House, but Ash is likely to pop up there and create a scene. Then everyone in the house is going to be all up in my business—and honestly, I just don't want to talk about it. Not yet, anyway.

God, what a fucked-up night. I can't stop thinking about my conversation with Ash. He's a spy—or, excuse me—a *consultant* for the CIA? And David is supposed to be some kind of evil mastermind? If any of that is true, then they clearly have the wrong guy. David couldn't be less threatening if he tried. And why would he have any reason to work with Russia? It doesn't even make sense.

And the most alarming part of all of it was that I didn't see any pictures of David up on Ash's wall. They were all of *me*. If he was supposed to be spying on David, then why is *my* face wallpapering his office?

God, why did I allow myself to get sucked into Ash's chaos? Why did I go against my gut instincts telling me not to go anywhere near him? If I'd just stuck to my original plan and pursued David, I'd be planning a wedding right now—not reevaluating my life choices.

As I walk up to the front door, I inwardly cringe. Spending time with her isn't ever fun, or soothing. She'll pepper me with a million questions, not listen to my answers, then go on to talk about her latest boyfriend. Or husband. Or fiancé. Or breakup. I can never keep up.

Mom is in the kitchen when I walk in. She's never awake this early, which can only mean she hasn't been to bed yet. Not a huge surprise. Her sleep schedule has always been a bit chaotic. For a while, it was the cocaine she was doing, and then, I don't know, I guess it was all the parties she attended. Even now, she's out at all hours of the night. She's fifty going on nineteen.

"Alexandra, my darling," she calls out in a sing-song voice. "I didn't realize you were coming over today!"

She meets me in the living room, wearing a silky pink robe, her brown hair still curled perfectly. When she pulls me into a stiff hug, I can feel she's lost another five pounds. She's constantly complaining about her looks or her weight, so I wouldn't be surprised to hear that she's dieting again. She's too skinny as it is, but I know better than to try and talk sense into her.

"Sit at the table. I'll pour you some coffee."

A cloud of thick perfume precedes me as I follow her to the table. The second I sit there, I notice a guy sitting in the living room, wearing nothing but a robe. He's at least ten years younger than her with a dragon tattoo twisting up his neck. "Oh, uh, sorry, am I interrupting something?" I stammer.

"No, no," Mom says, "Don't be silly. Sit down. This is Dan. Dan, my gorgeous daughter, Alexandra."

I wave at the guy awkwardly and slip into one of the empty chairs. I lower my voice so only my mom can hear. "So, um, where's John?"

John is mom's regular boyfriend. I *think*. Or are they married now? I honestly can't keep up. She changes men like she changes her underwear, one for every day of the week, and then some. Even when I was a kid, she was constantly in a relationship with someone new. There was no sense of stability in our house. It was constant emotional chaos.

Mom pours me a cup of coffee, adds a little cream, and sets it in front of me. "John and I broke up three months ago, darling."

"Really, why? You guys seemed good."

Dan clears his throat fro the living room and then stands up. "I'm goin' upstairs to take a shower." He comes into the kitchen and kisses Mom on the forehead. "See you up there, babe. Nice meeting you, Alexandra."

I flash him a tight smile. "Yup."

Mom slips into the chair next to me with her own cup of coffee. "John was getting dull," she says when Dan has disappeared.

"Mom, he was *nice*, and even better, he was age-appropriate."

John is in his mid-fifties. Comfortable financially. Not handsome, per se, but cute in a nerdy kinda way. And his biggest flaw was that he didn't floss. What the fuck is wrong with any of that?

"Alexandra, there's more to life than finding a *nice* man." She does a little shoulder shimmy. "You want someone who will light your fire."

My thoughts instantly land on Ash. He lit my fire in more ways than one, and look where that got me. I promised myself a long time ago that I'd never take advice from mom. In fact, I've made it a point since high school to do the *exact opposite* of whatever she tells me to do, and it's worked out so far. Well, until Ash. He's a perfect example of a man my mom would fall for, and look where *that's* gotten me.

I shake my head. "Fire is great until you get burned," I say. "A little thrill isn't worth the pain."

My thoughts are cast back to Ash and his ridiculous claims about spies and Russia and the CIA. Probably all contrived to make me doubt David.

It doesn't matter.

I shake myself mentally. Ash and I are over, and I need to move forward with David. That's the only way I'm going to avoid my mom's destructive cycle. I need to settle down with a nice, stable man. Fuck Ash and his magical dick.

I yawn and glance at the time on my phone. I've been up for way too long. "I need some sleep. Can I take the guest room?"

"Of course," Mom says, lifting her swollen, collagen-filled lips. "Just don't mind us and our…bedroom activities. The walls are thin, but there's a white-noise machine in that room if we get too loud."

Gross. I stand up and head toward the living room. "Thanks, Mom," I say dryly. "Very considerate."

As I head up the staircase to the spare bedroom, I unlock my phone and text David.

I'm sorry about tonight. The whole evening was a bit of a bust, but Gwen got her material. Thank you for getting us in. I'm at my mom's place now, but I'd love to see you. Dinner tomorrow night?

I wait, but there's no immediate reply. It's five in the morning, so I'm sure he's asleep.

With a sigh, I shut myself into the guest room and turn on the white noise machine as loud as it will go. I strip off my dress and find a pair of old pajamas in one of the dresser drawers. Then I brush my teeth in the adjoining bathroom and lie down. As I stare up at the ceiling, listening to the sound of ocean waves crashing, I deliberately shove all thoughts of Ash Grayson out of my head.

Tomorrow, I'm going to seal the deal with David. Call it a new beginning. The *right* choice.

Chapter 26
A Roofie Over My Head?

IT'S EARLY EVENING. I SHOW UP AT DAVID'S DOOR WITH A bottle of champagne in hand, hoping it will help break the ice. I haven't seen him since that less than auspicious date, when I ended up super drunk and left with another man. Thank goodness he's not aware of any of those circumstances.

This morning, when David replied to my text, he said he would order in from a fancy local restaurant. He wanted to take me to Isca again, but I steered him away from that. There's no way I'm going to chance running into Ash in his own domain. The speed with which he found me in the sex club is still fresh in my mind.

And besides, I haven't been to David's house yet. It's in a fancy Brentwood neighborhood with a gated driveway. Spending time here will give me a chance to get to know him a bit better, hopefully.

David's housekeeper greets me at the door and takes my bottle of champagne to chill. She says David would like me to meet him on the patio. From the large living room, I can see through the french doors that there's a table formally set with a lush tablecloth. Full place settings for two sit right at the edge of a gorgeous, glistening pool. I smooth the goosebumps from my arms and breathe in the cool evening air, listening to the water trickle over the fountain rocks and into the decorative pool.

All this could be mine...and more. I bite my lip. Maybe tonight's the night he'll finally put a ring on it. Or had it all been a dream? That night at the restaurant all seemed so surreal. As if it had happened in a dream. For a second, I thought Ash's theory about David drugging my drink might be true. But given the litany of lies and manipulations I've caught Ash in recently, I'm now certain his accusations were just another way to control me.

David isn't out here yet, so with a virtual *fuck you* to my ex-whatever-he-was, I pull out a compact and check my makeup before slipping it back into my purse. I'm excited to see David again.

On the table, candles flicker in the early evening light. The food, still covered in decorative chafing dishes, smells amazing. It occurs to me that I'd never once shared a dinner with Ash at either of his residences. Nothing so intimate. Had that been on purpose? Wishing I could put Ash out of my mind entirely, I hear the French doors open onto the patio.

I continue to watch the play of evening light on the surface of his swimming pool, suddenly wishing I'd brought a swimsuit. Or maybe not. Skinny dipping is always an option, right?

His hands are on my waist, and I jump a little, to make him think he startled me.

"Oooh!" I yelp.

His mouth moves immediately to my neck. "Hello, beautiful. I've missed you."

I swallow when he presses his body against mine, his hands coming around to cinch me against him. He presses the obvious bulge of his arousal against my ass. My eyes pop wide open.

Whoa. Is he drunk? I turn my head to get a quick whiff of his breath. No discernible alcohol.

He's never really been forward with me, physically. That was yet another thing that completely set him apart from Ash, who could never keep his hands off of me. David was one to let me be the one in control of physical intimacy. And admittedly, that hadn't been very much of late.

All because of Ash.

I force myself back into the moment by closing my eyes and letting David touch me. I let his hands roam from my hips to my waist and higher. If we're getting engaged soon, it's high time this happened, right? I was ready to crawl into his bed weeks ago. The same bed Ash had been waiting in instead...

Shit. I have to stop doing this to myself. It's *David* who's kissing my neck. It's *David* who has his hands on my breasts, roaming over my curves...

"Hey." I turn around slowly in his arms, and he kisses me deeply on the mouth, his hands sliding to my ass. Suddenly, I'm uncomfortable with this change in his demeanor. It's just flat-out weird.

"Mmm, I'm so glad to see you. But I'm starved!"

He smiles and lets me slide out of his hold. "Let's eat, then. We can get it out of the way..." He lets that dangle with a certain look in his eyes, and I swallow, looking away.

Well, I've come here for this, haven't I? David is my ticket to forgetting that other guy. Ash was a temporary diversion, an unwanted distraction, and now I'm moving on.

Tonight I'll sleep with David and Ash will be forgotten—as he should be!

Dinner is from the local high-end Italian bistro down the street. It's absolutely delicious, and he's ordered all my favorite things. But we're nearly halfway through our meal when David slaps his head. "Damnit. I decanted the wine to let it breathe and then forgot to pour it." He gets up from the table and goes inside, returning with two over-full glasses. "Let's make up for lost time."

I eye the wine at my setting and then promptly ignore it, starting on some humorous story about my academic advisor at Caltech. He sips at his wine, nods, occasionally darts his eyes to my glass, then away.

Once we've finished our main course, and I fold my napkin, he says, "You didn't touch your wine."

"Oh." I shake my head. "I'm not a big fan of red." He frowns, as if searching his memory for my having told him that before. I have, a couple times. But I try not to be annoyed that he's forgotten.

Then, I stand up. "I'm, um, I'd like to freshen up a bit. Would you mind?"

Like the gentleman he is, he also stands and smiles widely. "Absolutely. Down the hall and the first right. I was, ah, thinking that we could take dessert over in the gazebo. Or if you'd rather wait, we could have a swim first."

I force a smile. "I don't have my swim—oh." I laugh when it's clear he's meaning we don't really need our suits. I glance at the high-walled garden all around us. It's very private here and there's no danger of us being seen.

I duck inside and head for the bathroom, hoping for a moment to collect myself. Of course, I am serious about freshening up, and I also want to adjust my sexy underwear to maximum effect. Of course, he won't get much of a look at it if we strip naked to go skinny dipping.

When I run into the housekeeper who's walking out, a purse hanging on her arm; however, I remember the bottle of champagne I brought. Much more palatable than the heavy red wine he wanted us to drink.

"Oh, hi, can I get that champagne—?" She turns on her heel, as if headed to fetch it for me, but I stop her. "No, no. I'll open it up. If you just let me know where it is? And where you keep the champagne flutes?"

She smiles. "Thank you, miss. That is kind." She gives me directions to the kitchen, pointing the way and explains which cupboard the flutes are kept in.

I continue down the hallway to the bathroom. On my way, I pause to admire some beautiful wooden benches, silk flower arrangements and paintings on the wall. Suddenly, I realize what it was that was bugging me about David's immaculate mansion. There's nothing personal here at all. No pictures, no sentimental tchotchkes. Not even bookshelves with dog-eared books. It's giving me a very artfully decorated but sterile vibe. Like an Airbnb.

I frown. That's odd. Maybe David isn't a very homey type or doesn't spend much time here? Well, that will definitely change when he settles down with me, no doubt. I smile, my white-picket-fence vision of our future suddenly renewed. I eye the rest of the place while taking mental notes on how I'll redecorate it. I'm almost to the kitchen when I stop short. There's something rather personal—and out of place—sitting untidily on the floor at the end of the hallway. A gym bag.

David's gym bag?

Cocking my head, I bend to get a better look. I'm not above being a little nosy. Especially when it comes to my potential future husband. There's a laminated badge pass hanging off of the bag's handle. I recognize the name and logo of the gym inside Exeter House. Of course, he'd do his workouts there, as eager as he is to get membership.

I'll have to steer him away from Exeter House in the future. No sense running the risk of bumping into Ash. Talk about awkward. I only hope that David remains as malleable as he's been up to this point, so I can have that influence on him.

Tilting my head, I peek into a side pocket of the bag that's partially unzipped. I spot the unmistakable shape of a foil packet of condoms. It's a string of them, actually, and it's pulled out of its box as if the end has been ripped off hastily and pocketed. I blink. Has he used those recently, or are those for tonight?

There's something else in the bag. A package of prescription medication. Before I even realize what I'm doing, I reach in and pull out the packet.

What the...? Is this some kind of Viagra-type drug? I skim the label. *Flunitrazepam.* Pulling the medication out of the packet, I see that they are white tablets in blister packaging with two tablets missing.

Blinking, I'm now gripped with curiosity. Like, what if he has an STD? Do I want to go anywhere near that—even if he's wearing a condom? Or three? *Gross.*

I grab my phone out of my pocket and snap a quick picture of the package and hastily replace everything as I found it. Then I slide back into the bathroom to Google whatever the hell it is.

My fingers are shaking as they hover over the touch screen, and my mind is racing over what to do or say if it is, indeed, STD medicine. Like, maybe we can wait until he's in the clear? How do I even bring it up?

My stomach tightens in knots of anxiety over the thought of such a confrontation when the Google search comes back, and I start frantically skimming the results.

That's when I almost drop my phone in shock. Flunitrazepam is a generic for Rohypnol, the date-rape drug. Also known as the roofie drug.

Holy. Shit.

Ash was right.

CHAPTER 27
RUSSIAN AROUND

I'M STARING AT THE GOOGLE RESULTS TELLING ME THAT THE medication in David's gym bag is a standard generic for the roofie drug. Since pills from the pack are missing, it goes without saying that the weird effect I suffered from the other night at the restaurant is now explained.

I blink, mind racing, thinking about that glass of wine he poured that I haven't touched yet. Is he trying to do it again?

I'm conscious of the fact that I've now been gone for a while. I told him I was going to "freshen up" and he's likely to get suspicious soon if I don't get back out there.

For that matter, do I even want to join him, knowing what I know now? I could duck out the front door this minute and get myself a ride home with the luxury of making my excuses via text once I'm miles away.

My heart races as fast as my thoughts. I don't have the time to think this through. But my anger gets the better of me. I felt so awful the morning after that restaurant date. I was already feeling the effects of the drug when David popped his question. But why roofie someone in public and then ask them to marry you? What the hell was he trying to accomplish?

I'd shown him before that point that I was more than willing to go to bed with him.

And on top of all of these questions, I wasn't sure whether I was angrier about him drugging me or Ash being right after all.

With determination, I make my way back to that fucking gym bag and pop two tablets out of the blister pack. I palm them and continue on my merry way to the kitchen.

The champagne is chilling in the fridge, right where the housekeeper told me she'd put it. I snatch it out and grab the flutes from the cabinet.

Then, I pop the cork and pour the glasses so quickly they start to foam over. I almost spill one of them when I hear the French doors open followed by his footsteps across the elaborate Spanish tiles.

"Lexi? Baby? You get lost? Did someone pop a cork?"

I jump so hard I almost lose the tablets before dropping them into the champagne flute. By the time he's rounded into the kitchen, the tablets have just barely fizzled into dissolution.

"I-I brought champagne with me. You seemed a little sad that I didn't like the wine. I thought we could do champagne, instead."

"How thoughtful," he says with a stiff smile. "Why don't I carry those out?"

"No," I say too quickly. "I, um, I've got them. It's fine."

He smiles again and nods, then turns to lead us back toward the patio. With shaky hands, despite holding the flutes, I follow him.

While I'm fighting with myself to keep my hands steady, I'm willing myself to remember over and over. It's the drink in the right hand that has the roofie in it.

It would be just like me to roofie myself on accident.

Do I even know how to do this? Did I give him enough of the medicine? Or enough alcohol for the medicine to take effect? I make a mental note to grab the rest of the champagne if necessary.

How long will it take? I had no time to Google any of it.

"What shall we toast to?" David asks, a grin hovering on his mouth. I see his eyes dart to the untouched glass of wine at my place setting. Thank God I didn't drink it.

"Let's drink to my new study-abroad assignment." I'm totally winging it, but what the hell. With any luck, he'll be unconscious soon.

He hesitates when I clink his glass, eyebrows darting up. "Study-abroad opportunity? What's this?"

"Oh, yes. I've been meaning to tell you that I got an opportunity to study for six months in Moscow. I'm so excited." I flash him a wide fake grin.

His eyes light up in surprise. I can almost see the wheels turning behind his eyes, as if he's trying to figure out what to do with this new information. "Well, that's interesting news. When will you go? And what will you be studying there?"

"Cyber security, actually." I have to mentally thank Ash, or curse him, for giving me that. David's eyes narrow slightly, but I plow onward. "Drink up, then!" I press my flute to my lips and watch him warily as he takes a sip and then another and another. *Thank God.* I down mine quickly. Then I giggle and blink flirtatiously.

We end up finishing the bottle in short order. Then he suggests we go for a dip in the pool. As much as I would like that, because I'm feeling flushed and extremely nervous right now, I can't chance him falling unconscious in the middle of a swim. As angry as I am, I'm not ready to drown him. And to be honest, after three and a half glasses of champagne, I'm a bit too buzzed to be swimming myself.

I tell him I'd rather get cozy on the lounge seat beside the pool, and he follows me there. I have no idea how far I'm going to have to take this before he eventually passes out. And shit. What if he *doesn't* pass out? Do I still have to sleep with him? I'm now finding the idea revolting.

He sinks down on the couch beside me and immediately his mouth is on mine. He's not holding anything back. His mouth moves over mine while his hands pin my head forcefully against his. When he finally comes up for air, I'm breathing heavily.

I'm also a little bit angry that in order to tolerate this, I have to imagine he's Ash. Even though he kisses nothing like Ash, tastes nothing like Ash, and feels nothing like Ash. He's not Ash. *Damnit.*

"Have you given any more thought to what I asked you last week?" David presses his mouth to my ear, kissing all along the rim. My heart is racing, though it's not desire I'm feeling. It's cold hard fear, mixed with anger. I cling to those feelings like armor. In my head, I'm formulating a thousand plans to get out of this.

I really need him to pass the fuck out already.

"What question was that?" I put forward coyly. Why not be a little infuriating right now?

"The one where I asked you to marry me. I wasn't joking about that, baby. I know I didn't have a fancy ring to put on your finger. I'd rather purchase one that you really want." He pulls back to look in my face but seems to be having trouble focusing his eyes.

"Well, I'm not sure what's going on with me," I hedge. "Given this new study-abroad opportunity. My options are up in the air.

I'm *so* excited about Russia. Do you speak any Russian?" Good God, I'd make the world's shittiest secret agent. Ash said he thinks this guy is a Russian asset or spy or hacker or whatever. Here I am signaling it like a giant red flag.

David frowns. "What makes you think I speak Russian?"

Is it wishful thinking or is he slurring his words?

"Oh, I guess because of your last name. It's Russian, isn't it? I just thought maybe you had Russian relatives or something."

He puts his hand to my chin to smooth my cheek with his thumb and says, "You're a verrrry, silly girl, Lexi…verrrrry…ssssilly." The cadence of his speech is obviously impaired.

Instead of replying, I grab his face and start kissing him. I don't want to talk anymore. I just want to kiss him until he passes out—and not in a good way.

It feels like hours until his body finally slumps against me. I pull my mouth away and study his face. His full weight is now pressed against my shoulder, eyes closed and his head is drooping.

"David? David? Is everything okay? Are you awake?"

No reply.

Just to test it out, I shake his shoulder. Vigorously. No movement. Not even a groan. To further test it out—and maybe blow off a little of my frustration—I give him a good hard smack on the face. Not even a flinch. It feels better for me than it does for him. That shit's going to sting when he wakes up.

I double-check to make sure he's still breathing, then sidle away from him. Bending, I carefully lay him down on the couch.

New questions have popped into my mind. How long will he be out? If I wanted to find some clues, where would I look?

Maybe I just leave and block his number, never to hear from him again.

Something tells me that's the coward's way out, so I decide to at least give this place a quick once-over before I take off. It would help my peace of mind to know what David's up to with his stupid roofie meds and his random marriage proposal. And what the hell is this thing between him and Ash?

I assume this is, in fact, a rental, but quickly deduce that he'd probably keep all his papers and anything else important close to him. However, my first destination is the gym bag.

I don't find much that's useful among the stinky gym clothes, shoes and the aforementioned prophylactics and drugs. However, in a side pocket, I do find a very tiny flash drive. I tuck it into my pocket, then turn and dart up the stairs.

I meander down a long hallway, opening doors as I walk by. Each of the spare bedrooms looks completely untouched. There's one room at the end of the hallway, the master, with an attached bathroom. It's huge and beautifully decorated, but the bed is unmade. There's a laptop on the desk with a scattering of papers and other debris.

For a moment, I wonder where his phone is, then roll my eyes at myself. It's probably down on the patio with him, tucked in his pocket. Before I run back down there to grab it, I give myself a chance to look around a little more.

I bend to get a closer look at the papers on his desk. They're covered with notes, scrawlings really, that I don't understand. But clearly, some of it is in Russian. I blink, straightening. Holy shit. No wonder he had such a weird reaction when I asked him if he spoke Russian.

For a moment, I consider snagging his laptop but realize I have nothing to hide it in and it would be very conspicuous.

My eyes skim over the rest of the surface, but there's nothing really of value here. Next, I open the desk drawers, and when I register what's in there, I gasp. There are two pistols and several boxes of ammo, one of which is half empty, which implies one or both of the pistols is loaded.

My throat tightens, and I swallow, not even willing to touch them. Was David going to use one of these on me if I didn't cooperate? And what, exactly was I supposed to cooperate with?

For that matter, what the fuck am I even doing here going through this stuff? I'm not a spy!

Beside the guns, underneath some more papers, I find a phone. But it doesn't look like the phone I've seen David use before. A burner phone, possibly? It's small enough for me to smuggle out, so I grab and pocket it. With my heart racing in my throat, I shut the desk drawer and move on to the nightstand. There's a watch, a half-drunk glass of water, a box of tissues, and a condom, still in its wrapper. This is probably where he was hoping the night would end up. And that condom might have been meant for me.

But who knows? Russian spies probably get around a lot more than I give him credit for. My stomach twists at the thought. I almost slept with him. *Gross.*

Okay so…what the fuck do I do now? I'm breathing so fast I risk passing out from hyperventilation. I'm definitely feeling a little giddy, and I struggle to get control of myself.

I've got a flash drive and burner phone in my pocket. Should I look for more stuff? Or get out while I'm ahead? My eyes fly to the clock. I've been snooping around inside the house for about a half hour since David passed out and have no idea how long that stuff is good for.

I pull out the top drawer of the nightstand as my one last search. Inside, there is a small book. It's a notebook small enough to tuck into a jacket or trouser pocket. I thumb through it. Every page has notes on it. Mostly illegible. A code of some kind? At least four different languages. Some of it looks Russian.

I grab it, just to make sure. The last thing I see of interest inside the drawer is a file folder. To see if it's worth bothering with, I pick it up and thumb through it.

My blood runs cold the minute I look at the first sheet of paper. Inside, there's the name and address of Hill House. *My* address. Beneath it, there's a list of all the residents. Me, my roommates. A line is drawn through Maddie's name as if she's no longer an option.

What the hell did he have this for? Underneath, there are notes about how Maddie has been seeing and recently engaged to Evan Kohl. As I page through the other sheets of paper within, I see more things about me and my roommates. *Personal* things. There's a page for each of us with our full birth names, hometowns, our dates and places of birth. Even our Social Security numbers. There are pictures, too, and financial information, what we're studying, our hobbies. Everything.

What the hell is he doing with all of this?

Incensed, I double the folder in half and shove it under my arm. I'll make it fit into my purse even if I have to sit on it, damnit. I'm not leaving all this with him!

Now I wish I'd slapped him harder.

Sobered by the thought that nearly an hour has now passed, I decide the prudent thing to do would be to take off. No telling what he'd do to me if he found me up here snooping in his things.

Besides, I'm so terrified right now, I'm about to pee my pants. Definitely time to go!

I run back downstairs, barely avoiding tripping by leaning heavily on the wall. I find my clutch in the entryway on the table where I left it and quickly shove everything inside. Too bad I hadn't brought a shoulder bag with me or I could grab that laptop, too.

With a groan, I realize that I left my shoes out on the patio underneath the lounge where David is now unconscious. Damnit. Okay, so I have to head out without my shoes, then. He could wake up at any moment. So instead, I beeline out the door, down the walk, out the gate and to freedom.

But am I any safer out here?

I make a mental list of all the things I need to have with me. My purse? Check. My phone? Check. At the curb, I'm standing with my bare feet. What will happen when David finally wakes up and realizes that I've ransacked his stuff and taken things?

I keep a wary eye on the front door the entire time—which feels like eons, by the way—I wait for my Uber to arrive.

Damn it all.

Only when the driver arrives do I realize that I've keyed in the address for Exeter House as my destination. I guess it makes sense. It's closer than getting a ride completely across town. And it won't be the first place David will suspect I go.

Above all else, I want to avoid going home with all this stuff and possibly putting my roommates in danger.

I'm halfway to Exeter House when I whip out my phone to call Ash. He picks up after the first ring.

"Ash, I need you. I think I'm in a lot of trouble. I really, *really* need your help."

CHAPTER 28
DEFEAT

LESS THAN A HALF HOUR LATER, THE UBER DROPS ME OFF at Exeter House. I'm in the front but can't help remembering the last time I was dropped off here, at the side entrance, practically hidden for Obscura, the sex club.

I swallow, forcing my mind away from that memory lest it take me down a path I don't want to go down. I don't want to remember what happened there between me and Ash, even though the images and sensations are easily called up into my thoughts regularly.

With a shaky breath, I glance up at the tall towers in front of me, heart in my throat. My dinner is a lump of stone in my stomach, and I'm running on pure adrenaline right now.

I double-check the back seat of the Uber before I get out, making extra sure not to leave anything behind. Especially no top-secret Russian spy evidence, if it turns out to even be anything Ash can use.

Looking down at my bare toes, I sincerely hope that Exeter House doesn't have a no shirt, no shoes, no service policy. Then I remember Ash's necklace. Even though I've taken it off and no longer wear it, I couldn't bring myself to tuck it away. Like an idiot, I carry it with me in my purse, tucked into my wallet as some kind of weird good luck charm. I guess, in this case, it might not be far from the truth.

I reach into my clutch and pull out the necklace and step off the warm asphalt, making my way down the front walkway to the entrance.

The doorman, a familiar face now, has only to look at the necklace for his eyes to alight with recognition. He studiously ignores my bare feet and waves me in, holding the door open for me.

"Shall I notify Mr. Grayson that you've arrived?" he asks with a tilt of his head.

"He's expecting me. Thank you." My eyes scan the spacious entrance of the elegant tower, skimming over the gleaming marble and bouncing off the shiny chrome. My anxiety suddenly triples being back here.

Why the heck did I even come here? Should I have gone to the police instead?

No, I don't want to be involved. And if I go to the police, I'll be irrevocably entwined with whatever the fuck this is. I just need to give the evidence to Ash, then I can wash my hands of him, David, Russian spies...*all of it.*

But with a firm resolve, I tighten my fists at my sides and decide I'm not going to be anywhere alone with Ash. I already know I have zero willpower when it comes to him. So I'm not going anywhere near his apartment, *nowhere* near his bedroom. And *definitely* nowhere near his bed.

I'm only in the lobby for a minute when an elevator chimes. It's from the side bank, where the private penthouse elevators are. Out of it strides Ash, long-legged, confident. He carries himself with a take-charge attitude and a no-nonsense look on his face.

He's wearing suit pants and the white long sleeve button-down shirt he likely wore under his suit for work. *Sexy as hell*, as always. The man couldn't be unsexy if he tried.

"Lexi," he calls across the lobby as if I haven't already noticed him and have my attention focused completely on him.

Suddenly, I'm shaking like a leaf and only seconds from bursting into tears. The second he's within reach, he takes me in his strong arms and holds me tightly against him. I press my face against his solid shoulder and breathe him in, savoring his smell.

Calm instantly washes over me, and I sink into his embrace. This feeling of being in his arms and tightly held against him brings sudden relief and a complete feeling of safety. I'm at once overwhelmed and angry at my own reaction. I press my face hard against him as if that will dam the tears that are already poking at the backs of my eyes.

"Princess, are you alright? What can I do? Tell me what happened."

"Is-is there somewhere we can talk? Alone?"

He opens his mouth to reply, but before he can even say a word, I interrupt again. "Not your apartment. Somewhere more public, please."

I think he might have argued with me had my voice not trembled on those last words. With a sharp nod, he takes me by the elbow and guides me gently mentioning to the front desk that he needs to use one of the private meeting rooms on the ground floor. With the wave of a hand, a person appears and guides us there. It's not far from the entrance to the restaurant and it's elegantly appointed, as everything is here, a basic room with a desk and seating area specifically for people to talk business or have more private conversations without having to enter the members-only areas of the club.

Once inside, he shuts the door and pulls me back into his arms. He kisses my temple, my cheek, and my ear. "Princess, tell me what's wrong. What happened? Is this about David? Do I need to fucking kill him? *Because I will.*"

I take a deep breath, then sigh, letting myself relax a little. "It's fine. I'll be okay. I just need you to take this off my hands. I need—oh, Ash, I don't know what I need!"

"Well, start at the beginning then. This has something to do with David, doesn't it?" he asks again.

Without looking into his eyes, I nod. I can feel the tension rolling off of him. His wound up tight, like a coiled spring. He is most definitely not pleased.

When I feel myself waiver on my feet, Ash guides me to a chair and sits beside me. Then, he smooths my cheek with his long fingers.

"You were just with him?" I can feel that tension ratchet up inside of him. He asks the question between his teeth like he's fighting with himself to keep from erupting in anger.

The way he asks it, I know he's asking about more than just being in David's presence. He wants to know if I slept with him. I swallow, suddenly feeling guilty that it was my intent to do just that. I have no idea why I feel guilty, though…

"I was just with him, but not in that way. He invited me over to his house for dinner."

Some tension appears to leave his shoulders, and he nods.

"You chose not to listen to my warnings about him. Why?"

I looked up at him, meeting his gaze. "I-I needed to move on. I needed to forget you, us. I needed *something,* so I thought…"

"You should have listened, Lexi," he growls sternly.

I nod. It's all the acknowledgment I'm willing to give him. Then, I clear my throat, lick my lips, and prepare to tell him the entire thing. Which I do, from start to finish, in a flat voice, as if I'm narrating someone else's story.

When I get to the part about finding the guns in his desk drawer, I can't help the tears streaming down my face. I'm reliving the terror of finding them and the complete fear that freezes me still. What if he uses that gun to come after me tonight?

Ash has his arm around my shoulder and he's pulled me against him. He dries my tears with his large thumb, leaving kisses where those tears once were. He whispers reassuring words to me, and it calms me and makes me feel safe. So I let him do it, even though my heart and my head are at war right now.

"This is what I found, and I don't know what to do with them. I-I just want to give them to you and be done with this whole thing." I reach into my clutch and pull out the items in question— the flash drive I snatched from David's gym bag, the burner phone I found with the guns, and the small booklet with the notes scrawled inside.

He removes them gently from my hands and sets them aside. "I'll take them, it's fine. I've got this, Princess. Now come upstairs with me and we'll talk about a plan for your safety."

It's only when he says this that I push away from him, shaking my head vigorously. "No," I say, my breath almost completely depleted from my chest so that I can barely force it out. "No," I repeat more forcefully. "I won't go home with you. It's over, Ash. I told you that before. You need to respect that."

His expression sobers. "I need to know that you're safe. That's all this is. Nothing will happen that you don't want to happen."

But I shake my head. That's the problem, I know what I *want* to happen, deep down, and that's not what's good for me. My heart and my body want him and want to be with him again. Only my head is telling me differently. And right now my head is in control, thank God. But who knows for how much longer?

"I mean to have you back, Lexi." His statement is quiet, determined.

My eyes dart back to his and I see the conviction mirrored in his gaze as well. "That's not going to happen, Ash. We're *over*. I told you that. Please don't make me keep repeating it."

He reaches his hand up to touch my cheek, but I pull my head away before he can connect. His gaze intensifies. "Don't let this color what we had. You know how good we are together."

I do know. But I know also that my heart has been crushed by everything that's gone on between us. From finding out that he was the one who set up our "accidental" hookup that first night. That I was his intentional prey, his mark. His asset. I just can't stomach that thought. I can't trust anything he says.

With my hesitation, he speaks again. And he uses that tone of voice, the tone of voice that could get me to do anything. I recognize it immediately, and I silently shore up my defenses against it. "Princess, let me take care of you right now. I need to protect you."

I'm so swayed by the words that I almost fall into him once more, into his waiting arms, but I just can't. Instead, I force myself to stand up and push away from him. I face him and with my fists clenched at my sides, I look at him with as much conviction as I can muster. "No, Ash. We are *done*. We're done *forever*. I don't want to be involved in any of this. You used me to get what you needed. Now you have it. I have my own life to get back to, and it doesn't involve any of this."

He stands as if he's going to walk after me, but I hold up my hand and I yell a little louder than I should, "No! Do *not* follow me."

Then I run all the way out to the curb, bare feet slapping across the marble floor. My mind races for what to do, but not for long. I fumble for my phone to summon an Uber, but before I can submit the request, the doorman approaches. He lets me know that Mr. Grayson has asked him to order one of the Exeter town cars to take me home.

With relief, I let loose a long breath and accept this last favor from him.

But I don't turn around. I don't want to see if he's standing there. I don't want to see him. Not ever again.

In minutes, the car is ready, and I slip into it, my bare toes wiggling on the coarse carpeting of the car. In a moment of weakness, I look up.

I see Ash standing, watching the car pull away from the curb. His hands are in his pockets, and there's a determination in his eyes that terrifies me.

That look tells me that, as far as he's concerned, this defeat is only temporary.

Chapter 29
Daily Reminders

THE NEXT FEW WEEKS PASS IN A SORT OF HAZY BLUR. I GO about my daily life and consciously push all thoughts of Ash out of my mind. I block his number and refuse anything he sends me.

Because he sends me things. Every *single* day. Sometimes it's flowers, sometimes it's something more. But I send everything back. I can't stand the thought of keeping something that might remind me of him.

Not that I need any physical reminders. My mind does that well enough.

The days are easier. I fill them up with my studies, reading, research, even running errands for my friends or physical exercise. Gwen keeps me busy, pulling me around town to bookstores and libraries for her story. I staunchly refuse to visit any more sex clubs, and I'm relieved when she doesn't even ask. She seems to be on the trail of something big but won't give me details.

In the quiet moments each day, I fill myself up by watching mindless internet videos or listening to podcasts. Anything that keeps me occupied and away from where my thoughts naturally tend to drift.

Because they always come back to Ash.

The nights are worse. I lie in bed willing myself to fall asleep, without much success. I remember how it felt to be lying next to him, having him reach for me, even waking up in the middle of the night with him already engaged in some delicious sexual act. Try as I might, I can't forget the pleasure I experienced at his hands. And now it feels like I'm detoxing from an intense addiction.

I'm not sleeping well, and I tend to get cranky and short with my roommates. Especially as new gifts arrive, each one more elaborate than the last.

First, it was a bracelet, intricate, gold filigree studded with small emeralds. Then it was a necklace with diamonds. Then, he sent me another tiara with a note, of course, that said I'll always be his princess.

That one almost made me cry.

But I'm strong and I don't let the tears fall.

I'm all out of patience the afternoon that Gwen barges into my room with what I assume is today's gift. I'm in the middle of taking notes on an old lecture that I don't even need anymore, but it's just something to occupy my mind.

I'm not proud of it, but I yell at Gwen, "Stop it. Just send them back. I don't need to be told every time he sends something."

But Gwen ignores me. She's breathless as if she's just run full speed up the stairs and straight to my room. "Lexi, turn on your TV. You're not going to believe this."

Without even waiting for me to follow her directions, she grabs the remote and turns on my TV, flipping through the channels until she gets to a network that's broadcasting the news.

I gasp at the close-up shot of David. He's being led, handcuffed, by two policemen and escorted into a police car while a voice-over narrates what's going on. He's being arrested on suspicion of espionage, working for the Russian government. There are details about a plot to take down part of the country's virtual network grid, making it vulnerable to Russian cyber-attack.

What the…?

My mouth drops. I knew David was up to no good—and that it involved the Russians—but I'm still stunned. Ash had warned me *multiple times* that David was dangerous, and I hadn't listened. The guy had successfully roofied me once and had likely tried to do so a second time. And here he was, on his way to prison.

I can't believe this is the guy I thought I was gonna build my life with. The guy I thought would be the perfect husband for me. I can't believe my judgment is so terrible that I'd have married him blindly. Hell, if he'd asked me, pre-Ash, to go to Vegas and elope, I would have done it. He would have completely played me, and easily, because he fit my "ideal husband" criteria.

I watch the footage and as the ramifications sink in, my whole life turns upside down.

When they move on to another story, Gwen turns the TV off and sinks onto the bed beside me. She's quiet for a moment as if waiting for me to absorb the shocking new info. She's quietly watching me until I turn my head away. I'm just numb—I've *been* so numb.

"So, what does all this mean for you?" she asks.

I turn back to her with widened eyes. "What do you think it means? It doesn't change anything."

Her confusion is clear on her face. "How can you say that? I mean, it proves that Ash was right. And that he's sincere. Why else would he still be sending you gifts and wanting to hear from you?"

I blow out a breath and give her some serious side-eye. "Ash doesn't need you to speak for him, Gwen. I've been taken in by *two* different men and I'm not willing to believe *anyone* anymore. I'm done with all this man stuff. At least for a while, because honestly, I don't know who to trust anymore. No one told me the truth for months. I've pinned hopes on two men who were both lying straight to my face while using me."

The empathy in Gwen's eyes is obvious. But it's the pity I fear. I don't want to be pitied. Pitied like my mother, always trusting the wrong man, always betting her life and future on the wrong horse. But really, who am I to say? My own judgment seems to be just as shitty as hers. The apple really doesn't fall far from the tree, as they say.

"Lex." Gwen's voice is soft lacking any sort of judging tone. It still sets me on edge. I let her talk anyway. "Ash has no reason to use you anymore."

I blink at her. "Did you just hear yourself? *Anymore.* That's the key word, isn't it? He has no reason to use me *anymore.* You have to say that because he actually *was* using me. The entire time. He might still need me for something. Or maybe he's just trying to soothe his own guilt. Not that I think that highly of him. I doubt he has the conscience that would make him feel guilty."

"But—"

"No, you need to drop it. For the sake of our friendship, we need to agree not to talk about this anymore. Ash is in my past. David is in my past. I'm moving on. And if you were a true friend, you would help me."

Gwen blinks, hesitates, opens her mouth as if to say something, then shuts it again. She nods slowly and, in a quiet voice, says, "Okay, you've been very clear. I'll respect that, as your friend. Just know I love you, Lex."

A bit later, we hug it out and all is well again. She wanders off to go work on her story and I'm back to my extraneous busy work. Hopefully, life will get back to normal. And soon.

Only it doesn't.

It takes me a little over a week to realize that I'm being followed. That's either how good they are or how clueless I am. I have no idea *who* is following me, though. Is it David's people? The Russians? The feds? I have no idea. They don't come anywhere near me, but they don't attempt to disguise themselves either, which leads me to think that this isn't covert. They're not spying on me. Am I being guarded? Some type of witness protection?

One day, when I go to the coffee shop, I decide I'm going to sidestep them by exiting through the back door. Most likely, losing them will only be temporary. Since they know where I live, they'll always know where to find me.

So I don't even try to shake them off. Instead, I double back around to the front, maneuvering so I can get close enough to them to get a clue about who they are. With my phone at the ready, I snap a couple of pictures before they catch sight of me, turn around, and act nonchalant like they have no idea who I am.

Later, when I'm at home, I get a chance to look at the photos a bit closer. I enlarge them and notice the tie pin. It's a brass-colored symbol and one I've seen before. It takes me an hour or two of mulling it over to remember where it's from. I've seen the pin on the suits of security personnel at Exeter House.

Could they be Ash's people? Maybe they're following me to report my movements back to him? Maybe they plan to force me to talk to him? Or maybe it's something less sinister. They could just be protecting me from retaliation. I'm pretty sure my part in David's arrest wasn't insignificant. It may have even been instrumental.

With the picture blown up as big as I can without it being too fuzzy to recognize, I take a screencap. Then I call Maddy and explain the situation to her. I text her the photo, and she quickly confirms it's Exeter House security. She's been escorted by them many times, to certain functions. Her guy, Evan Kohl, is over-the-top protective, so it makes sense.

"Yeah, the security guys all have those pins. It's the logo of their business. They also provide video surveillance, all the bells and whistles to keep the premises safe."

"Thanks, Maddy. I really appreciate you confirming that for me."

"Is everything okay, Lex?" Concern is clear in her voice. "Is there anything I can do? Or ask Evan to do for you?"

I clear my throat. "I'm good for now. I'll be okay. Thank you so much, Mads."

She hesitates a moment as if she isn't fully convinced by my reassurance. "Promise you'll let me know. And, you know, since Evan and Ash are close friends, I've had a chance to get to know him, too. Ash is actually a really good guy. And I just feel like I should put in a good word for him."

Good thing she can't see me roll my eyes. I wonder if she and Gwen are tag-teaming. "Did he ask you to say that to me?"

"No, he didn't. And I wouldn't do that just because he asked. I know something of what it's like. How hard it is to love these men. They don't make it easy. His friend is not too different from him. And you know I had my own struggles when Evan and I were first together."

I nod, even though she can't see me on the phone. "I get it, I do. But things with you and Evan were always on the up and up, weren't they? It's not like he lied to you, or used you. For the two of you, it was a business agreement. A contracted relationship from the very beginning. Things just grew openly and honestly from that."

"Well," she laughs. And then laughs again, as if remembering things that only she knows, things she hasn't shared with me. "It wasn't *quite* as easy as that, but I do understand that the circumstances are very different with you and Ash. I respect that."

That's what I need to hear. That right there.

"Thank you, Maddie. You are a really good friend. I promise, if I need your help, I'll ask."

"Thank goodness." She lets out a long, relieved sigh. "And if you need me to ask Evan to do anything, let me know. If Ash is doing anything to make you feel uncomfortable, please tell me. Because you know, even though I just spoke up for him, I'm on *your* side. You're my friend, and I really love you."

Tears clog my throat at her honest empathy. I'm so moved by it. I keep my cool until I can tell her goodbye and then end up shedding more tears shortly after.

With the next few days come more gifts. Each morning, a fresh dozen red roses, half bloomed. Every afternoon, a box of chocolates, or a basket of muffins. Those were confiscated by my roommates before I could even get the chance to reject them and send them back. In the evenings, more intimate gifts still.

Sometimes a piece of jewelry, sometimes a beautiful piece of clothing. A dress, a sexy negligee.

Every single thing I can send back, I do.

I'm a rock. I'm determined not to feel anything. And each night, I go to bed hoping that the next morning I'll wake up with no feelings.

And each morning, I wake up realizing the feelings are still there. But they might be fading. Or maybe it's just wishful thinking? That they can fade...even if just by a micron a millimeter each day.

Maybe after a hundred years, I won't feel anything at all.

Chapter 30
Being Brave

Only days after I double-crossed my so-called security detail at the coffee shop, I manage to ditch them again. This time for close to a full day. It's not easy, but I devised a plan, because I know the Caltech campus a whole lot better than they do.

And it's only a matter of going out a back door they didn't know about.

I congratulate myself on my own cleverness. It actually makes me feel a bit triumphant like I'm taking back some control. And it's a good day, too.

Until that night, when my binge-steaming of *Friends* is interrupted by someone pounding on the front door of Hill House. Whoever it is sounds like they're seconds from just busting the door down and walking in. Clearly, they're angry about something.

I know on instinct that it's not a coincidence. I'd ditched Ash's people earlier that day. Now they're back to reestablish their beat.

Or worse, it could be Ash himself.

Minutes after the pounding stops and, presumably, someone answers the door, there's a light knock at my locked bedroom door. Gwen identifies herself, allaying my fears that it might be Ash. I crack the door open and peer through it.

"What is it?" I whisper crankily.

She grimaces, almost apologetically, as if anticipating my response before she even speaks. "It's Ash. He *really* wants to talk to you."

"*No*. No way. That isn't happening. Tell him to go away. He knows I don't want to see him. He needs to respect my boundaries."

Gwen blinks at me, and when she might protest, I raise my eyebrows at her as if to silently remind her of the promise that she'd made to me a few days before. That she'd respect my decisions when it came to Ash. That's all it takes. Breathing a sigh, she nods and turns to leave. I shut the door, and just in case Ash gets any ideas of going alpha and barging in, I make sure to lock it.

I open my window so I can hear what's going on in the front. As my room overlooks the side of the house, I'm safe from being seen by him. I can hear the distant rumble of his voice as he speaks to Gwen. I can't deny the reaction it evokes deep inside of me. Squeezing my eyes shut, I fight to keep myself from opening up that door and running down the stairs to him.

But I'm strong and I can do this.

Minutes later, Gwen is back at my door, and after she's assured me that she's alone, that Ash has now gone, I let her in.

"What's up?" I ask.

She steps in, almost gingerly, and waits until I sink back onto my bed before she takes my desk chair and faces me. "Can we talk for a minute, please?"

I stare up at the ceiling. "What did he want?"

She clears her throat and busies herself by arranging her skirt around her thighs. "He wanted to see you. He seemed pretty upset."

I blow out a breath. "That's because I ditched his goons today. He doesn't like not having complete control. He doesn't like not knowing everything."

"I don't doubt you're right about that but…has it occurred to you that he also doesn't like not being able to protect you? I mean, David's people, whoever they are—the Russians, I guess—they're still out there. They could come after you in retaliation. I'm sure Ash isn't just having you followed for the hell of it."

"He doesn't need to protect me," I say in a voice that doesn't sound one-hundred percent convinced of what I'm saying.

"I disagree. I've been following David's case. The reporting of it, the court proceedings, and all that. He's being federally prosecuted, Lex. Most of the charges and most of the documents have been redacted. We're talking high-level stuff. Ash wasn't bullshitting you. David really is a bad guy, and Ash was intervening to get you out of it. Just think…if you'd gone further with David, where would you be now? You could be at the bottom of Malibu Bay wearing cement shoes."

I give her some serious side-eye. "Gee, thanks for the visual."

"I'm just saying, Ash's intentions are not wholly impure. He really *does* care about you or he wouldn't be doing all this."

"He just doesn't want to lose his star witness," I quip cynically.

"You don't even know if they're gonna subpoena you. What would you even be a witness for? You gathered some stuff at his house. I would imagine the evidence is more than enough to put him away without even needing you. I think Ash just wants to make sure you're safe, especially since you were in so much danger—or at least *potential* danger."

"You don't have to speak on Ash's behalf." I sigh, hoping she'll drop it. Hoping I won't always feel as swayed by those words as I do right now.

"Actually, I do. Because you're refusing to listen to him. You're turning this into a game, running away from his security. Besides that, you're absolutely miserable. You *do* love him, but you're questioning your own judgment. That's because your mom has shown some really bad judgment in the past. And you're so determined not to be like her that you're sabotaging your own happiness. Yes, you got in over your head with David. But Ash isn't one of those con men your mom gets tangled up with. I have a strong intuition about these things. He's going above and beyond to let you know that he's there for you and that he still cares."

"I don't really care about fancy gifts, flowers, jewelry—all that elaborate bullshit."

Gwen shakes her head. "He's just trying to tell you that he really cares, and he wants you in his life. Since he can't, you know, tell you to your face."

I turn and look at her directly for the first time since she came in. "I don't even know what would motivate him to want that."

"For real?" Gwen's eyes widen as if she can't believe my cluelessness. "You have no inkling of what could possibly be motivating him right now? Has it not occurred to you that he's being motivated by *love*?" Gwen frowns as if carefully choosing her next words. "It's interesting how selective you're being. How you judge what's coming out of his mouth as truth and what you are labeling as lies. Everything negative and awful about him, you deem the truth. Everything that could possibly clue you into his honest intentions and true love is a lie. Don't you think that it's a little illogical to be applying that filter so inconsistently?"

I put my palms to my forehead and rub it in frustration. "I don't understand why it's so important to you whether or not I believe Ash."

"What I want, as your friend, is your happiness. And I know you love him. And I know you're strong, Lexi. I know that you were such a badass when you had the courage to drug David and ransack his room. You were the key to locking him up. And while I know Ash is more than grateful, all of *this* isn't gratitude. He loves you, you love him, and I just want to see you happy."

I heave a sigh. I don't really want to give Gwen's words any credit, but I let her say her piece nevertheless. She has been a good friend to me and I know that she truly does want me to be happy. But that doesn't mean I agree with what—or *who*—will give me that.

When I say nothing, she continues, "I'm just saying that you have been so brave with how you handled the David thing. You should be brave again and give love a chance."

The silence between us grows for so long that Gwen might even suspect I've fallen asleep. My mind races, replaying memories—the way Ash touched my cheek, the way he looked into my eyes, the way he held me. It wasn't just about the sex, as hot as that had been. There was more. It couldn't have been a complete act, could it?

Or else he was the greatest actor in the world to look at me that way, to hold me that way. But...

"I never heard those words from him."

"You've never heard those words from him because he never spoke them out loud. But he's been writing them to you every single day. Every delivery of cards says it." She pulls something out of her pocket and hands it to me. It's a stack of cards, all small, like the cards that come from a flower shop.

"I told you to send the flowers back," I say flatly.

She nods. "I did, but I kept the cards and asked that they deliver the flower arrangements to the nursing home the next block over."

"And you snooped through them?"

She gives me a small smile while her eyes dart away. "Well, you know, I'm protective too. And I wanted to know what the hell he was writing to you."

I leaf through the cards one by one. The messages are short. One says how much he misses me. One says how much he wants to see me again. One says how much he would love to give me just a kiss or hold me in his arms again.

My heart starts thumping in my chest. I read through every card. There are at least a dozen here. Almost two weeks' worth of flower deliveries. The last ones just say *I love you*, no name, no other message.

I don't even realize I'm crying until the tears are streaming down my cheeks.

Gwen emits a sound of comfort the minute she notices them. She grabs the tissue box and plops herself next to me on the bed. Without a word, I grab a tissue and start dabbing my cheeks.

Gwen murmurs to me, "I didn't want to make you cry. I just wanted you to realize that this isn't a man who's trying to pull a con on you."

I blow my nose and give her a look. "I'm still having trouble forgiving him for the first one. It's not a matter of love. It's a matter of *trust*."

"Well." She looks out the window, her hand idly fiddling with a thread on my worn comforter. "All I have to say to that is, you'll never learn to trust him again if you don't at least give him a chance, right? At least you should let him talk to you again."

I shake my head, rejecting that idea instantly. "I don't trust myself to talk to him again face-to-face."

"You could always find some other way to communicate with him. Do it for yourself, if not for him."

To that, I only nod. My mind is racing through possibilities. Maybe I do have more to say to him. Maybe he has more he should hear from me.

But I'm exhausted and I don't want to think about it anymore, not right now, and not with Gwen here.

"Enough talking about me and my crazy life problems. Tell me…how's your article coming? Any closer to getting it written?"

She gives me a smile as if understanding that I'm done talking about the previous subject and with a nod answers, "I think I'm onto something,"

I lift a brow. "Another sex club?"

She laughs and it makes me feel better to see her laugh. I'm already feeling lighter. "No, no. I found a new lead. Something intriguing. My source at the club…Domino."

"Was that Mr. Delicious's name? Domino?"

She laughs. "A pseudonym, surely. I suspect most of the members use them while they're there."

I narrow my eyes. "Can you trust him?"

She shrugs. "No more or less than any other source for a good inside story, I suppose."

My eyes widen. "Are you sure your editor will take something different than what you pitched?"

She shrugs but won't give me any more details about this "new lead" even though I ask her a few more questions.

"I'm not ready yet. It might not even pan out, anyway."

Half an hour after she leaves, I finally find the strength to get off the bed, go over to my desk, and pull out a piece of stationary. I haven't written a physical letter in a very long time. But for some reason, this feels like the way I should reach out. The things I need to communicate are too big for a text message, or even an e-mail. So I pen the letter by hand.

In it, I say all the things I need to say to him. How betrayed I feel, how I can't trust him again. However, I can't resist; I also end my message with those same three words he used on that last card he attached with the flowers.

The next morning, I go about my day as normal. When I notice my usual tailgate, I realize these are the same guys I'd ditched the day before. So when I near the place where I'd ditched them, they get a little closer than they normally do. They're clearly afraid that I may try to do so again.

But instead of trying to give them the slip, I do an about-face and walk toward them.

I almost laugh at the startled looks on their faces, but they don't pretend or turn away. I should apologize for yesterday…I'm sure Ash chewed their asses for losing me. Hence their vigilance today.

All this makes it easier for me to walk up to them and hand them the envelope with Ash's name on it.

"Here," I say. "Give this to your boss."

CHAPTER 31
HIS PRINCESS

ONLY DAYS AFTER MY DRAMATIC GESTURE OF HANDING the letter to my unwanted security detail, Maddie invites Gwen and me to have dinner with her at Isca. Gwen is practically vibrating with excitement.

"This can only mean that she wants to ask us to be her bridesmaids! Can you imagine? Oh-em-gee. I can't even *begin* to imagine what her wedding is going to be like. How much money does a billionaire spend on his wedding? Maybe it will be an exotic destination wedding. Hawaii or the Caribbean or, God, Tahiti! I could use a trip to someplace warm."

"Geez, Gwen, calm down. She hasn't even asked us yet. She could just want to see us. You know, like friends do. Let's just take it down a notch or ten, please."

"Don't be a wet blanket, Lexi. A bridesmaid in a billionaire's wedding could be the only fifteen minutes of fame I'll ever get," she says.

"Not true. You're on your way to becoming a brilliant journalist."

Honestly, I'm a wet blanket about everything, lately. My life is on autopilot. I get up, eat breakfast, go to campus, eat lunch, study, come home. Typically, I ignore my security detail or pretend they aren't there. I've given up on the idea of fighting against them or even trying to lose them. If I'm being honest, I feel safer with them around, anyway.

On Thursday night, Gwen and I dress nice—not date nice, but definitely eating-out-with-girlfriends nice. I wish I'd thought to try and talk Maddie into another location for this meeting. I really don't want to run into Ash at Isca. So, I strike a compromise and ask Maddie if we can sit at a patio table, beachside. That way, we won't have to enter the restaurant through the main entrance.

In all likelihood, if I'm not stupid enough to wear that damn necklace again, Ash won't be notified of my presence. I'll just be any other girl blending into the woodwork.

But my plans are foiled when we're dropped off at the front entrance. I start to lead Gwen around the building toward the beach, but she grabs my arm and tugs me back toward the main entrance.

"Maddie said we need to go through this entrance, for security reasons."

Security reasons? What the hell is that? Did someone call in a bomb threat or something?

My heart thumps a thousand miles a minute, but I reassure myself that there are hundreds here in the building and Ash is probably still at work. Or maybe out with some other woman. *No,* that thought is too painful. I know we're over, but I still can't bring myself to think of him moving on with someone else, living his life like what happened between us didn't mean anything at all.

We make it through the entrance and step into Isca. The public has full access here, so the restaurant *should* be bustling.

But the lights are dimmed, and it doesn't look like it's even open tonight.

I turn to Gwen. "Did Maddie say anything about the place being closed? Did she text you? When was the last time you checked your phone?"

I turn and scan the lobby for Maddie. Maybe she knows what the hell is going on.

Without a word, Gwen grabs my hand and pulls me forward.

I push out a breath. "Gwen, what the fuck? It's—"

I cut words short as we move deeper into the restaurant. Every table is empty, the lighting dim. But there are so many tall, white pillar candles lit in a large restaurant space, it glows golden. Every available surface is decorated with fresh white flowers of every variety—roses, chrysanthemums, lilies. The tablecloths—like everything else—are white. It's like it snowed in here.

I dart a glance at Gwen. She's smiling wide, and I know instantly that she's up to something. I'm starting to suspect this doesn't have anything to do with meeting Maddie for dinner.

I stop in my tracks and pull out of her hold.

Before I can unleash the lashing on the tip of my tongue, I'm aware of someone else nearby.

When I look up, I see Ash. He's wearing a black suit that fits his muscular form, tailor-made just for him, a three-piece suit with a black tie and a crisp white shirt. He's so devastatingly handsome the breath catches in my throat.

He stands as still as a statue, or one of those cardboard cutouts of a perfect man that you can pose with in Instagram shots. He never takes his eyes off of me. And I'm frozen in my place. I hardly notice when Gwen's presence fades from my side, but the moment he steps toward me, I know we're alone.

I hold up my hand to stop his advance. "No, Ash. Please. Don't come any closer."

Obediently, he halts, hands working at his side. I can't take my eyes off of his. As much as I want to turn and run, I know I can't. I know I *won't.* There are too many unanswered questions between us.

Maybe this is a chance at closure for both of us. Maybe, after this conversation, after he responds to the things I expressed in my note, we can close the door on *us.* He'll set me free. And then I can go back to my normal life.

To the way I was before.

God, the thought of life without Ash makes my heart *physically* hurt. But it's for the best, right?

There's a table nearby. It's the only one that's set with elegant fine china and crystal goblets, gold-trimmed silverware. The settings reflect the amber light all around us. At one of the place settings, there's a tiara. It's the one he sent me, that I'd rejected and sent back to him. The diamonds pick up the ambient light and gleam like a pirate's treasure hidden in a cave for thousands of years, waiting for me to discover it.

When I return my gaze to Ash, I note, with gratitude, that he's kept his distance. I don't think I could handle it. I take a deep breath and finally speak, "What are you doing here?"

A stupid question, I know. But on the other hand, I have no idea what his intentions are.

He fixes his steadfast gaze on me, all seriousness. "I'm doing what I should have done weeks ago. I'm talking to you face-to-face. I'm opening up to you. I'm telling you now what I couldn't tell you *then* when I was forced to hide everything from you. It was eating me up inside, Lexi. You've only been in my life for a very short time, but you've changed everything. It's made me realize how fucked up everything was before you. If I could take it all back and do it over, I would. In a heartbeat."

I blink, aware of the sting behind my eyes, threatening tears. I try to summon up my anger, channel it as if it might somehow give me the strength to resist him. But I can't.

I lace my fingers together in front of me tightly. He still doesn't make a move toward me.

"Lexi, I'm sorry I couldn't be a better man for you..."

I shake my head but he keeps talking. Almost faster.

"I'm not asking you to believe me. All I can do is offer you the truth. When I saw you in the bar on that first night, you were a means to an end. My asset. And I'll never forgive myself for dragging you into this and putting you in danger. I'm not proud of that, and I'd give anything to change it. But everything I've done since that night was to protect you...because you're *everything* to me, Lexi."

I suck in a sharp breath, but it hurts to breathe. I can't move. He keeps talking through all of it, and I can't help but hang on his every word.

"I was so arrogant, I thought I could rise above it. I fought my own feelings. But why do you think I kept telling you to stay away from David?" He takes one step toward me. "I didn't just want to keep you safe. I knew you were mine. From the second I tasted you, I knew I could never let you go. I need your forgiveness, Lexi"—he dips his head briefly, before looking back up at me—"and in return, I vow to always be truthful with you.

Regardless of the circumstances. Because…I love you, Lexi Anderson."

The words "I love you" rush through me. Ash Grayson *loves* me. Despite my resistance, just hearing those words cracks my heart wide open.

My heart is beating loud in my ears, and my cheeks are now completely soaked with tears. His words are so beautiful, I want to believe them with everything that's in me. It's like a dream. I can't imagine taking another breath away from him. But I'm still so scared.

I shake my head and his hopeful expression fades. Then I ruin the moment with a huge sniffle and finally choke out what I want to say. "I'm too scared. I love you, too, but how could I possibly trust you?"

His jaw tenses, and he nods slowly. "I know. I understand. But believe me when I say that I love you more than anything, and I'll spend every single day of the rest of our lives earning that trust back."

Without realizing it, I've been stepping toward him. We're now only inches from each other. My head is tilted back, and I'm looking deep into his dark eyes. He doesn't even dare to reach out and touch me. Not until I speak.

I swallow. "I have conditions."

"I agree to them all," he says quickly.

I can't help but laugh. I'm half-tempted to give him some really ridiculous demands but we're not ready to joke about this yet.

"The condition is that we always, *always* tell each other the truth, even when it hurts. Even when it's inconvenient."

He nods, and the corners of his mouth turn up. "I've already promised you that. You'll only ever get the truth from me." Then he reaches up to smooth a strand of my hair away from my cheek, where it stuck because of my tears. He tucks it behind my ear. Then, under his breath, with the most emotion I've ever heard from any man, his voice trembles. "The days and weeks without you have been fucking agony. Promise me you won't ever walk away again. Whatever it is, we'll work it out together." He takes my chin between his thumb and forefinger, tilting my head up gently. "Promise me, Lex."

I lick my bottom lip and nod. "I promise."

Then, I sway into him, and his arms wrap around me tightly. He lifts me off the ground, and I'm pulled so tight against him I can hardly breathe. I have no true sense of how long he holds me like this, but it feels incredible. Like everything I ever wanted to feel when I was forcing a relationship with another man, but didn't. Here I have the man who not only sets my body on fire but makes me feel safe, secure, *loved*. Cherished.

He whispers into my ear, "*My* princess."

The rest of the night passes in a blur. After I wipe away the tears, I manage to choke down a little bit of the elegant dinner. The entire restaurant is ours for the evening, so we're completely alone, except for the staff.

We don't spend too much time eating, however. When the pianist begins playing "Can't Help Falling in Love," Ash stands, buttons his jacket, and offers me his strong hand. I stare at it for a second. Maybe it's just the wine, but it feels symbolic. If I take his hand, I take it forever. If I take his hand, I'm choosing to push past the fear and let him into my heart.

He waits patiently until I finally slide my hand into his. Then, with that panty-melting smile, he pulls me toward a cleared section of tables and holds me close as the painfully romantic melody flows through us. I rest my head on his chest, and everything else just fades away. All the lies and deceptions. None of it seems to matter anymore. Just this moment, the two of us, and our new beginning.

When the song ends, he pulls back slightly, and I look up. Without speaking, he dips his head and touches his lips to mine. It's just a kiss, not meant to be arousing or stimulating. But it's the most intimate, vulnerable, honest expression of feelings between us. His mouth, my mouth, our tongues entwined. We taste each other. We give and take.

We open up to each other and communicate on a level beyond words.

Eventually, he makes the suggestion to go up to his room for dessert, but I tilt my head back and tell him, "No, actually, I was thinking we could go back to my place. You could stay with me there, if you want."

The smile on his face turns up a notch, and he dips his head to lightly brush his lips across mine again. "I'll go anywhere you want, Princess. I'm all yours."

And that's just what we do.

CHAPTER 32
SUBMIT

A FEW WEEKS LATER, WE'RE MAKING OUR WAY BACK TO Ash's penthouse after a lovely dinner at the members-only restaurant on the fifth floor. I've spent the evening teasing him, eating my food in a suggestive manner and taking advantage of the long white tablecloths to hide the very naughty things I'm doing to him with my foot.

By the time dessert is finished—and I lick the last bits of chocolate mousse off his fingers while his eyes smolder into mine—I can tell that he's as hungry for it as I am.

We barely make it back to the front door of his penthouse before he has half my clothes off. While we're in a frenzy to get inside and get naked, we're also not wanting to stop long enough to unlock and open the door. He's got my clothes half-pulled off and me sandwiched between the hardwood of the door and his own...*very* hard wood.

I'm just hoping one of his colleagues doesn't walk by while I'm out here with my shirt off, my bra pulled askew, and Ash's mouth and hands roaming everywhere.

Since it was finals week, I'd had to stay at Hill House for the previous ten days to get my work done, because this guy can't keep his hands off me. And I just might be guilty of the reverse.

We'd agreed that we'd spend our time apart efficiently, but we'd talked on the phone for hours every night.

Tonight, this special date night after the time away has gone amazing. And it's just getting started.

Once inside the penthouse, Ash removes the remainder of my clothing while my hands roam over his solid chest, his hips, his ass, anywhere I can reach.

He drops my clothes to the floor and then steps back to admire my naked body. I half wonder if he's going to just drop us and go at it right here on the floor for our first time in a week and a half.

The way I'm burning for him, I'll be thrilled if he does just that.

Instead, his eyes flick up to mine after sliding down my naked form.

"Don't move," he says, and my arousal kicks up a notch or three. I swallow, my throat tight with anticipation, my core heavy and aching with desire.

What delights does he have in store for us tonight?

I wait for what feels like hours. I never know what to expect with Ash, and that's both frightening and exhilarating. Finally, he strides back into the room, a pair of black leather handcuffs dangling from his hand—not the usual red rope he prefers to tie me up with.

Once he's within reach again, he holds the handcuffs out to me. They dangle from his fingertips for a few seconds before I realize he wants me to take them from his hand.

I do, but I'm totally confused. Am I supposed to put them on myself?

"What am I doing with these?" I ask. My heartbeat is thumping at the base of my throat, and my mouth is dry. I'm so close to breathless that it's almost hard to talk.

Without a word, Ash begins stripping off his clothes—his shirt first, followed by his socks, shoes and finally his trousers, adding each article of clothing to the pile where mine are. He stands before me, completely naked.

My gaze roves over his chiseled body, and I lick my lips, imagining them pressed against his hot, salty skin.

And then something completely unexpected happens...Ash kneels on the floor in front of me and holds out his wrists.

I blink at him for several seconds before realizing he wants me to put the handcuffs on *him.* His gaze holds mine for long seconds, and suddenly the air feels tight in my lungs. The energy between us is electric, and I have to remind myself to breathe.

I have this amazing man at my command. This strong, confident man is submitting to *me* and just the erotic idea makes me heady.

Lifting my chin, I point to the bedroom, and imitating similar commands he's made to me many times, I say, "Go in there and lie on the bed."

I follow him into the bedroom and watch as he, without any protest or hesitation, obeys my command. I swallow, my heartbeat ratcheting up a notch. "Put your arms above your head."

Again, without once taking those beautiful dark eyes from mine, he obeys. I move to the headboard and secure his wrists there with the handcuffs. He's lying on his back, his glorious body stretched out, his cock hard, reaching out for me...

Cupping his balls in my hand. I roll them gently, watching his face. His expression is unreadable, but his hands are clenched and the muscles in his arms are tense, strained. I explore him further, gripping his steel cock and wrapping my fingers around his thick length.

Slowly, I pump his cock, dragging my grip from base to tip and then back down again. He sucks in a sharp breath in response, moving his hips in time with my rhythm. A drop of precum wets the tip and I can't help it, I lean down to lick it off, swirling my tongue around the soft head. He tastes salty, earthy.

"Holy fuck, Lexi," he breathes. "Put your lips around my cock. Suck me hard, Princess."

"Uh-uh," I tease. "You don't get to tell me what to do. I'm the one who decides."

He arches his back, growling in defiance, straining against the cuffs. I smile a

little at his resistance. He needs control—craves it like most people crave water, as if it's essential to his survival. And yet, he has surrendered that control to *me*.

Releasing his cock, I allow my hand to trail up his torso, over the ropes of muscle that line his stomach. His body is glorious, chiseled perfection. Like the figures of ancient Greek and Roman gods in museums.

My gaze locks with his, and my chest suddenly feels tight. This man would go to the ends of the earth for me—to hell and back. He's done whatever it took to protect me.

Ash pulls against his restraints again, his muscles bulging. "God, Lexi, I need to be inside you." He pushes his head back against the headboard in frustration. "I'm so damn hungry for your pussy."

Lifting my leg over his torso, I straddle him, my wet core pressed against his pelvis, right below his belly button. I lean down, the tips of my breast brushing across his chest. "I want you to beg," I whisper in his ear.

Why not? He's made me do the same before. And I've done it. Enthusiastically. When I lift my head to look down at him, his eyes are narrowed and his jaw is clenched.

"Please," he hisses between clenched teeth.

Realizing it's as good as I'm going to get, I lift up slightly, gripping his cock and guiding him to my entrance, wetting the tip with my juices. A deep, guttural groan escapes from his throat. He juts his hips upward, pushing his cock into me greedily.

I lower myself all the way down until we connect and I'm fully seated on him. He stretches me wide, and I moan. "Oh, God, Ash."

He's so big, and he fills every inch of my channel. Every nerve is electrified. I grind my hips against him.

He growls. "You feel so fucking good. If you don't slow down, you're going to make me come in that sweet little pussy."

Lifting his hips up off the mattress, he thrusts into me—hard—taking what control he can.

Our bodies move in unison as we both hurdle toward climax. Pleasure crashes through me, and I pick up the rhythm, jerking against him in a fevered blur of motion, my hands pushing against his wide, solid chest for leverage.

"Christ, Lexi!" He arches his back up off the mattress, every muscle coiled tight. I can feel his cock pulse as his come pumps into me, filling my core. "*Fuck*. God! Fuck!"

I release a muffled cry as my own climax hits me like a tidal wave, drowning me in hot, exquisite pleasure. My head falls back and my fingers find my nipples, pinching hard to draw out the orgasm.

"Ash!" I cry out. "God, yes!" My orgasm rolls on and on, stealing the breath from my lungs. I gasp for air as I ride the last spasms of his cock, greedily milking every last drop of come from his glorious body.

When we both finally float back down to earth, I reach over and unfasten the handcuffs that are securing his wrists to the headboard. His hands fall and immediately cup my backside, squeezing hard.

"Ready for another round?" His voice is husky with desire.

I laugh and slide off of him, curling against his side. "Will you ever be satisfied?"

"When it comes to you? Probably not."

He pulls the comforter over us, brushing a kiss across my forehead. Warmth and contentment spread through me. This is how it was meant to be—just the two of us, naked and tangled up together, securely in each other's arms.

I have no idea how long we drift off like that, not even bothering to move. Suddenly, we're abruptly interrupted when my phone starts blaring in the other room where Ash dropped it with my clothes.

I blink hard in the darkness, my eyes gritty. It's late. Or early. I have no idea.

"What time is it?"

"After three a.m.," comes Ash's hoarse reply. He sounds as exhausted as I feel. I don't bother to move. It's probably my mom again. She always forgets the late hour and calls me whenever she has a stray thought.

I moan my protest as I let it ring.

Ash gets up to go fetch my phone. It stops ringing by the time he gets there, and I call out that I'm sorry. By the time he's headed back into the bedroom, it's already started ringing again.

Suddenly, I'm fully awake and sitting up in bed, taking the phone from him. I glance at the screen. It's Cassie, my roommate at Hill House, and I have at least three unread texts from her, too. Without hesitation, I click to answer, reaching out to squeeze Ash's hand in silent thanks.

It has to be some kind of emergency or she wouldn't be spamming me like this.

"What's up, Cassie? Is everything okay?"

I'm greeted on the other end by frantic breathing. She sounds hysterical, almost like she's sobbing. I gulp in fear. "Cass? What's wrong?"

"I'm fine. But it's Gwen. I'm really, *really* worried about her."

I frown. "But I saw her earlier tonight. She and Maddie and I got together for happy hour at Isca while I was waiting for my date with Ash. She told me she was going to spend the evening working on her story. Didn't she come home?"

"She didn't, and it's bad, Lex. We've spent the last couple of hours retracing her steps. I don't think she ever made it past the perimeter of Exeter House."

My insides run cold. "What do you mean?"

Cass is breathing heavily again, and I can tell she's crying. "All we know is that she sent me a text at about nine p.m. It had me worried to begin with and then…nothing. I kept texting her. Tried calling her. She never answered back. I used the Find My

Phone app to stalk her phone. I saw it was near the beach right next to Exeter House, so Sam and I hopped in her car and headed over to get her."

More whimpering ensues and there's some whispering as if Sam is asking her a question and she's answering.

I'm dying, and my heart is racing. Ash sinks down on the bed beside me, brow wrinkled with concern when he notices how upset I'm getting.

"Cass? What happened when you got to her phone?"

"It was in a ditch by the side of the road near the beach. Along with one of her shoes."

"What? What the fuck? Oh my God, Cass."

Ash smooths a hand down my arm but otherwise waits patiently for me to end the call. By this time, I'm practically hyperventilating.

"What did Gwen's text say? Tell me the exact words," I bark.

"It said, *Some guy's following me.* Then a few minutes later she sent, *I'm gonna try to lose him.* That was the last time I heard from her. If that was even her sending the text."

My head spins with anxiety and worry. I frantically search my texts to see if maybe she had sent me anything, but I come up empty. I put the phone back to my ear. "Cass, I'll check with the Exeter House staff to see if they've seen anything."

I hang up and then frantically turn to Ash.

"Tell me what I can do, Princess." So relieved that I'm with him when I got this news, I fall against him, giving him my full weight.

After I explain everything to him, he texts his assistant to tell him to cancel everything on his calendar for the next day. Then, he puts the phone to his ear to call his connection at the CIA, asking them to see what they can find out.

Within minutes, we're dressed and on the road back to Hill House, ready to do whatever it takes to get Gwen back safe. The math is running in my head. She may have been taken. All signs point to it. And she's been missing for nearly ten hours now.

We aren't even back to Hill House when the CIA calls back and informs us that Gwen disappeared near one of those "black holes" of surveillance where there was no camera even close to catch what could have happened.

Ash runs his hand through his hair and turns to me. "They don't have anything. It's like she's vanished into thin air."

My blood runs cold. We have to find her no matter what it takes.

CHAPTER 33
GWEN

PANIC CLOGS MY THROAT.

Darkness surrounds me.

I can't see *anything*, not even through the cracks in the trunk lid. I've given up counting to give myself a sense of how much time has passed. My phone was snatched out of my hand. I have no watch. And I'm fucking terrified.

And worse? It's getting hot in here, harder to breathe.

When the two strange men first shoved me in here, I tried to make mental notes about which way the car was going. For a while, I think I had a sense of where I was. But time just dragged on—for hours, it seems—and somewhere along the way, I lost my bearings.

How long can I even survive in here? I have no idea. I just know that I'm *really* thirsty, and I'm dripping with sweat.

I'm curled up in a fetal position, and I've already tried pressing against all four edges of this box surrounding me. I can't help feeling like I'm in a coffin. Just the thought of that makes me hyperventilate. It takes several minutes for me to get a handle on my breathing.

Breathe.

In. Out. In. Out.

I need to shove my emotions aside and stay in control. I can panic *after* I get myself out of this fucked-up situation.

I'm slightly calmer now, so I focus on finding a spot I can press—maybe a button that opens the trunk to the back seat? Or maybe I can punch my way through the tail lights of the car? *Anything.* I remember reading a random article about this somewhere—how to escape if you're ever kidnapped and trapped in the trunk of a car.

Kidnapped.

Fuck, I've been kidnapped.

And I have no idea how this will end. Will I be taken to a dark field, told to kneel on the ground, then executed from behind, my body left in the desert somewhere? Maybe never to be found. Fear crawls back up my throat. *No*, I can't go there.

Breathe.

In. Out. In Out.

It won't end like that. It can't. I'll find a way out of this.

I have friends. I have a family. I have people who care about me, who are probably already looking for me. I did send Cassie those texts…

My mind races through all the things that have happened in the last few hours.

It all started when I left Exeter House after having dinner with Maddie and Lexi at Isca. When I walked outside, alone, to Isca's ocean-front patio, I noticed a tall, dark-haired man watching me. I was afraid he might approach me, so I decided to leave and head back home. Maddie and Lexi had already left, so I called an Uber.

As I waited for my ride, the man followed me and stood a few hundred yards away. Now, in retrospect, I know what I *should* have done. I should have alerted the Exeter House staff and asked someone to wait with me. But I didn't want to inconvenience anyone. Instead, I'd just decided to change the Uber pick-up to an area a few blocks down. I turned and headed down to the beach to take a shortcut.

There are usually a lot of people on the beach, but it was well after sunset, so it was empty. And dark. I took a deep breath, swallowed my fear, and headed parallel to the beach road. I stared down at my phone, watching as the Uber inched closer to my location on the map.

It didn't take me long to figure out that the man had followed me down to the beach as well. From the corner of my eye, I could see *two* men approach. The man from Isca now had a tall, beefy buddy. They appeared out of nowhere, it seemed, trapping me—one advancing from ahead and one closing in from behind me. In a moment of panic and desperation, I darted toward the water.

I have no idea what I was going to do when I got there—jump in? Start swimming toward Japan? Even during the heat of summer, the Pacific is frigid. I probably would have become hypothermic pretty quickly, but at least it would have given me a *chance* to get away.

I never got that far. The dark-haired man grabbed me and held a hand over my mouth, muffling every scream, every question, every word. With me in a choke hold, hand over my mouth, he dragged me back toward the road.

I'm such an idiot. I'd literally fallen right into their hands. Since they'd grabbed me at the shoreline and in the dark, there wouldn't be any security cameras that could pick that up.

The next thing I knew, I was unceremoniously dumped into this trunk. I've tried banging. I've tried screaming. But there's been no response. I'm completely alone. And I've realized that if I want to get out of this, I'll have to rely on myself.

We've been rolling along the streets of Los Angeles—or what I *presume* is still Los Angeles—for hours. Or maybe we've left Los Angeles. Hell, we could be at the Mexican border by now for all I know.

Who the fuck are these guys? More importantly, who do they work for? Because I don't believe for a second that the two men who kidnapped me are the masterminds behind this. They moved too robotically, too stoically, to have any personal stakes in my kidnapping.

I search my memory for any clue, any indication of who could be capable of something like this. And yet, in the pit of my stomach, I think I already know the answer to that question.

I don't have any solid proof yet, though. And in the end, does it even matter? For now, all I need to do is focus on staying alive. I'm way too young to die.

Images of my poor mother creep into my mind. News of losing me would destroy her, and that thought alone sobers me. Whatever comes, I have to fight.

Fuck, I should never have pursued that story lead. But I'd discovered some shocking secrets, and as I dug deeper, I became obsessed with uncovering the truth. I *had* to pursue it to the end. I'm stubborn that way. But look where that stubbornness has gotten me?

Even the biggest story of my life isn't worth losing it.

BIOGRAPHY

Evelyn has been telling stories in her head for as long as she can remember. She lives on the west coast with her family, and a menagerie of pets. She loves lattes, all things Disney, gaming, and writing dark, wildly sexy stories that give readers all the feels.

Sign up for news and updates:
evelynaustinbooks.wixsite.com/my-site/newsletter